"I want that torc, Mr. Jackson."

"Understood, sir."

"Good enough." The man turned and headed up the stairs, but stopped before he'd gotten more than a few steps away. He turned to face Jackson once more.

"This woman, the one with the sword. Do we know who she was?"

Jackson nodded. "An American archaeologist named Annja Creed." He took a photo out of the file folder in his hands and passed it to his employer. The picture had been taken at the dig site and showed Annja's still and bloodied face.

The other man stared at it for a few seconds, then passed it back.

"She was a pretty thing, wasn't she?"

Titles in this series:

ROGUE ANGEL

Alex Archer

TEAR OF THE GODS

A GOLD EAGLE BOOK FROM

WORLDWIDE.

TORONTO • NEW YORK • LONDON
AMSTERDAM • PARIS • SYDNEY • HAMBURG
STOCKHOLM • ATHENS • TOKYO • MILAN
MADRID • WARSAW • BUDAPEST • AUCKLAND

First edition July 2011

ISBN-13: 978-0-373-62150-7

TEAR OF THE GODS

Special thanks and acknowledgment to
Joe Nassise for his contribution to this work.

The
LEGEND

...THE ENGLISH COMMANDER TOOK
JOAN'S SWORD AND RAISED IT HIGH.

The broadsword, plain and unadorned,
gleamed in the firelight. He put the tip against
the ground and his foot at the center of the blade.
The broadsword shattered, fragments falling
into the mud. The crowd surged forward,
peasant and soldier, and snatched the shards
from the trampled mud. The commander tossed
the hilt deep into the crowd.
Smoke almost obscured Joan, but she continued
praying till the end, until finally the flames climbed
her body and she sagged against the restraints.

Joan of Arc died that fateful day in France,
but her legend and sword are reborn....

1

Myrrdin sat high astride his horse and stared down the slope of the hill at the Roman army amassing in the valley below. What was left of his command was gathered at his back, but it was pitifully small compared to the enemy presence before him.

It was hard to believe that things had gone wrong so swiftly.

Less than a week before, he'd been war leader to Queen Boudica herself and had led an army of more than eighty thousand souls across Britannia, carving a path of destruction in their wake. They had destroyed the colony at Camulodunum and had marched against first Verulamium, and then Londinium itself, sacking each city and slaying as many of the invaders as they could find. Blood flowed like a river wherever they went, appeasing the anger of the gods at the presence of the Roman invaders and bestowing blessings upon the Iceni as a result.

Nothing, it seemed, could stand in their way.

Nothing, that was, until the coming of Gaius Suetonius Paulinus.

Even thinking of the Roman's name was enough to make Myrrdin curse aloud and spit on the ground. He longed to carve the man's flesh from his bones and feed it the crows. He prayed to the gods that he would get his chance before the battle was over.

What a difference seventy-two hours made.

Less than five thousand men remained of the army that had met Paulinus and the soldiers of the XIV *Gemina* on the field of battle three days before. Few, if any, of his senior commanders still lived, for they had stood their ground and fought on even when the battle had turned in the Romans' favor. Myrrdin would have gone down fighting alongside them if the queen hadn't ordered him to retreat, to ensure that someone still remained who could rally the remnants of the Iceni and see to it that their people's sacrifice was not in vain.

How he wished he had never left her side!

He reached up and fingered the torc he wore about his neck, the one Boudica had entrusted to him before the battle. She'd always claimed it to be the root of her power, that the metal from which it was formed, the metal given to them by the very gods themselves, protected her time and time again. But Boudica was dead now, poisoned by her own hand while in Roman custody rather than be handed over to Paulinus's troops as a plaything for their amusement. When word reached him earlier that morning of her fate, he wept, wondering if he'd condemned her to death simply by taking the torc.

Not that it mattered now; what was done was done.

Myrrdin was a good enough tactician to know that at

this point there was no way the Iceni could win. They were outnumbered and the Romans were not only better armed but better armored, as well. If he hadn't been able to beat them with eighty thousand warriors at his command, there was no way he was going to be able to do so with only five thousand. But there was no question of retreat. He would rather die on the field of battle, sword in hand, than be hunted down like a dog in the weeks to come.

And perhaps, Awran willing, he could take a few Romans with him as an offering before it was his time to die.

He let his gaze roam over the soldiers gathering on the field below. Unlike his ragtag band of warriors, who often wore as little into battle as possible, the Romans were all dressed in identical coats of chain armor worn over a short jerkin with thick-soled leather sandals on their feet. They each carried two iron-tipped spears, pilums he'd heard them called. The short swords were designed primarily for stabbing in close-quarter combat. The soldiers also held large rectangular shields, big enough to cover a man from ankle to chin.

The legion's standard, a charging boar on a field of crimson that was so dark as to be almost purple, flapped in the afternoon breeze, the Romans arrogantly claiming this land on behalf of the Emperor.

Myrrdin turned and surveyed the men assembled behind him. What a sharp contrast to those they were about to face. Where the Romans were tall and muscled from years of disciplined labor, his men were smaller and wiry in nature, built for speed and dexterity. Where the Romans were armored and carried multiple weapons, many of his men were naked or nearly so, their fair skin decorated in blue woad. They clutched swords made of iron and carried small, round shields of leather stretched over wooden frames.

Of his illustrious horse soldiers, less than fifty remained. They sat stiffly in the saddle off to his right, weary from the days of fighting and the long chase they had endured so far, yet none hesitated to return his gaze or gave any sign they would shy away from the confrontation to come.

As he turned away, one thought was prominent in his mind.

We don't stand a chance.

Myrrdin shook his head, clearing it of such defeatism. The simple fact was he no longer had any choice; there was nowhere else to run. He'd never get his men through the bogs on the other side of the hills before the enemy could catch up with them. He had no choice but to stand and fight.

Like all good commanders, Myrrdin wanted that fight on his terms, not the enemy's, which was why he'd assembled his men along the crest of the hill while the Romans attempted to set up camp in the valley below. He hadn't been able to choose the field on which they would meet, but he'd be damned if he wouldn't choose the time.

And that time was now, before the enemy got themselves organized and settled in.

He brought his horn to his lips and blew a long blast. The sound echoed across the valley, like a great voice shouting from the hilltop, and Myrrdin smiled in defiance as he watched the Roman soldiers milling about in response.

Behind him, his men took up the call to battle, pounding the flats of their swords against their shields, calling up a frightful racket, letting the spirits know that there would soon be newcomers, friend and foe alike, entering the land of the dead. Bare-breasted women moved among the ranks, screaming in hatred at the Romans massed below and whispering words of encouragement to their men, stoking the twin fires of courage and power.

Myrrdin let it build for a few minutes, allowing his men to whip themselves into a killing frenzy, and then, when he judged the time was right, he raised his right arm above his head, his fist clenched for all to see, and then brought it slashing downward.

Like a breaking wave his army surged into motion, pouring down the hill toward the enemy, shrieking their war cries as they went.

With a joyous shout, Myrrdin spurred his horse and joined them, thundering down toward the rapidly forming enemy line. Behind him came the rest of his horse soldiers, their voices raised in harmony with his own.

Ahead of them the Romans stood shoulder to shoulder in a long, unbroken line, waiting with disciplined ease for the enemy to make contact, their oversize shields held before them to form a wall. As the Iceni warriors closed in, the Romans unleashed a blistering rain of stones and spears from behind the protection of that wall, hoping to blunt the force of the attack. The Iceni had faced the Romans before, however, and they were ready, having expected just such a move. Almost as one they bent low over their mounts, their heads sheltered by the animals' long necks, and as a result the majority of them made it through the storm unscathed.

Mere yards separated the two forces and Myrrdin felt his lips peel back from his teeth as he bared them at the enemy like a wild animal defending its den. Heart racing, blood pumping, he let out another shout of defiance and drove his horse right into the ranks of the enemy, smashing aside that wall of shields, trampling those foolish enough to stand firm in the face of the attack under the hooves of his battle-hardened mount. Beside him, his horse warriors did the same, smashing aside the Roman line, creating a breach for their foot soldiers to exploit as they caught up with the charging cavalry.

In seconds the orderly nature of the Roman defense had dissolved into chaos.

The air was full of the coppery scent of fresh blood, the smell of leather and sweat, the screams of the injured and the dying. Myrrdin slashed about him with his sword, hacking at anyone who got close enough, striking down as many of the enemy as he could, driving his horse relentlessly forward, doing all he could to widen the gap, to give his people a fighting chance at survival. If they could break through the other side of the Roman battle line, some of them might survive to fight another day.

A tall Roman rose up on his right side, his battle-ax already in motion, but Myrrdin took the blow on the buckler strapped to his left arm. The shield shattered, smashed to pieces by the force of the blow, but it served its purpose, giving Myrrdin time to thrust his sword deep into the other man's chest, killing him where he stood. The Iceni chieftain turned in the saddle, searching for his next foe.

The spear came out of nowhere, whistling through the air with all the grace of a weapon of war doing just what it had been designed to do. It struck him high in the right side. As luck would have it, he'd been in the midst of turning and the projectile drove into the narrow gap his mail coat failed to cover at his armpit, burying itself deep in his chest.

It was like being buried in an avalanche of ice, his sword falling away from fingers gone suddenly numb, his grip on the saddle loosening as he lost the feeling in his legs, and he tumbled from his mount to lie in the mud of the battlefield as the fight raged on around him.

As his vision began to narrow and the darkness closed in, Myrrdin could have sworn he felt the torc about his neck pulse in time with his heartbeat.

2

Annja Creed studied the decapitated heads on the table in front of her.

Two of them had their eyes closed, as if they'd died peacefully in their sleep, but Annja knew better than to trust in simple appearances. There had been nothing peaceful about their passing; the fact that they were sitting on the table minus the rest of their bodies was proof of that, she thought wryly. The eyes of the third were open and surprisingly free of detritus from the bog. From her position in front of the table, the dead man's eyes seemed to stare directly back into her own, as if he were as intently curious about her as she was about him. It would have given most people the creeps, but after all she'd been through over the past few years since inheriting Joan of Arc's mystical sword, she barely even noticed.

The heads had been unearthed in an isolated peat bog several hours north of London in the West Midlands.

She'd been invited to the site just over a week earlier by an old friend from the British Museum, Oxford University professor Craig Stevens.

From what he'd explained over the phone, a pair of farmers had reported seeing a head staring up at them out of the bog while they were out hunting. Further investigation revealed that the two men hadn't been hunting at all, but rather running an industrious little business on the side selling cut peat for fuel. They hadn't wanted the police to know that the section of the bog they were harvesting didn't belong to either of them.

"Of course, when it comes to decapitated heads, the police tend to be a bit pushy," Craig said with a laugh, something Annja didn't have any trouble believing.

The detective in charge had seen enough bog mummies to know the difference between a recent murder and one that had happened a few centuries before. He dumped the head in Craig's lap, given his specialty in Iron Age Celtic cultures, in an effort to avoid as much paperwork as possible. Craig was more than happy to take care of the problem.

It had only taken a few days at the site before a second head turned up and that had been enough to get Oxford University to fund a small dig to see what else might be present. Annja had worked with Craig on a previous dig in Wales and he'd called to let her know that he was looking for a few experienced hands to help him out. Did she think she could make it?

It had been a while since she'd had the chance to work an actual dig. The cable television show she cohosted, *Chasing History's Monsters,* had kept her incredibly busy for the past few months, rushing around the world to highlight one legend after another. As had her unofficial role as protector of the innocent and the bearer of

the mystical sword that once belonged to Joan of Arc.
A week or two with her hands in the mud doing honest-
to-goodness science was just what she needed.

But when she'd called her producer, Doug Morrell,
in New York to get the time off, he'd gone ballistic.

"Are you insane?" he cried when she finished laying
out her request. "We're talking decapitations, human
sacrifices and bog mummies here! How can you think
of leaving us out of it?"

Quite easily, she'd thought at the time, but she knew
if she stiffed Doug now he'd only get even with her
later. He'd saddle her with hours of editing work or,
even worse, handle it himself. And if he did that, who
knew what would show up in the middle of one of her
episodes? She still hadn't forgotten the bloody mechani-
cal shark incident….

In the end, they'd cut a deal. The show would pay
for her airfare and her expenses while on-site and in
return she'd deliver enough material to put together a
special double feature on bog mummies, druids and
ancient Celtic culture. It was as good as she was going
to get and she quickly got Doug off the phone before
he decided the episode wouldn't be complete without
a full-scale reenactment of a druidic ritual, preferably
with plenty of special effects and a well-endowed blonde
as the sacrificial centerpiece. If it drove ratings, Doug
was all for it, science be damned.

She'd landed at Heathrow the day before, headed to
a hotel and slept off the jet lag. This morning she rose
early and set out for the dig site in a rented Land Rover.
The dig was pretty remote; it took her until early afternoon to reach the landing stage where the rest of the
vehicles were parked and then another hour of hiking
up and down a series of hills thick with birch groves

before finding the camp on the far side, down near the edge of the bog.

Annja bumped into one of Craig's graduate students, a curly-headed guy named Zeke, just after arriving at the site and Zeke had been kind enough to offer to let "Dr. Stevens" know she was here. While waiting, she spotted the heads through the open flap of a large canvas tent, like those used by army encampments the world over. She wandered in to take a look.

Up close she could see that each head was held upright in a frame of clear polymer, designed no doubt to protect the artifact while at the same time allowing the scientists to study all three dimensions at once. It was a clever piece of equipment, one she hadn't seen before, and she was moving in for a closer look when a cheerful voice boomed out from behind her.

"At last, she arrives!"

Annja jumped in surprise; she'd been so intent on her examination of the heads that she hadn't heard him come up behind her. Working with bog mummies was an entirely new and exciting experience for her.

Craig looked much as he did the last time she'd seen him—a bear of a man with a thick beard and a mop of unruly hair the color of pine sap. He towered over her at six and a half feet and she could have easily hidden behind his nearly three-hundred-pound body if she'd ever had the need to, but his imposing size was a complete contrast to his open and general ebullient nature.

"Now we can do some real work!" he said, a twinkle in his eyes, before crossing the space between them in that smooth gliding gait that always looked so out of character on such a large man. He wrapped her in one of his trademark hugs.

When he finally released her, and she double-checked

her ribs to be certain they were all still intact, she couldn't help but smile at him in return. One thing about working with Craig: his good humor was infectious.

"You've got an interesting interior decorator," she said, nodding at the heads on the table behind her.

Her fellow archaeologist beamed. "Marvelous, aren't they?" he said, and then stepped around her to squat in front of the center head.

"This was the first," he said, "the one the police sent over. Isn't it beautiful?"

His voice held a note of awe, the kind reserved for those who've just had some kind of religious epiphany or incredibly mind-blowing experience, and Annja almost laughed in response. She wasn't sure that *beautiful* was a word she would ever use to describe a decapitated and mummified head, but it was certainly striking, she'd give him that. The victim, if that was indeed what he was, appeared to have been a male in his late twenties, maybe early thirties, with sharp cheekbones and a prominent nose. His skin had the look and appearance of well-tanned leather. His hair, still held in a ponytail with a short piece of braided rope, was a fiery orange, just short of red.

"It's certainly something," she replied. "I'm amazed at the level of preservation. I thought bogs were basically swamps."

Craig nodded. "Yes and no. It depends on where they are in their development."

He stood and faced her, doing his best to explain. "When moss dominates a low-lying section of land, the soil becomes waterlogged and acidic. Since bacteria have a difficult time surviving in such conditions, it isn't present to break down the dead moss and other vegetation. Instead, the stuff just piles up and eventually becomes peat."

Annja got the implication right away. "So the acidic nature of the water itself actually protects the body rather than destroying it. No bacteria means no decomposition."

"Right," Craig said, smiling. "And the tannins produced by the moss add an extra level of preservation, turning the skin to something like leather and keeping it from tearing in response to the pressure from above as the peat grows deeper."

"Is that why their skin is so dark, because of the tannin?"

Craig nodded. "And why their hair is red, too."

"You mean that lovely color isn't natural?" she asked curiously.

"Not even close. In fact, I'm pretty sure all three of them were Romans, which means their hair was probably darker than either of ours."

"Romans? Seriously?" She'd never heard of Romans being uncovered in a peat bog before.

"Yeah, I know, it's unusual to say the least. But it's hard to argue with the evidence. Here, look." Moving to the head on the right, he reached out and turned the frame around, pointing at something on the back of the man's skull.

At first Annja couldn't figure out what it was, but after staring at it for a minute and mentally smoothing out the skin while doing so, she finally got it.

"It's a tattoo, isn't it?"

Craig's eyes twinkled. "Yes, but a tattoo of what?"

Annja leaned in closer, trying to puzzle it out. "It's an animal of some kind, I think. A dog, maybe? Or a wolf?"

"Close," he replied. "Look at its mouth. See anything unusual?"

She peered at it harder, trying to sort out the details of the tattoo from the natural lines of the aged flesh. It looked like…

"Is that a tusk?" she asked without looking up.

"Right! Which makes that," he said, pointing at the tattoo, "a wild boar."

He beamed at her, as if the presence of the boar explained everything. But Annja wasn't seeing the connection.

"Okay, so it's a boar and not a wolf. So what? I still don't see why that makes him a Roman rather than a Celt."

Craig led her across the tent to where another table held two laptop computers and a combination printer/scanner. He sorted through a stack of papers next to one of the laptops until he found the page he was looking for and then handed it to Annja without a word.

She found herself looking at a scanned image of a battle standard photographed from a museum collection somewhere. She could even see the edge of the glass box in which it was housed. But what really caught her eye was the image of the charging boar that dominated the center of the standard. It was the exact same design that was tattooed on the back of the bog mummy's head.

"XIV *Gemina,* or the Fourteenth Legion," Craig said. "Under the command of Gaius Suetonius Paulinus, it was ordered back to Britannia by the emperor in A.D. 67 to quell the Boudican rebellion."

Boudica was the warrior queen of the Iceni clan, Annja knew. She'd inspired and led one of the largest uprisings against Roman rule in the history of the empire. The Roman historian Cassius Dio wrote that she was "most tall, in appearance most terrifying, in the glance of her eye most fierce"—a description that made Annja smile the first time she'd read it. Annja'd been called fierce once or twice in her day, too.

She had to give Craig credit; it was a nice piece of detective work. But it raised more than a question or two in her mind. "I thought Boudica made her stand near Mancetter?" That was at least fifty miles south of where they now stood.

"She did. And that's where the story ends for most historians. But there's a small group, myself included, that believe a portion of her army escaped the battle that day and tried to make it to Anglesey by cutting overland across the moors. If they had, and if Paulinus pursued them as I believe that he did, then it's not inconceivable that they met again in battle and that we've stumbled on evidence of that very encounter. If you examine—"

Craig's explanation was cut short by the sound of running feet. He and Annja turned to face the entrance just as the flap was thrown open and Zeke stuck his head in through the opening.

"Dr. Stevens!" he cried, his voice full of excitement. "We've got another one!"

3

After delivering his message, Zeke turned and took off at a run back across the camp. Annja made as if to follow, but then hesitated. Given his size, there was no way Craig would be able to match the younger man's pace.

He must have guessed what she was thinking, for he waved a hand at her in dismissal. "Go on! Quickly, before he's out of sight. I'll meet you at the excavation," he said with a chuckle.

That was all she needed to hear. Annja was five feet ten inches tall, with chestnut hair and amber-green eyes. She had an athlete's build, with smooth, rounded muscles and curves in all the right places, and it took her only a moment or two to sprint along until she had the eager grad student back in her sights.

She kept her eye on Zeke as he left the camp behind and moved at a quick pace through the trees for about a hundred yards, following a path worn into the earth from the passage of the dig team over the past several days. Ten minutes later Anna emerged from the trees to find herself standing on the gentle slope of a small hill, the dig site laid out before her.

The site was roughly half the size of a football field and was located in a hollow between several small hills like the one she stood on. There were two significant features that set this particular valley off from dozens of others in the nearby area. The first was a large rock cairn that had been erected at the base of the slope on which she stood, its stone face now overgrown with moss and lichen but still recognizable for what it had once been. The second was the skeletal remains of an ancient oak tree standing near the middle of the site, a jagged black scar of a lightning strike clearly visible even from a distance.

Although Craig's team had only been here a short while, Annja could see that they'd been busy. A grid had been laid out on the valley floor in colored string, dividing the space into individual sections that Annja knew from experience were roughly two feet square. Work had begun in several sections, with the top layer of the peat removed, revealing the rich substrata beneath. Sifting stations had been set up beneath canopies to the right of the grid and there was a plethora of shovels, rakes and handheld trowels scattered about.

Most of the team was clustered around a single grid square, obviously the location of their most recent find. Annja made her way down the hill and across the dig site to join them.

The smell hit her as she moved closer, the unmistakable scent of scorched earth that accompanied a peat bog of any decent age. She resisted the urge to cover her nose; the human body only recognized an odor in the first few minutes of contact, after that it was as if it didn't exist.

Two grad students were on their hands and knees near the corner of the grid, using hand tools to clear the debris away from the blackened face that was peeking out of the peat. While this one wasn't as well preserved as the others, the similarities were still obvious. It was clear that the four men had the same ethnic background; the prominent nose and high cheekbones were as easy to see in this specimen as they were in the others. And like the others, this head had been severed and lay by itself in the peat that preserved it.

Who were they? Annja found herself wondering. And what happened to their bodies?

It was mysteries like these that had helped her fall in love with archaeology in the first place. She couldn't wait to get her hands dirty.

Craig finally caught up with them then, his face red and his chest heaving from his hike through the woods, but it did nothing to stem his enthusiasm for what they'd uncovered. Being the excellent teacher that he was, Craig let his people continue unearthing the find, guiding them with encouraging comments here and there rather than taking control of the process for himself as Annja knew others she'd worked with in the past would have done. It was what made Craig such a good student of archaeology; he cared more about the artifact and what it could tell them than the academic reputation associated with whoever unearthed it.

For the next two hours Annja lost herself in the simple joy of doing what she loved, helping Craig and his students excavate the mummified head from the peat surrounding it and then carefully packing it into a foam-lined carrying case for transport back to the campsite for further examination. Several of the students recognized her from *Chasing History's Monsters* and it wasn't long before she was surrounded by a small group of her own, dispensing advice and stories of former digs just as Craig was doing with the others a few yards away. It was such a welcome relief from the recent craziness in her life that Annja found herself relaxing for the first time in weeks and enjoying the simple pleasure that came from doing something you loved in the presence of others who felt the same way.

By the time dusk fell over the campsite, Annja felt like she'd been working with the team for weeks.

"Not a bad first day, huh?" Craig asked her as they helped the others cover the site with tarps to protect it in case of rain later that evening.

"It was wonderful, Craig. Truly," she said with a smile. "Thanks for inviting me."

He grinned. "Don't thank me yet. You haven't tasted what passes for cooking around here."

Once they were finished at the dig site, Annja was introduced to Sheila James, a fellow American, who gave her a tour of the camp, showed her the tent she'd be using for the duration and introduced her to some more of the students over dinner that night.

Worn out from the hard work and the lingering effects of the jet lag, she thanked them all for their hospitality and headed off to bed.

Annja found herself walking in the woods beneath the silvery light of a full moon, though she knew she was not herself. The hand at the end of her arm was decidedly male. She was part of a group of four warriors carrying the body of a fifth on a funeral bier made of wood, fashioned together with rope and vines. Around

her came a host of others, warriors mainly, but some
women were scattered amid the company here and
there, as well—all of them moving through the trees in
a long, snaking procession. Torches threw flickering
light across the scene, highlighting the faces of those
around her, revealing the geometric designs painted
on their faces in blue woad—whirls and spirals and
circles that interlinked and crossed one another so that
it was difficult to discern where one ended and the next
began.

The body on the bier was that of a tall warrior with
long red hair. He was dressed as he'd been when he'd
fallen on the battlefield, his tunic and mail stained with
blood, both his own and that of his enemies. His arms
were folded across his chest, his hands grasping the
hilt of the sword that he'd carried into battle, the blade
broken off halfway down its length.

Annja's eyes were drawn to the necklace of gleaming
black the dead man wore around his neck. It was made
from a substance that she couldn't identify, at least not
from this distance, and it reacted to the light the same
way an oil spill does, reflecting myriad colors back
at the viewer. She felt the need to reach out and touch
it....

The moonlight suddenly grew brighter, breaking her
reverie, and she looked up as the group emerged from
the trees into the open. They stood upon the crest of a
hill that sloped gently downward until it met the edge of
a wide marshland. A spit of land jutted out into the bog
for a short distance and a white robed druid stood upon
it, waiting for them. Behind him a massive oak tree rose
out of the depths of the bog, its branches spread wide,
forming a living canopy over that part of the swamp.

The procession descended the hill. When they

reached the narrow spit of land, the rest of the group came to a halt while Annja and the other pallbearers continued forward. The druid directed them to place the bier on the ground at his feet. They did so and then, as a group, stepped off to one side to wait for further instructions.

The druid raised his hands to the sky and began to chant in a deep voice, his words rolling out across the night air. The words were spoken in a language Annja didn't understand—Welsh or Gaelic or some derivative thereof—but she was familiar enough with ancient burial ceremonies that she knew the general gist of it. The druid was asking for the blessing of the four elements and calling upon the gods to look with favor upon the one they were committing into their care that night.

When the chant was finished, four male prisoners were led forward from the rear of the procession. They were naked and bound at the wrists with thick hemp ropes. Their movements were sluggish, their expressions unfocused, and it was clear to Annja that they'd been drugged.

She understood why a moment later, when the first of them was made to kneel at the edge of the bog with his head resting sideways on the stump of a tree Annja hadn't noticed before now. The man's eyes roamed over them, seeing but not seeing, and the real Annja breathed a sigh of relief when it was clear that he didn't understand what was to come. As if on cue, the druid approached the prisoner, a gleaming sickle-shaped blade in his hands. There was another chant, this one much shorter in length, and then that blade rose and fell in one swift, sure motion.

The druid turned to face the procession, the Roman's

severed head held aloft by the tangle of its own hair, and at the sight of it a shout went up from the rest of the onlookers. Inhabiting a body not her own, Annja found herself shouting along with the rest of them.

The cry was repeated three times—a ritual response, Annja realized—and then the druid turned to face the dark waters at his back. Another prayer flowed forth, a request to Arawn, god of the underworld, to accept the blood offering they were making on behalf of their slain chieftain, most likely, and then the slain prisoner's head was flung outward into the night.

Annja heard the splash as it hit the water and watched as the bog swiftly sucked it out of sight.

The first prisoner's body was dragged away and the second victim was brought forward. The ceremony was repeated, and then twice more with the final two victims. The stink of blood filled Annja's nostrils by the time the druid was finished, so thick that she could almost taste it on the back of her tongue.

At a sign from the druid, she and the other pallbearers hefted the bier back up again. Following the druid, they marched out into the bog.

Much to her surprise the bog did not swallow them whole. Her feet instead found the hard surfaces of stones laid just beneath the waterline, a hidden walkway extending out across the marsh to the base of the sacred oak. They carefully placed the bier under the tree's sheltering boughs and returned to the shoreline.

Annja and the rest of the pallbearers rejoined the main procession, leaving the druid standing alone on the small strip of land where the ceremony had taken place. As she watched, the high priest raised his arms toward the heavens and shouted in a voice full of power.

In the sky above him, thunder raged and lightning cracked, answering his call as the funeral bier of the last of the Iceni chieftains sank toward the bog's heart.

ANNJA AWOKE WITH a start. Lightning flashed, lighting up the sides of her tent for a moment before the darkness returned to smother the camp in its embrace.

Just a dream, she told herself. Just a dream.

But dream or not, it took a long time for her to fall back to sleep.

4

Annja rose the next morning with the dream still fresh in her mind, which was unusual for her. More often than not, she forgot her dreams upon waking, but something about this one stuck in the forefront of her mind and wouldn't leave her alone. All through breakfast her mind worried at it, the way your tongue will worry a loose tooth.

It was as if her subconscious was trying to tell her something.

While the others were still finishing their food, she excused herself and made her way through the trees and down to the excavation. Once there, it only took a few seconds for her to understand why the dream was bothering her so much.

The location of the ceremony in her dream matched the location of the dig.

The bog, the rock cairn, even the remains of the massive oak tree were right where they'd been in her dream.

A glance at the excavation grid showed her that the four heads had all been found in the same general locations as she'd seen the High Druid toss them in the dream.

Her dream, it seemed, had come to life.

Now hang on a minute, she told herself. Don't get carried away. You saw the site yesterday; you spent several hours working right in the middle of it all. Is it any wonder that you saw it again in your dream?

Of course not.

She'd taken her excitement about the day in the field, her first in weeks, and carried it with her in her dreams that night.

That was it; it had to be.

Still she lingered, her eyes going again and again to the shell of the ancient oak rising in the middle of the peat. In her dream, someone important had been buried nearby.

Ignoring the voice of reason that was quietly protesting in the back of her mind, she grabbed a shovel from the pile of tools nearby and headed for the oak.

That's where Craig found her ten minutes later. She'd eyeballed the distance from the tree as best she remembered it from her dream, telling herself she was crazy all the while but unwilling, or unable, to give it up without at least looking first. After all, she told herself, what harm could it do?

Craig, however, had a different opinion.

"Annja! What on earth are you doing?" he shouted in dismay when he saw the trench she had begun digging into the peat. "I can't believe that you, of all people, are ignoring procedure like this! We haven't photographed or measured that section of the site, and we're not even close to being ready to begin excavations…."

Craig's tirade suddenly fell silent. Annja followed his

gaze to where he was staring at the ground a few inches from her left foot. A shout of triumph almost passed her lips when she saw what he was staring at.

A hand was thrust upward through the peat, as if reaching for the light of the sky above.

THERE WAS ROOM for three of them to work the find so Craig brought in Paolo Novick, a professor from the University of Turin and an expert on pre-Roman Gallic cultures, to help them. Most of the rest of the team gathered about to watch. Little by little, the peat was peeled away, exposing another inch of the man's remains.

It took them almost four hours to bring the chieftain's body into the light of day for the first time in millenia. Unlike the remains they'd uncovered to date, this one was completely intact. Everything from the shoes on his feet to the tunic he wore beneath his long coat of mail was in excellent condition, seemingly none the worse for wear after their years of submersion in the bog. Even the small piece of twine that bound his long red hair in a ponytail had survived.

A quick measurement put his height at seventy-four inches, and that was after the bog's natural preservation process had shrunk the body slightly. In life, he'd probably been closer to six and a half feet tall, which Annja knew was a literal giant for that day and age. His size, combined with the massive knot of red hair that still hung from his skull, quickly earned him the nickname Big Red.

Photographs were taken, covering Big Red from every angle possible so that a record would be preserved of how and where he had been found before the laborious process of removing him from the peat could begin. The previous night's thunderstorm had Craig worried that the weather would take a turn for the worse soon, however, and he didn't want the body left exposed to the elements. The decision was made to cut a block out of the peat, body and all, and move that back to the camp where it could be studied and worked on at leisure, away from the potential damage the elements could inflict.

As Craig sent several members of the team back to the camp to organize the tools they would need to pull off their plan, Annja bent over the body with a set of hand tools. She was still shocked that Big Red had been there at all; she'd almost convinced herself that everything she'd seen in her dream had been just that, a dream. Obviously it had been something more. She wondered just what part Joan's sword had played in it all. It wouldn't be the first time its powers had surprised her, that was for sure.

Using a miniature pick and a small brush, she began to work at the peat still covering the front of Big Red's throat. She remembered the strange gleaming necklace the chieftain had worn around his throat during the burial ceremony and wondered if that, too, had been real.

A chunk of peat cracked and fell away from the rest, partially revealing the gleaming surface of the tribanded necklace Big Red was wearing around his throat.

"What have you got?" Professor Novick asked from his position at her side.

"Looks like a necklace, maybe a torc of some kind," she said, and leaned back to let him take a look.

He whistled at the sight of it. "What is that? Obsidian?"

She shook her head. "I don't think so. It looks metallic to me. It seems too shiny but maybe it's iron. We'll have to wait until we can get him into the lab to examine it more closely."

As the day wore on and the hard work of removing Big Red from his resting place got under way, Annja was forced to forget about the necklace and concentrate on the task at hand.

The damage, however, had already been done, though Annja didn't know it.

The block they cut out of the peat reminded Annja of one of the stones used in the building of the pyramids; it looked that big. It was also heavy enough that they had to use two different winches to get it up out of the earth and into the front of the Bobcat they'd had brought up from London to serve as their transport vehicle. Once the peat slab was secured in place, the Bobcat made its way up the hill and down the path through the woods to the camp that part of the team had spent the afternoon clearing.

A new tent had been erected in their absence—a thick tarp rolled out in the center of the floor—and it was on this that the peat block was finally placed. Seeing Big Red's body partially protruding from its surface reminded Annja of *Star Wars;* Han Solo encased in carbonite was far less interesting to her than this ancient Gallic warrior, however.

She, Craig and Paolo worked through the afternoon, slowly chipping away at the heavy peat surrounding Big Red's body, freeing him inch by inch from the preserving matter. By the time they called it a night, the sun had long since set and many of the camp's other residents had gone to bed.

As they were leaving, Craig pulled her aside.

"How'd you know?" he asked. "How did you know to dig there, of all places?"

She answered him as honestly as she could. "I saw it all in a dream."

He laughed. "Right," he said. "And I suppose tomorrow you'll wake up and tell me you've discovered the location of Genghis Khan's long-lost tomb."

Annja smiled. "Nah. Been there, done that."

The look of shocked surprise on his face was the perfect end to a perfect day.

5

Shortly after midnight a man slipped out of a tent in the middle of the camp and quietly made his way across the clearing to the tree line just beyond. At the edge of the woods he stopped and turned, looking back the way he'd come. He waited, one long moment, then another, watching, listening, making certain that no one had followed him.

Assured that he was unobserved and alone, the man disappeared into the woods, following a faint path through the trees until he reached the deadfall he'd selected as a landmark. There he turned and traveled for another hundred yards before stopping beside a huge boulder that had probably been there since the last ice age.

Again he paused, listening, sweeping the path behind him with his peripheral vision, searching for anyone who might be on his tail. While it was unlikely, it never hurt to be careful, and with something like this he didn't want to be wrong.

Finally satisfied, he reached into a cleft in the rock and pulled out a satellite phone. Switching it on, he waited for it to power up and then dialed a number. When it was picked up on the other end, he said, "It's Novick. I need to speak to him."

There was a pause. Novick figured the man on the other end of the line was considering the wisdom of waking their joint employer at this hour of the night, and so he said, "It's about the torc."

That seemed to convince the other man, for he said, "Just a moment," and put the receiver down.

Several minutes passed.

Finally Novick heard the phone on the other end being picked up.

"You have something for me?"

Novick swallowed the sudden hesitation he felt at the sound of that voice and answered him. "Yes. At the new site in the West Midlands. We found a body in the bog this morning, an Iceni warrior."

"And?"

"And he was wearing a torc that fits the description of the one you've been seeking for the past several years."

"You're certain?"

"Absolutely."

"What about the test?"

Sneaking into the artifact tent with the device in hand had been easy. "It was positive."

There was a long silence as the other man considered the implications, then he said, "Very good. I will dispatch someone to meet you tomorrow afternoon."

With thoughts of the reward money he'd been promised for finding the torc dancing in his head, Novick said that he understood and ended the call.

6

David Shaw rose the next morning with anticipation thrumming through his veins. He'd been searching for the Tear of the Gods for more than a decade. Many had scoffed at his dedication and focus. It's just a legend, they'd told him. Nothing more than a myth, like the Holy Grail or King Arthur's Excalibur. You'll never find it because it doesn't actually exist. But Shaw had believed differently and now, in less than twenty-four hours, he was going to be holding that so-called myth in his own two hands.

Shaw was in his mid-forties, with brown eyes and a sharp nose set in a narrow, aquiline face. The combination of his facial features and his shoulder-length dirty-blond hair often resulted in others mistaking him for the actor Sean Bean, a suggestion that Shaw would publicly chuckle over but which infuriated him to no end. That he could be mistaken for an actor, of all things, was an insult to all he'd worked to achieve since graduating

from Oxford at the top of his class and founding the
Vanguard Group.

To say Shaw was driven would make one guilty of
a gross understatement. He had ambitions and dreams
the likes of which not even his board of directors were
aware and obtaining the Tear of the Gods was just the
first step in a process he'd been planning for years.

After a leisurely breakfast he had his driver take him
to the Vanguard offices. Several men were seated outside his office waiting for him, as he had known they
would be. His executive assistant had sent word to them
all the night before, requesting their presence in the
office by nine this morning, and if there was one thing
his people knew, it was not to disobey his orders.

Shaw pointed to one of them, a man named Trevor
Jackson, and the former SAS commando and current
Red Hand Defenders strike team leader followed him
into his inner office, shutting the door behind them.

"I've got a job for you," Shaw began as he took his
seat behind his desk and waved Jackson into the chair
before him. "A particular artifact was uncovered at an
archaeological dig in the West Midlands last night. I
want it."

He handed the other man a thin folder. Inside were an
assortment of documents, including aerial photographs
and topographical maps of the surrounding area, dos-
siers on Stevens, Novick and other personnel they could
expect to encounter at the dig site, as well as a snapshot
of the torc that looked like it had been taken quickly
with a cell phone.

"The photo was taken by my source on the ground,"
Shaw explained. "It's not perfect, but it should be good
enough to let you verify it when you arrive on-site."

Jackson glanced through the materials, lingering

on the photograph. "What kind of opposition can we expect?" he asked.

"Little to none," Shaw replied. "They're a bunch of academics. Somebody might have a gun with which to shoot snakes, but that would be about it, I'd think."

"So we go in, recover the necklace and get out again. Sounds simple enough."

But Shaw was already shaking his head. "You need to take any steps necessary to ensure that no one knows the artifact was recovered from the site."

Jackson had worked with Shaw long enough to know what the other man was talking about. "And the bodies?"

Shaw shrugged. "Dump them in the bog, for all I care. Just be sure there aren't any survivors. I don't want someone turning up at a later date to counter the official report."

"What about your man on the inside?"

Shaw didn't hesitate. "Get rid of him, too."

"Fair enough," Jackson said with a smile. "Consider the problem solved."

WITH THAT TASK behind him, Shaw could turn to the other major item he had on his agenda for the day—informing the Committee about the discovery of the torc.

The Committee was a group of wealthy collectors that he'd put together slowly and carefully over the past several years. Each of them was interested in the discovery and acquisition of ancient artifacts for one of two reasons—either to add to their own personal collections or to sell them on the black market to the highest bidder in order to fund some other project or ideology. Shaw didn't care which it was, provided he was paid on time and in the proper currency as agreed. Whenever Shaw found an item worthy of their consideration, he called a meeting of the group and presented it to them. A bidding war would usually ensue, with Shaw taking ten percent of the asking price plus expenses to cover the costs of acquisition.

There were five members of the Committee—six, if he considered himself. Conrad Helmut was a German financier with a gift for the international commodities exchange who saw the artifacts solely for their monetary value. He had no interest in the past, whether it was yesterday, last year or last century. He treated artifacts recovered from tombs untouched by human hands for more than four thousand years the same way he'd treat something picked up at a rummage sale. It was all just merchandise to him—something to be bought and sold but never desired.

Allison Brennan was the opposite extreme—a fanatic who made no bones about her intention to craft a truly legendary collection. She was always trying to get a leg up on the others, beat them to the choicest prices. Standing in her way was the Frenchman, Roux. Just thinking of the man brought a scowl to Shaw's face. The arrogant bastard didn't use a first name; it was always just Roux. As much as he disliked him, Shaw had to admit that Roux had access to some first-rate intelligence and had helped them find some choice items over the years.

Sebastian Kincade had inherited his fortune at the ripe old age of nineteen, when his parents had died unexpectedly in a car crash. He'd added to it through a series of almost breathtakingly audacious financial moves in the decade since. He was as ruthless as Genghis Khan himself and twice as greedy. Rumor had it that the accident that killed his parents hadn't been an accident at all; Sebastian had supposedly wanted access to his part of the family fortune before dear old mom and dad were ready to give it to him.

The fifth, and final member of the Committee, Saito Yamada, owned one of the largest telecommunications entities in the Asian market and, like the others, was regularly listed as one of the top fifty most wealthy individuals in the world. Shaw knew that Yamada's legitimate fortune was dwarfed by his illegal one; as one of the major yakuza bosses in all of Japan, Yamada had his hands in a lot of different pies. He didn't buy all that often but when he did it was usually for big money.

It was going to be an interesting morning.

Shaw stepped over to his desk and settled into the high-back leather chair behind it. Glancing at his watch, he saw that it was time for the meeting to begin. He purposely waited several more minutes before activating the videoconferencing link.

When the link was established, four windows opened on his monitor, each one showing the video feed from the four committee members who were on the line. Brennan, Roux, Helmut and Kincade stared out at him. Only Yamada was absent.

Four out of five's good enough, he thought. Something so European probably wouldn't have appealed to the yakuza boss, anyway.

Shaw put a smile on his face, activated his own camera and said, "It's a pleasure to see you all again."

Thanks to the wonders of modern technology, each of the Committee members could see and hear Shaw through the conferencing link. Their identities were kept secret from one another, however. They could hear when others chose to speak, but they didn't have access to the video feeds and could never be certain just how many others were on the call with them.

Fear, uncertainty and doubt, Shaw thought. The key to any successful sale.

Since the Committee was well aware that Shaw only scheduled meetings when there was an item in play, he got right down to business.

"Near the end of the first century, Rome nearly lost control of Britannia when a warrior queen named Boudica staged a revolt," Shaw began. "Despite being outnumbered and underequipped, Boudica's forces overwhelmed the Roman legions.

"Some say it was because she caught the Romans napping. Others, that she was a military genius the likes of which the Romans hadn't ever encountered among the tribal Celts before or since. But there are those who believe that Boudica's power came from an external source, a strange and unusual necklace, or torc, that she wore about her neck at all times."

The Committee members had long since learned how to keep their emotions off their faces, but Shaw had been studying them carefully over the past several years and thought he'd identified some of their tells, those non-verbal cues that they couldn't control when they were excited about something. Like the way Helmut's right index finger would tap on the arm of his chair a few times before settling down again. Or the way Brennan would cross her legs in one direction, then quickly switch them to another position, as she was doing now.

"The Tear of the Gods, as it is known in certain circles, has been lost to history for almost two thousand years. Lost, that is, until today."

He tapped a key and the photograph Novick had sent to him last night appeared on the screen in front of each of the callers. He left it there for only a few seconds—just a short, tantalizing tease—then sat back and waited for a reaction, knowing that he who spoke first ultimately ceded power to the others.

Brennan was the first to break the silence, as Shaw knew she would be. The chance to add something actually carried by one of Boudica's chieftains, perhaps even by Boudica herself, was a prize too good to pass up for a woman who considered herself a modern-day warrior queen.

"It looks just like every other torc I've ever seen," she said derisively. "What makes you think this is the—what did you call it? The Tear of the Gods?"

Shaw smiled. Her interest was so obvious. Did she honestly think she was fooling anyone with her feigned disbelief?

"The torc was found around the throat of a Celtic warrior who'd been ceremonially buried in a bog in the West Midlands region," he told the group. "Four sacrificial victims surrounded the body, proof that the warrior was more than just an ordinary soldier or low-ranking chieftain, for such sacrifices required the presence of a druid, perhaps the High Druid himself, and would not be wasted on anyone less than the royal family or their close companions."

Brennan frowned, apparently uneasy with Shaw's quick answer. "But that still doesn't prove that this is the torc you are claiming it to be," she said stubbornly.

Shaw surprised her a second time by agreeing. "You're correct. That alone is not proof enough. Which is why we turn to more, shall we say, personal sources?"

He pulled a book off his desk and held it up to the camera. "A copy of Tacitus's *Agricola,* which I'm sure we will all agree is a reasonable source."

Turning to a marked page, he began reading. "'This necklace, or torc as it is known among the Britons, was fashioned of the most unusual metal, unlike any other I have seen in all my years. It gleamed in the darkness, as if lit by an internal fire, and in the light it reflected the many hues of the rainbow. It was neither gold nor silver, copper nor bronze, iron nor cold hard steel, but something new and different under the sun. Three bands it was made of, twisted about one another like the coils of a snake, though no wider than a man's first two fingers at its thickest point.'"

Shaw snapped the book closed and looked at the group with a triumphant smile. "Given what we've seen today, I'd say that's pretty conclusive, wouldn't you?"

Roux caught Shaw's attention with a quick lift of his finger. "You have the artifact in hand?" he asked.

Shaw lied without missing a beat, the smile still plastered on his face. "Of course," he said. "It is being packed up for transport to my offices as we speak."

The Frenchman looked skeptical, but sat back as if satisfied enough by the answer.

"Bidding will commence within the next forty-eight hours through the usual methods, with a minimum starting bid of ten million dollars. You will be notified via cell phone five minutes before the auction begins and bids will be accepted for just seventy-two hours."

Shaw looked at each of them in turn, trying to gauge their reactions, to figure out just who would bid and who would not. Helmut was listening to someone offscreen, so Shaw took that as a lack of interest in this particular piece, but he was pretty sure that both Brennan and Kincade were in. Brennan for sure, he thought. Roux, on the other hand, was as inscrutable as always.

It didn't really matter, though. The auction was just

a front to raise some extra cash for the final phase of his plan. He had no intention of turning over the torc; if the legends were right, it would be far more useful to the Red Hand Defenders and his ultimate cause if it remained in his possession. By the time the winning bidder realized that he, or she, had been had, he'd be long gone with both the money and the torc. Shortly after that, England, and the world itself, would have far more pressing issues to concern themselves with.

After reminding them that they'd only have seventy-two hours to cast their bids once the auction began, Shaw wrapped things up and ended the call, a smile of satisfaction on his face.

WITH THE CLICK of his mouse, Roux ended the video-conferencing session, but left the tunneling program he'd activated while in the middle of the call running in the background. That particular piece of software had cost him a small fortune, but it had been worth every penny he'd spent on it so far. By creating a virtual private network between the two computers via the videoconferencing link, it turned the other computer's microphone into a two-way listening device. The connection would be severed when Shaw turned off his monitor, but until then, Roux was privy to everything being said inside Shaw's London office.

He'd first begun spying on Shaw to get a leg up on the various artifacts and items of interest that he uncovered. The man was a cretin, no doubt about it, but he had an uncanny sense for locating some truly unique treasures and Roux wasn't shy about using that to his advantage. Lately, however, he'd begun to suspect that Shaw was involved in something darker than illegal artifact smuggling. There was something there, just beneath

the surface, like a shark in blood-infested waters, and
Roux was determined to expose it to the light.

Hence, the eavesdropping worm.

So far, though, it had yielded little in the way of
worthwhile results. He'd caught a few snatches of conversation here and there, but nothing that helped him
narrow down what Shaw's overall plans were or the true
nature of whatever it was he was involved in. The minute
Shaw shut down his monitor, the bug went inactive, so
its use was by nature limited.

Today was one of those days. Roux could hear Shaw
shuffling things around on his desk, heard the snap of
a briefcase lid closing down and then nothing more as
the monitor was switched off on the other side.

But after living through the centuries, Roux had
learned to be patient. Shaw would let something slip
one of these days, and when that happened Roux would
be ready for it.

7

While Craig and Paolo got back to work the next morning excavating Big Red from the midst of the block of peat they'd cut from the bog, Annja turned her attention to the necklace that she'd removed from around the warrior's neck the night before. The artifact had been soaking in a chemical bath overnight and she went directly to it after breakfast, removing it from the solution and washing it under a gentle flow of cold water. Slowly, bit by bit, the dirt, silt and hardened peat that had encrusted it began to fall away, revealing the artifact to the light of day for the first time in almost two thousand years.

It *was* a torc; she'd been right about that. The braided strands of metal were easy to see now that the gunk had been cleared away. What struck her as strange, however, was the fact that this one hadn't been fashioned from gold, as almost every other one she'd ever seen had. Rather, this one was made from some kind of darker metal that threw off a scintillating array of colors when the light was shined on it just so. She'd thought it might be iron at first, but closer examination revealed that it was much too refined for that.

Perhaps a combination of various metals?

There really was no way to tell until they had a chance to get a sample of it into a gas spectrometer to analyze the component elements. And that wouldn't happen until they got the necklace back to Craig's lab at Oxford. For now, she'd just have to wonder.

Annja didn't know all that much about torcs; Iron Age civilizations hadn't ever really been her specialty. That was one of the reasons she was so excited to be taking part in this excavation. The chance to break ground, literally, on a new site coupled with the opportunity to learn more about a period of history she wasn't all that familiar with was like winning the lottery for her. She did know that, in general, the wearing of a torc was usually a sign of nobility or high social status. The time and cost in creating them almost made it so by default. That fit with the events she'd witnessed, if she could call it that, in her dream from the other night. Big Red had clearly been a warrior of some renown; otherwise, they never would have had such an elaborate burial ceremony. But exactly who he was or why he'd been honored in such a fashion might never be known. It was up to Annja and the rest of the team to try to answer those questions, and others like them, as they worked with the body and the artifacts that had been buried with it.

As the cleaning continued, Annja noticed that each end of the torc was adorned with a small sculpture in the shape of an eagle's head. The ornaments were made from a hard white substance, perhaps bone or even ivory, and it looked as if the beaks once fit together in a certain way to form a clasp that kept the torc secured around the wearer's neck. Annja marveled at the design; it was quite ingenious.

They broke reluctantly for lunch and were back at it again within the hour. More artifacts were turning up as Craig and Paolo continued the slow but steady process of freeing Big Red's earthly remains from the peat that surrounded them. A beaded necklace was first, followed by a pair of chain-mail gauntlets and an assortment of coins, their faces blackened from the tannic acid of the bog. As each one was unearthed, they were passed over to Annja for cataloging and cleaning.

Throughout it all, Craig and Paolo shared with Annja stories of prior digs they'd been on and she, in turn, told them about some of the remote places and legends the cable show had sent her to investigate. It was a companionable afternoon and Annja thoroughly enjoyed herself.

Late in the day they heard several shouts coming from the center of camp. The occasional raised voice was common in camp—friends shouting after friends, that kind of thing—but this went on for several minutes, which was unusual and caught their attention.

Craig frowned, then got up from his stool, setting the tools he'd been working with down on the table in front of him. "What's the heck's going on out there?" he said, though it was clear he wasn't expecting an answer from either Paolo or Annja.

He crossed the tent and disappeared through the flap, apparently intent on finding out. Paolo followed him a moment later.

Annja ignored the interruption and kept working, at least for a few minutes. But when the others didn't return, she began to get worried. The sense that something was seriously wrong stole over her, like a chill wind blowing through an open door, and she shivered in response. The shouting had stopped, but the silence that had replaced it only made her more concerned.

Something was clearly wrong.

She could feel it in her bones, like that sense of unease just before a sharp summer storm.

Annja stepped away from the worktable, intending to go and see what was happening for herself, when her gaze fell upon the torc. Something told her that leaving it behind would be asking for trouble, so she snatched it up and slipped it into her pocket before leaving the tent. On any other day she would have been appalled to treat an artifact so cavalierly, but she was somehow convinced that it was the right thing to do.

She could always put it back afterward, if it turned out to be nothing.

She drew back the flap of the tent, intending to step outside, but stopped short when a man with a pistol in hand stepped into view, leading two of the dig workers forward at gunpoint. They were headed for the center of camp, just as Craig and Paolo had done, and it didn't take a rocket scientist to figure out that there was probably more than one of the intruders in camp at that very moment. That realization kept her from immediately going to her coworkers aid; she didn't want to draw attention to herself until she knew exactly what was going on.

She waited for them to move out of sight, then slipped out and looked around. There didn't seem to be anyone else about. Even if she hadn't seen the gunman, that in itself would have been unusual. People were always moving about the camp. Now that she was outside and the tent walls were no longer acting as a sound baffle, she could hear several angry voices coming from the center of the camp. She cautiously made her way in that direction, slipping in and out between the tents rather than walking openly down the main path. As she drew closer to the center of camp, she crouched down beside one of the tents and peered around the corner.

From where she crouched she could see that most of the dig team had been herded into the open area in front of the mess tent. Craig stood alone in front of the group, facing a bearded man in dark fatigues who was pointing a pistol at Craig's head. Behind the newcomer were several more men, all dressed the same way and all holding firearms of their own, pointing them indiscriminately at the rest of the dig team. Annja recognized the guns as MP-5s, the stubby machine pistols that in recent years had become the weapons of choice for more than a few special-operations units across the world. They were effective little things, capable of firing eight hundred rounds per minute on full auto.

If the armed men opened fire, the archaeologists would be cut down in seconds.

Craig glared at the men in front of him.

"What do you want?" he asked.

The leader looked past Craig as if he didn't matter and addressed his words to the rest of the dig team huddled behind him. "I'm looking for a necklace. A black one. Surrender it now and there won't be any trouble."

Annja couldn't believe what she was hearing. How did they know about the torc? Craig hadn't even reported it to the trustees from Oxford overseeing the dig yet, never mind to anyone else.

Craig stepped forward, causing the gunman to turn his attention back to him rather than the others.

"I don't know what anyone has told you, but we haven't uncovered anything of value here. There's no gold. No treasure. Certainly nothing to make you rich."

The man laughed. "I want the torc," he said. "We can do it the easy way or we can do it the hard way. I don't really care. Now where is it?"

There was a look in the gunman's eyes that Annja didn't like. Almost as if he was eager for a confrontation.

Tell him, Craig, Annja thought. Tell him what he wants to know.

"I don't know what you're talking about," Craig replied.

The man shrugged. "That's too bad," he said.

Then he pulled the trigger.

The shot took Craig in the forehead, knocking him over backward to the ground. He was dead before the sound of the gunshot had finished echoing over the campsite.

Silence fell as the rest of the dig team stared in stunned horror at the body in front of them.

The gunman seemed to drink in their fear and terror like a fine wine. A slow smile spilled across his face as he watched them stare at the dead body in front of them and then, almost casually, he said, "Okay. Now that we've established that I'm not screwing around, I'll ask again. Where is the torc?"

The need to charge out and avenge her friend screamed through Annja's bones, but she fought the urge back down, knowing that to do so right now would be tantamount to suicide. Running out into the open and confronting the mercenary leader—for that is what she guessed them to be, mercenaries—would only get her killed. That would serve no one, least of all the people she needed to help. If she was going to get the rest of the team out of this alive, the next few minutes were crucial. She would need all her wits about her if she was going to succeed.

She slipped slowly backward until she was out of sight behind the nearest tent and then reached into the otherwhere, summoning her sword to hand. It slid smoothly into existence, appearing with the speed of thought, fully formed and ready for use, the hilt fitting her palm as if it had been made for her and her alone.

Sometimes she even thought that it had.

Her life hadn't been the same since that fateful day when she'd brought the broken, scattered pieces of the sword together again for the first time since their original owner, Joan of Arc, had been burned at the stake centuries earlier. The sword had miraculously reformed in a flash of power right before her very eyes and, in some strange way she still didn't quite understand, had chosen her to be its next bearer.

The role came with its own unique set of responsibilities, protecting the innocent seemingly first and foremost among them. Her own innate sense of justice seemed amplified when she carried the sword and she'd found herself forced into any number of situations that others would have simply walked away from as a result. Numbers didn't matter, nor did the odds, only that she acted whenever possible to defend those who couldn't defend themselves.

Like now.

Craig's death made the intentions of the intruders quite clear. There was no way they were going to let the other dig workers live after witnessing Craig being killed in cold blood. That meant it was up to Annja to get them out of this alive.

Despite knowing that they would never get there in

time, Annja pulled out her BlackBerry with her free hand and placed an emergency call to the regional police. She told the sergeant who answered her name and that the archaeological dig just north of Arkholme was under attack by armed insurgents. When he began to ask questions she hung up. She didn't have time to sit there and chat with him; people's lives hung in the balance.

As she slipped the phone back into her pocket, her fingers touched the torc. Something told her that it wouldn't be safe there; if she was caught, her captors would find it in seconds. She took it out of her pocket and slipped it inside her sports bra instead. That way, at least it would pass a casual search.

Then she took a moment to consider her next move.

Clearly she couldn't take them all on at once. But if she could even up the odds a bit, she'd have a better chance of succeeding in the end.

With that in mind, she faded back into the shadows, waiting for her chance at vengeance.

8

The gunman ordered his men to herd the rest of the dig workers into the mess tent behind them, and as they began doing so, Annja slipped around behind it and found a place to crouch down out of sight near one of the windows. From this position she could see and hear most of what was going on inside the tent, while potentially being ready to do something to help if an opportunity presented herself.

The lead mercenary stood facing the group, his gun still in hand.

"Where is Professor Novick?" he asked.

No one would look at one another, for fear of giving Novick away. They had seen what had happened to Dr. Stevens; it didn't take too much imagination to figure out what was likely to happen to Paolo.

For a moment, Annja didn't see him and she began to hope that he had slipped away in the initial confusion, but it was not to be.

"I am Novick," a man said from the back of the crowd and Annja watched as Paolo stepped forward.

"You," the man said, pointing at Novick, "come with me." He turned and faced the two guards who had entered the tent with him. "If they try to escape," he said, nodding back over his shoulder at the prisoners, "kill them."

Paolo and the mercenary leader walked out of the tent, leaving the entire workforce guarded by only two men.

This was her chance.

Annja slipped over to the corner of the tent and peered around it. From where she crouched she could see other guards moving around the camp, hunting through the tents, apparently searching for the torc. She thanked her intuition for making her grab it at the last moment; at least that would keep it out of their hands for now.

If she didn't call undue attention to herself, she should be able to make it to the entrance and slip inside the tent without anyone on the outside being any wiser.

Taking a deep breath to calm herself, she released her sword back into the otherwhere and did just that.

The guards had their backs to her as she strode inside. They were having too much fun terrorizing the dig crew, particularly the female students, and Annja was able to cross most of the distance to them before one of her fellow coworkers called out her name in surprise upon seeing her approach.

"Annja!"

The guards whirled around, reaching for the guns they'd let hang free on the straps around their necks, but Annja was much too fast for them.

Her right leg was already coming up in a perfectly

executed crescent kick that caught the first guard across
the side of the head, driving him to the floor.

She didn't let that stop her, though, using the momentum of the kick to spin herself around one hundred
and eighty degrees, delivering a stunning hammer fist
to the other guard's face and then, when the blow momentarily stunned him, grabbed either side of his head
in her hands and pulled it down toward her rapidly rising
knee.

As he fell Annja was already turning back in the
other direction. She'd seen the first guard trying to get
back on his feet and she lashed out with a powerful side
kick that knocked him into unconsciousness like his
partner.

The whole thing had taken less than ten seconds.

Annja didn't give the others time to think about what
had just happened.

"Quickly, this way," she said, rushing over to the rear
wall of the tent. She snatched a knife off a nearby table
and thrust it through the canvas, ripping downward with
all her strength as she did so to create a big gash in the
fabric.

"Run for the woods and get as far away as you can,"
she said to the others.

"What about Dr. Novick?" one of the men asked.

"I'll get him. Right now you have to get as far away
from here as you possibly can. When you're free, call
the territorial police. Hurry now!"

As they began to file out one at a time into the growing darkness at the rear of the tent, Annja headed in the
opposite direction. If they were going to have any chance
of getting away, she had to create a diversion, something
to keep the gunmen occupied. And she knew just how
she was going to do it. She summoned her sword.

As she drew closer to the entrance to the tent, the flap was suddenly pulled back and Annja found herself staring down the barrel of the gun held in the lead mercenary's hand.

She didn't stop to think, didn't look where she was going or what she might land on, just reacted on instinct and threw herself to the side.

He pulled the trigger.

The bullet that should have killed her merely grazed her instead.

It was enough to save her life, but not enough to keep her conscious.

The darkness claimed her before she even hit the ground.

9

Trevor Jackson was furious.

They'd been searching the camp for over fifteen minutes and still hadn't located the necklace that he'd been sent to find. Perhaps he'd been a little too hasty in dealing with the prisoners, especially their inside guy, Novick.

The professor had led them to the tent containing the bog mummy and the artifacts that had been found alongside it, but the torc wasn't there. Novick had sputtered in surprise, putting on a good act, but Jackson hadn't believed a word he'd said. When the man wouldn't reveal the location of the necklace, Jackson had grown impatient and put a bullet through his skull, figuring he didn't need the man and that he'd simply find it himself.

Now he was starting to regret that decision.

With Novick dead, Jackson focused his attention on the other prisoners, fully expecting one of them to tell him what he wanted to know. It only took a few minutes for him to realize that there was a problem, however; they really *didn't* know anything. The majority of them had spent the day down at the dig site and had only been rounded up when he and his men had shown up and forced them back to camp at gunpoint. Those who'd been in camp all morning said the same thing Novick had—the torc should be with the rest of the artifacts in the main tent.

Jackson had never been a patient man and at that point his day's supply exhausted itself. "Get rid of them," he'd told his men, and walked out of the tent where they were holding the prisoners just as the chorus of gunfire started at his back.

Now he stood in the center of camp, weighing his options. Shaw would be expecting him to report in shortly and Jackson didn't want to do that without having the torc in hand. Shaw was a harsh taskmaster; admitting he'd failed to secure the necklace might have some unhealthy consequences. No, the best thing to do was to hold off on making the call until he had the stupid thing in hand.

That would be better for all involved.

"Sir, I think we've got a problem."

The sound of the man's voice pulled Jackson out of his reverie. He turned to find one of his men standing nearby, extending a cell phone toward him. He took it, noting as he did that it was a recent-model BlackBerry much like his own, and then glanced at the screen. The number displayed there, the last number the phone's owner had apparently dialed, was the emergency line for the regional police.

His man was right; this complicated things considerably.

Jackson checked the phone's log and noted that the

call had gone through about twenty minutes earlier. He guessed the phone belonged to the chick with the sword; the call had been right before she'd done her best to throw a wrench in his entire operation and it made sense that she'd have tried to get help before moving to stop them on her own.

He wondered what she'd said. She hadn't been on the phone very long; the call had lasted less than a minute according to the log. How much information could a person relay to another in less than a minute? Had she had time to give the police their descriptions? Had she told them what they were looking for?

He didn't know. That meant he had to treat it like a worst-case scenario and go from there, hoping that he covered all the bases.

With that in mind, he considered what he knew about the regional police force's procedures in a situation like this. Their most likely response would be to do a quick flyby, probably via helicopter, to determine the reliability of the report itself as well as to assess the situation on the ground. If the flight crew deemed it necessary, a ground team would be sent in to investigate further.

The nearest airfield was more than fifty miles away. The report would have taken time to filter up through the channels as the initial responder tried to decide if it was an actual call for help or some crazy teenagers trying to have some fun. Since the call had come in on the emergency line, the origin point would have been automatically plotted and logged on the response board. It wouldn't have taken long for the duty officer to note that the call was coming from the middle of nowhere, increasing the likelihood that it was authentic. Their inability to get the caller back on the line would have tipped the scales that much further into the "believable" column and a response team would eventually have been dispatched to check things out.

From the time of the call to the point where the response team's transportation went wheels-up at the airfield would probably be fifteen, maybe twenty minutes, at most. Flight time was roughly another fifteen minutes, depending on course and airspeed, Jackson reasoned, so call it a good half hour, maybe forty minutes before they'd be over the site.

That meant they had anywhere between ten and twenty minutes left before company arrived.

Plenty of time, he thought.

He ordered several of his men to gather up the bodies of those who'd been killed when they'd first arrived and to dump them in the mess tent with the others. Three men were stationed inside the tent with orders not to open fire, no matter what happened, unless it seemed evident that they had no other choice in order to avoid discovery. Others were told to spread themselves out about the camp and to look busy. When the first response team arrived, Jackson intended to pass them off as the camp's legitimate personnel. All they had to do was convince the flyboys that everything was A-okay and they'd buy all the time they needed to finish up what they'd come here to accomplish. It was already late in the day; no one wanted to dispatch a ground team at night if they could help it and the recommendation would be to wait until morning if there wasn't clear evidence of a problem on the ground.

Jackson had every intention of showing them that things were just fine and dandy.

No sooner had they finished policing the camp and making certain the bodies were all out of sight than the sound of the approaching helicopter echoed through the trees toward them. Jackson stepped out into the open space at the center of the camp and waited for them to come into sight.

It didn't take long.

The chopper was a small, two-man unit, the kind of thing he could knock out of the sky with a few well-placed shots from the pistol he carried at his hip. He restrained himself from doing so, though, smiling up at them instead and waving with one hand as he used the other to shield his brow. They circled the camp once, then again, before coming back to hover a hundred yards or so above him.

The downdraft from their rotors was stirring up dust and starting to pull at the canvas of the nearby tents, so Jackson began waving them off, figuring that's what any good camp administrator would do.

To his surprise, it worked. The pilot gave him a thumbs-up sign and then quickly gained altitude before heading back in the direction they had come.

Leaving the inmates in charge of the asylum, Jackson thought with a grin. With the immediate threat taken care of, he and his men would have all the time they needed to dispose of the bodies and find that damned necklace.

SEVERAL HOURS LATER Jackson found himself standing in the foyer of Shaw's private estate, waiting for an audience with his employer. He'd been working for Shaw long enough to know that while he disliked incompetence, he hated those who shirked personal responsibility even more. Jackson stood a better chance of coming through this alive if he delivered his report in person, as backward as that might seem.

Surviving the next fifteen minutes was something he very much wanted to do.

Motion at the head of the stairs caught his attention and he stood straighter as he saw his employer come into sight. Shaw was still dressed; that was a good sign. That meant Jackson hadn't had the misfortune of waking him from one of his infrequent periods of sleep. In the back of his head, Jackson rated his chances of getting through this five percent higher than he had a moment before.

But only five.

"Do you have my property, Mr. Jackson?" Shaw asked as he descended the stairs.

Nothing to do to play it straight.

"No, sir."

That obviously wasn't the answer Shaw had been expecting to hear. Jackson watched as a series of expressions crossed the other man's face, everything from surprise to distaste, but thankfully outright anger wasn't yet one of them.

Knock that percentage up a few more notches.

"Pray tell me why not," Shaw said. His tone had gotten noticeably colder.

Like the good soldier that he was, Jackson laid out the events of earlier that evening in clear, concise sentences. Shaw didn't say a word until Jackson got to the part about the woman and the sword.

"She actually attacked you with a sword?" he asked, though Jackson couldn't tell if that was because Shaw didn't believe him or if he found the whole situation as weird as it sounded.

Settling on the latter, Jackson replied. "Yes, sir. While I'm no expert on medieval weaponry, if I had to hazard a guess I'd say it was an English long sword. Perhaps something they uncovered in the dig?"

Shaw waved the question aside.

"What did you do with this woman?" Shaw asked.

"I shot her, sir."

"Dead?"

Jackson thought about the way the woman's body had flopped when they'd tossed it into the bog with the rest of them. "Yes, sir." Though, now that he thought about it, he didn't know what had happened to the sword.

"A pity. Might have been an interesting conversation there. Go on."

Jackson explained how they'd tricked the team that had responded to the call for help, after which they searched both the camp and the bodies of the dead, but had been unable to find the torc anywhere. "Perhaps they packed it up and sent it back to Oxford before we arrived?" he ventured, looking for some reason, some excuse, why he was standing there empty-handed. He was not a man accustomed to failure and he particularly didn't like the way that this assignment had turned out. It was always the easy ones....

"Give me your assessment of the police response," Shaw ordered.

Jackson was prepared for the question and didn't hesitate. "They have to send a team out to the site in the morning, sir. It's standard operating procedure. They would have done so tonight if they'd had anyone reasonably close. The fact that the site is in the middle of nowhere played to our advantage."

His employer considered his assessment for a moment and then nodded. "I want you on the ground with that regional police unit when it arrives in the morning. If the torc turns up, I expect you to do what is necessary to recover it. Are we clear?"

Jackson nodded. There was a reason he knew so much about the regional police; he'd been on the active duty roster for the past seven years, ever since mustering out of the regiment. He'd expected Shaw to give that very order and had already made sure that he'd be assigned to the duty in the morning. With dawn only a few hours away, it meant even less sleep than he'd expected to get, but beggars can't be choosy. He was just happy to have escaped his employer's wrath.

"I want that torc, Mr. Jackson."

"Understood, sir."

"Good enough." Shaw turned and headed back up the stairs, but stopped before he'd gotten more than a few steps away. He turned to face Jackson once more.

"This woman, the one with the sword. Do we know who she was?"

Jackson nodded. "An American archaeologist named Annja Creed." He took a photo out of the file folder in his hands and passed it to Shaw. The picture had been taken on-site and showed Annja's still and bloody face.

The other man stared at it for a few seconds, then passed it back.

"She was a pretty thing, wasn't she?"

10

Annja came to with a start.

She was on her back, staring up into the sky. Light was just starting to peek over the horizon, which meant she been out for several hours, maybe more. Her head hurt something fierce and when she tried to move it she was nearly overwhelmed with a wave of dizziness that threatened to return her to the darkness from which she'd just come. She closed her eyes, gritted her teeth and fought it off.

The ground beneath her rolled gently, reminding her of how it felt to drift on an inflatable raft in a swimming pool, but in her pain and confusion she didn't pay it any mind.

Until she tried to sit up.

She put her hands down flat on either side, barely registering the cold, clammy feel of whatever she'd placed them upon, and tried to lever herself into an upright position. When she did, the surface she was laying on shifted dramatically beneath her, tilting to one side and dumping her face-first into a thick pool of muck.

In her surprise she panicked, flailing her limbs, feeling the muck pulling at her, dragging her down, but then her feet hit the bottom and she realized she wouldn't drown if she could just get control of herself.

She stopped thrashing, planted her feet firmly beneath her and stood up straight, bringing her head back above the surface. She gasped in a lungful of air and then breathed a sigh of relief when she realized that the muck only came to her waist.

Her relief was short-lived, however.

As she looked around, the dim morning light revealed that she was standing in the middle of an active bog, surrounded by the partially submerged corpses of her former colleagues!

What had happened the night before came rushing back—the sudden appearance of armed intruders at the dig site, the demands to surrender the torc, the deadly gunfire when the archaeologists had refused to do as requested and her own struggle to get as many of her fellow scholars to safety in spite of it all.

The last thing she remembered was staring down the barrel of a gun and her last-ditch effort to get out of the way of the bullet….

Her head throbbed, a not-so-subtle reminder that she apparently hadn't moved quickly enough.

She brought a hand up toward the side of her head, wanting to know just how bad the wound might be, but stopped herself when she saw the thick coating the peat bog had left on her limbs. There was already enough of it dripping from her head; rubbing it deeper into an open wound didn't seem like a bright idea.

Despite the early hour, it was already light enough

for Annja to see the bullet wounds and dark splotches of blood that stained the bodies around her. These weren't strangers; she recognized several of them. She recognized Paolo Novick from his curly gray hair. The bright yellow of an NAU sweatshirt identified another body as that of Sheila James, one of the graduate students who'd come overseas just last week. There was Matthew Blake and Dalton Ribisi and… She turned away, shaking off the feeling of despair that threatened to overwhelm her. Several of the dead lay with their eyes open, staring into nothingness, and Annja had the sudden urge to reach out and close them, pulling the blinds on the windows of the souls that had long since fled.

Knowing how close she'd come to her own death, and seeing the deaths of others she cared about, set a red-hot fire burning in her veins.

A careful look around showed her that the shortest route to solid ground was directly behind her, where thick tufts of grass were growing along the bank. But when she tried to move in that direction, she discovered a new problem.

Her feet had sunk into the thicker silt at the bottom of the bog and were now trapped.

Visions of being sucked down beneath the surface swam in her mind and caused her to try pulling her feet free with brute force, yanking upward first on one and then the other. Rather than loosening the bog's hold, however, all her actions managed to do was to get her feet to sink deeper.

She was stuck.

Annja opened her mouth, intending to call out, to see if there was anyone close enough to help. Surely someone else had survived the brutal attack. But then she thought better of it. While other survivors might be within earshot, so, too, might the very men who had slaughtered her friends. Calling attention to herself while she was trapped would just make her a target.

One that would be almost impossible to miss.

She was going to have to get out of this on her own.

Taking a deep breath to calm her already frayed nerves, Annja considered the situation. She knew she had to work with the bog's natural qualities rather than against them, if she hoped to get out of this alive.

She slowly began to wiggle her left foot, gently rocking it back and forth. Each time she did so it let a little more of the water within the bog slide between her foot and the thicker particles of peat that kept it trapped. Gradually she was able to loosen the bog's hold on her foot.

With one foot floating free she reached out and grabbed hold of the nearest corpse, using it to maintain her balance while she began to work on the other leg. The body was that of a blonde woman dressed in jeans and a flannel shirt, though Annja made a point of avoiding looking at her face, afraid of seeing the face of another friend. Her efforts pushed the corpse a little deeper into the bog, but it maintained enough natural buoyancy that she could still use it to support herself despite that fact that it was now mostly underwater.

After several minutes she was able to work her other foot loose enough that she could lift it when the time came.

With her feet free, she had to fight the urge to lean forward, to power through the muck with big strokes of her strong arms, for she knew that doing so was exactly the wrong thing to do and would only leave her trapped again, perhaps in an even more precarious position. She knew the surface of the bog would support her if she let it; the corpses floating around her were proof of that. With that in mind she leaned backward instead of forward, letting her head and upper back come in contact with the surface of the bog. When she felt its chill wetness lapping at her skin, she lifted her legs and spread her arms wide, allowing the bog to bear her weight.

It worked!

She floated on the surface and if she'd held still an observer wouldn't have been able to tell the difference between her and any of the other dozen corpses surrounding her.

So far, so good. Now comes the hard part, she thought.

Solid ground was only fifteen, maybe twenty feet away, but if she moved too quickly she'd sink and wind up trapped all over again.

Slow and steady wins the race, she told herself.

Using the nearest corpse as a lever, she pushed it firmly toward her feet. The act sent her own body gliding across the surface of the water, taking her a foot or two closer to the bank and what she hoped was solid ground.

Little by little, she made her way to safety.

When the water beneath her grew so shallow that she was having a hard time keeping her feet up, she rolled over and discovered that the bank was less than an arm's length away. Letting her feet down beneath her, she stood cautiously.

The bog immediately tried to tighten its grip.

This time she was ready for it. Rather than fight it, she simply let herself topple forward like a downed tree. Her upper body easily reached the bank. Sinking her fingers into the thick grass she found there, she pulled herself up onto firm ground and crawled away from the bog's edge on hands and knees.

Once she had her heart rate under control, she sat back on her haunches and thought about her next move. The sun was up now, its thin light breaking through the trees around her, and by its height she estimated that it was somewhere around 6:00 or 7:00 a.m., which meant that it had been at least that many hours since the attack had occurred. She had no idea if the killers remained at the camp or if they had fled once their job here was done, but it didn't matter either way. There were things she wanted at the camp and that was where she needed to go.

She stood and did what she could to wipe off the worst of the muck from the bog, which wasn't much. She purposely left the wound on her head alone; no sense messing with it until she had some way of cleaning it properly.

When she finished, she reached inside her sports bra and retrieved the torc from where she'd stashed it the night before. She had a bit of a bruise from where it had pressed against her tender flesh, but the torc itself was no worse for the wear. Not that she'd expected it to be; it had already survived a couple of thousand years in the bog.

Still, she was relieved that the killers hadn't found it. With it in hand, her chances of discovering what this was all about, as well as who was behind it all, went up considerably.

It also told her that the killers, whoever they'd been, made mistakes. The bodies should have been searched before being dumped into the bog. If they had been, those doing the searching hadn't been very thorough at all.

Not that she was complaining. A proper search would have shown them that she was still alive, so their poor effort had actually saved her life.

She stuffed the torc back into its hiding place and spent a few minutes searching through the tall grass at the edge of the bog until she found the trail the killers had used to get there. The added weight of the bodies they'd carried had pushed their footsteps deep into the soil and it was an easy matter to follow them back through the woods in the direction of camp.

It was cold and she was wet—not a good combination. Her first order of business was going to be dry clothes. After that she would figure out a more solid game plan. The authorities had to be notified, the bodies recovered from the bog, but before any of that happened she wanted a few minutes alone with whatever evidence the killers had left behind at the scene. It wasn't that she didn't trust the police to do their job; she did. This one just happened to be a bit more personal for her and she wasn't going to leave justice in the hands of someone who might not care as strongly as she did about seeing it served up properly.

Craig's smiling face flashed in her mind and she swore that she'd make those responsible pay for what they had done.

As the telltale flashes of color that marked the camp's tents became visible through the trees, Annja slowed down. It wouldn't do to just blunder into the middle of camp, particularly if the killers were still hanging about, so she stopped and listened instead.

Aside from the calls of a few morning birds, no other sound reached her ears. While that didn't mean the perpetrators were gone, it was certainly a good sign.

Still, it wouldn't hurt to be armed.

She reached out with her right hand and plucked her sword from the otherwhere. It flashed into existence in a heartbeat as it always did and just having it in hand was reassuring.

Cautiously she continued forward.

11

The camp had been ransacked. Several of the tents had been torn down entirely, while the contents of the others were strewn about, left to lie where they had fallen during what Annja assumed was the search for the torc.

She slipped from one piece of cover to another for the first several minutes, leery of suddenly running into any of the men she'd encountered the night before, but eventually she realized that the camp was deserted and that let her move about more freely in the open.

The killers, whoever they had been, had fled.

Her free hand touched the torc through her shirt. What was so important about it that someone would kill to possess it? she wondered.

The entire attack just didn't make sense. While she knew there was a burgeoning trade in black-market artifacts, she wouldn't expect a piece like the one she currently carried to be of particular interest. They'd only dug it up yesterday, for heaven's sake!

She knew the only way information could have gotten out about the torc was for someone on the dig team itself to have relayed word of the find to the outside world.

Which meant one of the people she'd been working with for the past two days was responsible for the deaths of more than thirty others.

It wasn't a comfortable thought. Realizing how close she'd come to dying sent a shiver down her back.

It also put a fire in her belly. She would find out who was responsible for this and bring them to justice, no matter what.

Annja came to her own tent and discovered, not surprisingly, that it hadn't escaped the attention of the intruders. She picked up her clothes from where they'd been scattered about and pieced together an outfit of clean jeans and a fresh T-shirt. An oversize Henley would help ward off the cold. Annja stripped, leaving her muck-covered clothes in a sodden heap on the floor of the tent. Goose bumps rose across her body as the chill morning air caressed her naked flesh and she didn't waste any time pulling on her new set of clothes. Her boots were unfortunately ruined, but some rummaging around in the other tents turned up a spare pair that was only a size bigger than her own. An extra pair of socks helped overcome the difference; it wasn't perfect, but it would do for the time being.

Feeling slightly better, Annja turned her attention to the rest of her belongings. Her iPod and BlackBerry were gone, more than likely snagged by one of the intruders, but she found her wallet, camera and laptop computer tossed into a corner. The computer screen had been smashed, what was left of it still bearing the muddy impression of the boot that had done the deed, but a few minutes with a screwdriver she scrounged from elsewhere allowed her to recover the hard drive that contained all her notes from the work they had done to date. Even better, the camera looked undamaged. That was the first good news she'd had all day; with the data on the drive and the torc in hand, she had a much better chance of identifying it.

Once she did that, she could narrow the list of individuals who might have been interested enough in it to kill to possess it.

Annja searched through the other tents, looking for a working cell phone, but came up empty. She briefly considered going back and searching the bodies of the dead for one, but then decided against doing so. Even if she got lucky enough to find one, it would probably be too waterlogged to operate properly, anyway. And the thought of pawing the bodies of those she'd been working next to only hours before made her wince with distaste. They deserved better than that and she'd see to it that something was done as soon as she got out of here.

She considered her options. Without a working cell phone, she couldn't call in help from the authorities. Nor was anyone expected to arrive at camp that day, which meant the assault could go unnoticed for days unless she got back to civilization and reported it. To do that, she needed to hike back to the staging area where she'd left her rental car.

It wasn't a bad hike, she knew, but it would get hot soon, so she looked around until she found a shoulder pack and a few bottles of water to go inside.

She stepped out of the tent she'd been rummaging through and that's when a sound caught her attention. It was faint at first, just a distant thrumming, but it slowly grew louder as it drew close to the camp. It only took Annja a few seconds to recognize the sound of an approaching helicopter.

She turned in a slow circle, trying to pinpoint the sound, or, even better, get a look at the approaching aircraft. She couldn't see it yet, but she knew it wouldn't be long. When it arrived, she had to be ready. If she could flag it down she could get the authorities on-site quickly before the elements had a chance to destroy too much of the evidence.

She glanced around, looking through the personal belongings scattered about the camp until she spied a bright red sweatshirt, then ran over and picked it up. It should be colorful enough to catch the attention of anyone looking her way, she thought.

The sound was loud now, filling the air with the steady rhythm as the rotors beat their way closer, and she moved into the center of the camp, only a few steps away from the spot where Craig had died. His blood had seeped into the ground, leaving a dark stain, and seeing it, Annja again vowed that she would make those responsible pay for his death.

She could see the helicopter now, moving in her general direction. Most of the body was black, with the section directly under the rotors painted a bright yellow, a color scheme she recognized as belonging to local law enforcement. She began waving her arms over her head, the red sweatshirt held aloft in one hand, doing what she could to attract the pilot's attention.

But as the aircraft drew closer, her waving hands faltered and then stopped. She had that feeling again, that sense that something was terribly wrong, and ever since taking up the sword she'd learned to listen to such things. Doing so had saved her life more times than she could count.

The helicopter altered course slightly, now headed directly toward the camp, and that sense of impending disaster rose up inside her like a wave about to break.

She had to get out of sight and she had to do it now!

Annja didn't stop to think, didn't consider that she might be turning her back on the only help for miles around. Instead, she turned and ran between the nearest two tents, getting out of sight as quickly as possible.

Once behind the tent she'd been standing in front of, she circled around to her left, dashing between several others until she found a place where she could watch the helicopter without being in the open.

The helicopter began its descent, the rotors pounding the air and whipping up a heavy breeze that tossed clothing and camp supplies about indiscriminately. Annja was forced to shield her eyes from the dust and dirt kicked up in its wake.

The aircraft settled to the ground in the center of the camp. Doors on both sides were thrown open and men wearing the uniforms of the regional police force climbed out.

For a moment, Annja thought everything was going to be all right. That feeling of foreboding must have been for something else. The police were here; she could breathe a sigh of relief and turn the investigation over to the professionals for the time being, at least until she'd had a chance to rest and get a better understanding just why someone would kill to possess the torc.

But as she moved to leave her hiding place, to call out to the police officers fanning out through the camp, her gaze happened to fall on one of the men at the back of the pack.

The last time she'd seen him, he'd just tried to put a bullet in her skull.

He was dressed just like one of the regional police officers, and from the easy way that he interacted with the rest of them, it was clear he wasn't a stranger.

What on earth was going on?

One thing was certain: any hope of getting help from these men was gone. With the killer an accepted member of their group, she couldn't trust that they wouldn't shoot her on sight.

Quickly and quietly she eased her way back from the tents and then slipped into the trees behind them, headed deeper into the woods.

12

When she felt she was far enough into the tree line to not give away her position, Annja picked up her pace, headed on a course that would take her directly away from the camp on the straightest line possible. She knew the police would be fanning out, looking for both the perpetrators and for any survivors, and right now she couldn't afford to be detained as either.

Once she was several hundred yards away from the camp, she stopped and took a moment to think about her next move. The staging area was out of the question; the cops would be all over the vehicles there in short order, if they weren't already. If she couldn't approach the cops and it was too risky to try and reach her rental car at the staging area, it seemed she had no choice but to travel overland until she found some alternate means of transport.

Squatting on her heels, Annja drew a quick map in the dirt in an effort to help her get her bearings. If the camp was here, she thought, and the staging area here, then the road must go like this. She drew a line in the dirt that traveled parallel to the camp for a short distance before angling sharply away toward the southeast. There was only one major road in these parts and that was it, if she was remembering things correctly. That meant if she turned south at this point, she should eventually run into it. She wasn't sure exactly where she would cross it, but cross it she would, if she just kept going south.

"All right then, south it is," she said.

With her pack over her shoulder, she started walking again.

It was hard going. The terrain was a mix of woods and marshland, which wasn't the best possible choice. She had a healthy respect for the danger the marshy bogs represented, given what she'd recently gone through, and so she was forced several times to change direction, skirting the edges of the bogs rather than attempting to find a path through them. Each time she cleared them she headed south once more, but after the first few hours it was clear she'd underestimated the task ahead of her.

By midday the sun was beating down and Annja had gone through the two bottles of water she'd snatched on her way out of the camp.

If she had to do this for much longer, dehydration was going to start being a problem.

The marshlands gave way to wooded hill country, which had its good and bad points. She was out of the sun more often than not, and no longer had to take these wide looping detours to avoid the bogs, but the constant hike up and down the hills began to wear on her.

As she crested another hill, the trees fell away before

her at the top and she found herself looking down a long grassy slope.

There, below her, was the road.

"About time," she said, with not a little impatience. She'd known it would be a long hike, she just hadn't expected it to take several hours. She was hot, tired, thirsty and more than a bit irritated. She almost felt sorry for whomever it was who eventually stopped to give her a ride.

Annja descended the hill and, once on the roadway itself, took a moment to brush the dust and leaves out of her clothing and hair. It was going to be difficult enough to get someone to stop out in the middle of nowhere; she didn't want to make it any harder by looking like she'd just spent the afternoon rolling around in the woods.

Satisfied her appearance was as good as it was going to get, she set off walking along the shoulder, hoping it wouldn't be long before someone came along to give her a lift.

The first two cars, both driven by women, passed her without slowing despite her efforts to flag them down. Stopping to help a fellow female stranded by herself on the side of the road was too much effort apparently. As they roared on past, their gazes averted so they could pretend to themselves they hadn't seen her, Annja took the time to memorize their license plates. If she ran into them again up the road, she wanted to be sure she could identify them properly, if only to show her appreciation for their kindness to a stranger. And just to show that she was a better person than they were, she waved cheerfully after them, laughing all the while. It felt good to blow off a little steam, even if it was over something as stupid as a stranger's failure to give her a ride.

Heaven knew she had enough to worry about.

She'd been on the road for almost an hour when she heard another car in the distance behind her. Her two previous encounters hadn't gone very well, so this time around she was prepared to try something different. As the sound of the engine drew closer, Annja hurriedly stripped off the long-sleeved Henley she wore to expose the thinner T-shirt beneath and stuffed the outer shirt into her pack. She gathered the bottom of the T-shirt in her hands and tied it into a quick knot, which had the dual result of exposing a bit of her tanned midriff while at the same time pulling the fabric of the shirt tight across her breasts. Stuffing the ball cap she wore in the back pocket of her jeans, she let her long hair fall down her back in a gleaming wave, fluffing it up a bit with her fingers as she did so.

At this point, her ears were telling her that the car was less than a hundred yards away.

Turning to face the oncoming traffic, she cocked one hip toward the road, stuck out her thumb and put a big smile on her face.

Please let it be a man, she thought, knowing she'd feel a bit ridiculous dressed like this if it was a woman who stopped for her.

The car was a beat-up old four-door Renault, blue-gray in color, and thankfully there was a man behind the wheel.

He was already slowing the vehicle as he got closer to her and so she was able to get a good look at him as he drifted past to bring the car to a stop just a few yards farther up the road from where she stood. He looked to be in his early thirties, with thick blond hair that didn't seem to want to stay where he put it and a tentative smile on his face that told her stopping for a hitchhiker, and a pretty one at that, was outside his usual behavior.

She hustled over and bent down to look in through the open passenger window.

"Car trouble?" he asked.

Wanting to avoid having to explain why he hadn't passed her car along the way, she answered, "Boyfriend trouble. The SOB dumped me on the side of the road three miles back."

He said something in reply, but Annja didn't really hear it, as she was staring at the Roman collar about his throat and taking in the uniformlike black shirt and pants he was wearing.

"You're a priest?" she said, surprised, though she didn't quite know why. For a second she even felt guilty about the thing with the T-shirt, but, then again, it had worked, hadn't it?

"Is that a problem for you?" he asked, genuinely concerned, and Annja realized she'd inadvertently offended him.

"Not at all," she said with a smile. "It's a relief, in fact. You can never be too careful nowadays."

He nodded sagely and Annja fought the urge to laugh.

"Can I give you a ride?" he asked.

Annja opened the door and slid into the passenger seat. "A ride would be great."

As she got into the car, another vehicle came roaring around the corner ahead of them, headed in the other direction, back the way she had come. It was a late-model Mercedes, black with silver trim, and Annja looked up to watch it go past. The windows were all tinted, so she couldn't see inside it, but she felt a chill pass over her as it sped by. In that moment she was thankful that she hadn't been on the road alone when the vehicle had appeared.

"Well, coming or aren't you?" her Good Samaritan called, breaking her reverie.

Annja laughed and got inside the car, the Mercedes already forgotten.

Concerned that the men who were hunting her might somehow catch up with them, Annja introduced herself as Amy, not wanting to reveal her real name. The less the good father knows, the better, she thought.

He, in turn, told her his name was Gary—Father Gary Anderson, to be exact—and he was a newly ordained Catholic priest working out of the Church of St. Ignatius, a small parish about twenty miles outside of London. He was returning from a clerical conference and was happy to take her to the parish rectory, where she could call a cab to take her the rest of the way into the city.

Gary was pleasant company and Annja found herself relaxing as he told her funny stories about the parishioners he'd met in his first few months at the church.

He must have been eager for company, for he barely let her get a word in edgewise, and she soon found herself listening with half an ear. That proved to be fortuitous, for when the growl of a heavy engine came roaring up behind them, Annja noticed. She looked back just in time to see the Mercedes they'd passed twenty minutes earlier closing on them rapidly.

It didn't look like the driver had any intention of stopping.

13

"Uh-oh," Annja said.

Gary glanced over in her direction. "Something wrong?" he asked.

Annja nodded. "You might want to hold on," she said as she braced herself against the dashboard with both arms.

A look of confusion crossed his face. "What's wrong?" he asked, easing up on the gas as the realization that there was a problem filtered into his consciousness.

Annja risked a quick look back and saw that the Mercedes was just a few feet off their bumper and closing quickly. It didn't take a genius to figure out that whoever they were, they were probably with the same group that had attacked the dig site. She didn't know how they'd known to look for her on the road—if, in fact, that was what they were doing—but at the moment the how really didn't matter all that much; they had and now she had to deal with it.

"Don't slow down!" she shouted at Gary. "Go faster!"

But her sudden exclamation had the opposite effect, startling him, and as a result his foot slipped even farther off the gas.

The driver of the Mercedes chose that moment to nurse his own engine and the big black automobile leaped forward and slammed into the back of the Renault, sending it skidding across the road as Gary fought to control the wheel.

"What the hell?" The young pastor cried out, glancing backward at the behemoth closing in again from behind. From the fear that was now plain on his face, Annja guessed that he'd never been involved in a car accident in his life, never mind a high-speed chase where the other guy's only interest was in driving you off the road.

Welcome to my life, she thought.

She reached over and shoved her hand down on his knee, forcing his foot down on the accelerator.

"I said faster!" she shouted.

This time he seemed to understand the urgency in her request and when she took her hand away his foot stayed right where it was, pinning the gas pedal to the floor.

The Renault bucked and jerked beneath them, not used to having so much demand put on its aging engine.

"What do they want?" he asked, glancing back and forth between her and the rearview mirror. His voice still had a slight tremor to it but Annja was pleased to see him getting his wits back about him.

Maybe there was hope for him yet.

"At a guess, I'd say they want to run us off the road,"

Annja said calmly, her gaze flitting around the inside of the car, looking for something she could use as a weapon. Mystical swords were all well and good, but they just weren't all that useful when you were tearing down a country road at sixty miles an hour trying to get away from the killer Mercedes behind you. It wasn't like she could stop and challenge them to a sword fight.

"Why would they want to do that?" Gary asked, and then before she had time to answer, followed that with a quick, "Hold on!" as he jerked the wheel to the right, avoiding the sudden rush by the vehicle behind them as it tried again to ram the back of their car.

Rather than attempting to explain the past twenty-four hours to him, Annja simply answered, "I have no idea."

He didn't believe her; that much was obvious. But he was too busy steering the car back and forth across the road to bother arguing about it, and for that Annja was grateful. It let her concentrate on how they were going to get out of this mess.

She opened the glove box in front of her and began digging around in it.

"What are you doing?"

"Looking for a gun," she answered.

"I'm a priest, for heaven's sake!" Gary said. "Do I look like the kind of guy who carries a gun?"

He had a point there.

Giving up on the glove box, she turned and glanced into the backseat. Her gaze fell on the two large cardboard boxes on the floor behind them.

"What's in the boxes?" she asked, hoping for something useful. A rocket launcher would be really nice right about now, she thought, knowing it was unrealistic but hopeful nonetheless.

"Hymnals!" he said.

Oh, for heaven's…

She suddenly had an idea.

Hymnals might just do the trick, after all, she realized.

She scrambled between the seats and fell into the back, being sure to keep below the level of the rear window as she did so. She didn't want to give their pursuers any idea of what was coming.

Annja looked inside the nearest of the boxes and found it filled with dozens of thick, leather-bound volumes.

These will do nicely, she thought.

She pulled a few of them into her lap and then turned around, positioning herself behind the driver's seat but still staying out of sight of the men in the other car.

"What are you doing?" Gary shouted.

"Giving them something else to think about," she answered.

She moved closer to the open window and watched as the Mercedes roared up behind them again, making another run at them. Their rear bumper was hanging off the vehicle now, the result of the past few times the two cars had collided. It dragged behind them, sending up a mass of sparks each time it bounced off the pavement, and from where she sat Annja could see that their trunk was half the size it used to be, crushed inward from the impact with the other car.

"Hold it steady and let them get close," she shouted above the window.

"Are you nuts?" he shouted back, but did as he was told, trusting her obvious command of the situation.

She waited, letting the Mercedes get closer.

Fifteen feet.

Ten.

Five feet.

As the other car surged forward, closing the gap between them, Annja suddenly sat up and whipped her arm out the window in a classic sidearm throw, sending the heavy leather hymnal in her hand flying directly at the windshield of the Mercedes.

The driver reacted just the way you'd expect anyone to react when something came flying at them at speeds in excess of fifty miles an hour; he ducked and jerked the wheel to the side. The book struck the center of the windshield, starring the glass there rather than directly in front of the driver, but it still had the desired effect. The Mercedes went careering across the road as the driver fought to regain control, the outer wheels actually leaving the pavement and bouncing through the scrub brush at the side of the road.

"Go, Amy!" Gary cried, pumping his fist in the air, but his joy was short-lived as the other car pulled back onto the road and raced up behind them again.

This time Annja didn't wait for them to get close but began flinging hymnals out the window as fast as she could. The big car swerved to avoid the first few and then hung back far enough that Annja couldn't reach them with the next.

The whole time Gary kept the pedal to the metal and raced down the center of the road without saying a word. Annja figured he was either praying that they didn't encounter another car coming the other way or cursing his luck for stopping for her in the first place.

Maybe even a little of both.

They drove another mile down the road before the men in the Mercedes decided to change the game. Annja was sitting up in the back, a hymnal in hand, ready to throw it, and so she had a clear view when the man in the passenger seat stuck his arm out of the window and pointed a gun at them.

"Oh, hell," Annja said softly. She'd known it was coming and was frankly surprised they hadn't forced the issue before now. After all, they'd killed more than twenty people so far to get their hands on the torc she carried. What were two more?

Two too many, Annja thought to herself, that's what.

"They're about to start shooting at us!" she shouted to Gary, ducking as she did so. As if in punctuation, her words were immediately followed by the crack of a shot and the crash of breaking glass. When she looked up again, the rear window had a hole in it.

Gary started swerving the car back and forth across the road, praying all the while. "Protect us Lord! Send Your angels to surround us! Lend us Your mercy and love…."

The gunman fired again, missing this time, but not by much. Annja knew it was just a matter of time before one of those bullets struck either her or Gary, and if that happened, it was all over for both of them.

Gary kept swerving.

Think, Annja! Think!

The gunman's third shot struck the rear of the car and the trunk suddenly flew open, hiding them from the driver's view for a moment.

There was no way they could outrun them; the Renault wasn't in the same class as the Mercedes and frankly never had been, even on the day it rolled off the assembly line. Nor could they keep doing what they'd been doing. Either the Mercedes would eventually force them off the road or one of the gunman's shots would finally hit something valuable.

Like Gary and me.

It seemed to Annja that their only choice was to bring the attack to the enemy. "Always mystify, mislead or surprise the enemy," the great tactician Sun Tzu had said in *The Art of War,* and Annja always tried to listen to her betters.

The trick was going to be convincing Gary of the necessity.

The trunk slammed closed, startling them both, and no sooner had it done so that a gunman opened up again, peppering the rear of the vehicle with several well-placed shots. Two of them struck the rear window, which finally proved to be too much for the old safety glass and it fell away behind them in one big cascading sheet.

The Mercedes crushed it beneath its tires as it continued after them.

"We've got to do something!" Gary shouted to her, and Annja took that as her cue.

She laid out her plan as quickly she could.

"Can't we just pull over and give them whatever it is they want?" he asked, not liking the sound of her idea at all. But when she explained that what they wanted was most likely their lives at this point, he saw the logic of her proposition.

They'd gone another half mile down the road and been narrowly missed by another flurry of shots before they were ready. Annja watched the other vehicle closely, knowing that the success of their plan depended heavily on the timing.

At her suggestion Gary eased up on the gas slightly, not enough to be obvious but just enough to let the Mercedes close the gap between them a little bit.

She watched.

And waited.

When the time was right…

"Now!" she shouted.

Gary stood heavily on the brakes.

Realizing at the last second what was going on, the driver of the Mercedes tried to do the same, but by then it was too late. The two cars slammed into each other, the big front grille of the Mercedes burying itself in the rear of the Renault so deeply that it was if the two vehicles had been fused together.

Having known it was coming, Annja and Gary had braced for the impact, but the two men in the front seat of the Mercedes had not. No sooner had they been thrown forward by the impact of the collision than they were bouncing back in the other direction as the dual air bags exploded in their faces.

For a moment they were both dazed by the impact and Annja took full advantage of the opportunity. The second the cars had stopped moving she was in motion, climbing through the open space of the rear window of the Renault and charging across the crumpled steel that had once been the trunk.

The air bags were already deflating by the time her foot hit the hood of the Mercedes and she saw the eyes of the man in the passenger seat go wide as he watched her coming toward them.

His right arm started to come up from where it was hidden below the dash.

That's the hand with the gun in it, a voice in the back of her mind told her, but it needn't have bothered; she was already prepared to deal with that very threat.

As she'd rushed across the hood of the Mercedes, she'd called her sword from the otherwhere. It blinked into existence inside of a heartbeat, and she thrust her arm forward just as the gunman attempted to bring his weapon to bear.

The sword passed through the shattered glass of the Mercedes's windshield like it wasn't even there, impaling the man on the other side through the center of his chest.

Life faded from his eyes almost immediately and Annja felt no remorse as she watched him go. He'd been trying to kill her, after all, and she was a big believer in doing unto others as they would do unto you.

As she pulled her sword free and turned to face the driver, she discovered that the crash had already done her work for her. The other man's head hung on his chest at an odd angle—the impact, or possibly the air bag, having snapped his neck.

14

"Where on earth did you get a sword?" Gary asked from behind her.

Annja turned, wondering how she was going to explain this. Something must have shown on her face, though, some vestige of the hardness that came over her during combat, for Gary took one look at her and backed away quickly, his hands raised in front of him as if to ward off a danger of some kind.

"You know what, I don't even want to know," he said. "I don't know who you are, or what you're really doing here, and right now I think that's for the best. I'm going to chalk it up to the Lord working in mysterious ways and leave it at that."

Annja could only stand there, mouth open in shock, as the young priest climbed back behind the wheel of his battered old Renault, threw it into drive and, with a wrenching shriek of torn and twisted steel, broke free of the other vehicle and drive off down the street as fast as the remains of his car would allow.

It was only after he was out of sight that it occurred to her that she could have claimed to be an angel of vengeance, complete with a holy sword, and he probably would have believed her.

She'd have to file that excuse away for next time.

Annja released the sword, letting it disappear back into the otherwhere. They hadn't seen another car in more than an hour but that didn't mean that one wasn't on its way. It would be just her luck to have the local constabulary come driving along at this point, catching her in the act, so to speak, so she didn't waste any time.

She dragged the bodies out of the car and laid them on the side of the road, hidden from immediate view by the bulk of the Mercedes itself. A quick check of their pockets didn't turn up any identification—not that she'd expected there to be any. The clothes were off-the-rack items with all the labels removed, which wouldn't prevent the forensics techs from identifying them but it would slow them down a bit. Clearly the two men were professionals. She found the same tattoo on each man, a red hand. The tattoo obviously meant something, but she had know idea what that could be. She assumed the driver must have been on his way to the dig site to rendezvous with the others and it was just her luck that he happened to see her as she got into the priest's car.

Both men were carrying pistols, 9 mm automatics, but Annja left them where they were. She was going to have to talk to the police at some point and she didn't want to have guns tying her to a roadside assault, never mind the deaths of two men, when she did.

A quick search of the car turned up nothing of

interest. The car was registered to a Mr. Steve Jones, which Annja knew was a fake without even having to check on it. These guys had taken the time to wipe out the obvious clues to their identities; they sure as heck weren't going to be driving around in a car registered in their own names. It was a fair guess that the license plates had been stolen from another vehicle, too. Still, she memorized the numbers, just in case.

Having found everything she thought she was going to find, Annja considered her options.

It probably wasn't going to be long before the priest decided calling the cops might be the best thing, after all—if he hadn't done so already. Given the investigation that was already under way at the dig site, she suspected they'd respond pretty quickly when he reported armed gunmen trying to run him off the road. He'd no doubt report the vehicle they'd been driving, as well.

All of which meant taking the Mercedes, if it even still ran at this point, was a pretty big risk. Still, it was a risk she was willing to take for it gave her access to transportation that could potentially put some serious distance between her and her pursuers. And right now that's what she needed most—room to figure out her next move.

She called forth her sword once more and used it to slash the air bags free of the dash, using one of them to cover the bloodstains on the passenger seat and tossing the other onto the floor of the backseat. Releasing her sword, she smeared some mud from the side of the road onto the rear license plate, stood back to give it a look and then nodded in satisfaction. It partially hid the number without looking too intentional, which was the entire idea. Sliding behind the wheel, she said a quick prayer and turned the key. The engine hissed and spat for a moment before turning over with a growl of power.

It looked like she was in business.

Before she left she rolled the bodies off the side of the road and into the ditch beside it. Eventually they'd be found, but that should buy her a little time at least.

Getting back in the car, she drove away from the scene of the attack without a backward glance.

The car sputtered and whined far more than she wanted, and it had a strong tendency to pull to the left if she wasn't paying attention, but it moved and that's all she really cared about. She pointed the car south, set the cruise control for two miles an hour over the speed limit and sat back to let the car do the rest of the work.

She almost made it, too. She was just entering the outskirts of London when the Mercedes began to buck and shake like a bull at the rodeo and she had to fight the wheel to get the vehicle over to the side of the road before it died completely.

Once it had, she was unable to get it started again. A grinding noise came from somewhere under the hood when she turned the key and it got progressively worse. Finally it let out a big screech and stopped making any sound whatsoever.

"Great," she said sourly. "Just great."

It looked like she was going to have to hitch another ride or go the rest of the way on foot.

Before getting out of the car, she used the edge of her T-shirt to wipe down the steering wheel and any of the other places she thought she might have touched since getting inside. She didn't want the police connecting her to the car or the two dead men who'd been driving it before her. She made sure to cover the door handle the same way when she opened it and got out once she was done.

Night had fallen an hour or so earlier, so Annja found herself standing on the side of the road in a run-down section of town. Traffic was minimal and after watching several cars drive past it was obvious that no one was going to be inclined to stop in this area. Maybe they would have in the bright light of day, but after dark was a different story apparently.

Still, that might work to her advantage. She'd been worried about the police finding the car, but in an area like this, the car might not be there long enough for the police to find it.

Especially if she left it unlocked with the keys in it.

She tossed the keys on the front seat, grabbed her pack out of the back and walked down the street, leaving the door open behind her, the interior light gleaming like a beacon in the night.

A few miles down the road she came to a run-down motel, the kind of place that would let her pay cash without leaving a name at the front and wouldn't say a word about the bloodstains on her shirt. Noting that the elevator was out of order, Annja deliberately took a room on the fifth floor. Without the easy access the elevator would provide, the fifth floor was high enough to discourage all but the most determined of human predators; the casual thief didn't want to deal with climbing five flights of stairs when there were easier pickings elsewhere.

She used the cash she'd taken from the driver of the Mercedes and paid for two nights in advance. When asked to sign for the room, a fit of mischievousness overcame her and she used the name of her well-endowed and wardrobe-malfunction-plagued cohost from

Chasing History's Monsters, Kristie Chatham. Imagining the look on Kristie's face when some paparazzo asked her what she'd been doing staying in a slum hotel in the north end of London nearly made her burst into laughter right there in front of the clerk and she vowed to herself that she'd leak the information the first chance she got.

Annja climbed the narrow flights of steps to her room. Once inside, she locked the door behind her and then dropped her pack on the bed. There really wasn't much to the place; a bed, a beat-up old dresser and a small nightstand were the only pieces of furniture in the room. There was a small safe set into one wall, but the scratches around the lock plate let her know just how safe it wasn't. Rather than risk putting the torc in it, she began looking for a place she could hide it for a little while. Her first thought was to tape it inside the toilet tank, but one look at it told her that opening it might require a hazmat suit and a week of detox, so that was out. She dismissed the air-conditioning vent for the simple reason that too many Hollywood movies had used it as part of their plots—it would be the first place someone looked, whether they were conscious of the association or not. Inside the ceiling tiles was out for the same reason.

Then her gaze fell on the thin piece of baseboard that ran around the perimeter of the room. A few pieces here and there were coming free from the wall and she could see a narrow space behind them.

That will have to do, she thought.

With the help of a hanger from the closet, Annja managed to pry one of the sections of baseboard free from the wall without damaging it or the nails that held it in place. Whoever had hung the baseboard on the walls had cut corners and hadn't taken them all the way to the floor but stopped instead, leaving a two inch gap between the wall and the floor, a gap just large enough to hide the torc. Once she had it in place, she replaced the baseboard and carefully pushed the nails back into place. Standing, she backed off a few steps and gave it a once-over, decided after she'd done so that the casual observer wouldn't know it was there.

Satisfied for the time being that the torc was in a safe place—or, at least, as safe as she could make it—she stripped off her clothes and took a quick shower. Under the spray of the water she took time to clean out the wound on her head, discovering as she did so that it wasn't all that bad. It had just bled a lot, as scalp wounds are wont to do. Padding naked out of the bathroom on bare feet, she picked up her clothes and returned with them to the sink, scrubbing them in cold water. A few minutes of effort got most of the bloodstains out. There were a couple of small spots here and there, but she'd didn't think they'd be noticeable. She'd buy something new the first chance she got, anyway.

Her chores done, she collapsed onto the bed, pulling the sheet up over her. Within moments sleep had claimed her for the night.

15

As Annja was falling into bed in a London hotel room, Detective Inspector Ian Beresford was arriving at the dig site outside Arkholme. The local authorities had just completed the difficult task of freeing the bodies of the deceased from the waters of the bog and transporting them back to the main camp for examination. The mess tent had been commandeered for the task; large tarps had been laid out across the dirt floor and the bodies carefully placed on the tarps in neat, orderly rows. Standing just inside the entrance, Beresford watched as teams of forensic personnel moved among the dead, photographing the bodies, cataloging personal belongings and trying to identify just who it was they were dealing with. This was complicated by both the predations of the local wildlife and the fact that some of the bodies had been in the water for more than twenty-four hours.

A twenty-year veteran of the Metropolitan Police

Authority, Beresford had transferred to the Counter Terrorism Command inside Special Operations just a few years before. In that short time he'd made a name for himself, cracking some high-profile cases and making the department look good, despite the fact that he had little to no interest in personal aggrandizement or celebrity. Beresford liked the intellectual challenge of solving high-profile crimes and he was good at it; that was all he needed to be a reasonably happy man.

That was why Home Office had roused him in the middle of the night and sent him to supervise the investigation when the Territorial Police hollered for help.

There was only one problem.

As far as he could tell, this had absolutely nothing to do with his primary mission, namely bringing to justice those engaged in terrorism, acts of domestic extremism and other related offenses.

He'd had a chance to review the initial report filed by his sister agency and recognized that it was more than likely going to be a political nightmare for the department. Among the presumed dead were a well-respected professor from Oxford, a dozen or more graduate students from the same university, a handful of foreign nationals and the host of a widely popular cable television show from the United States. It would be a three-ring circus for whoever had to coordinate all of the inquiries from the foreign police departments, but just because there were foreign nationals involved didn't necessitate calling in CT Command. So far, it was still just a homicide case.

A homicide with multiple and, in some cases, high-profile victims, but a homicide just the same.

Stop whining and get to work, Beresford, he told himself.

Knowing the techs had at least another hour, maybe more, before they could give him anything worthwhile, Beresford left them to their work and stepped back out into the night air. His assistant, Clements, was waiting.

"Well? What are the locals saying?" Beresford asked.

"To be frank, no one really has a clue. A million different theories, but nothing worth hanging our hat on."

Beresford grunted. That was to be expected. If they knew what had happened, they wouldn't have called him in in the first place.

"Give me the most likely scenario as you see it."

"Right," Clements said, and took a moment to gather his thoughts. The two had only been working together for a few short weeks and Clements was constantly, but unnecessarily, trying to prove himself to Beresford.

"Majority vote among the first responders, as well as our own people, is that it started out as a robbery and went wrong somehow. Rather than keeping their cool, the perps reacted before thinking it through and in the process hiked the charge against them from robbery to multiple felony homicide."

Beresford had been thinking the same thing. The black market in antiquities was alive and well, even here in merry old England. If the dig team had uncovered something seriously valuable, it wasn't beyond comprehension that someone else would take it into their heads to relieve them of their find.

"Seems a logical place to start. Take me to wherever they were storing the artifacts they uncovered," he told his partner.

Clements led him to a trio of tents a short distance

away. Like the mess tent, these were bigger than the others, capable of holding several dozen people at once. Beresford had been to a dig site on vacation once, where he had the typical process explained to him. Each dig was split into gridlike sections and the items recovered from each section would be collected and cataloged together so that they could be studied in reference to one another. The easiest way of organizing such a project was to set up rows of folding tables, with each row representing a certain area of the dig and each table designated for holding objects recovered from a particular grid square.

The scene that greeted them as they entered the first of the artifact tents was anything but organized. The tables had been overturned, the carefully cataloged objects they'd held scattered about the floor like so much trash. Mixed in with the pieces of pottery, clothing and various Iron Age weapons were several pieces of gold jewelry and even a large gold-plated cup that reminded Beresford of the chalice he'd drunk from at church last Sunday.

He stood in the entrance, taking it all in.

"Does it make any sense to you," he asked his partner casually, "that our would-be thieves would ransack the place looking for items of value and then leave the gold lying there on the ground in plain sight?"

Clements frowned and then shook his head. "Nope."

"Me, either. That means we can probably rule out simple theft as our motive here."

"Maybe whatever they took was worth so much that they could ignore the smaller pieces?" Clements suggested.

Beresford thought about that for a minute and then ruled out the possibility.

When his partner pressed him for an explanation, Beresford answered simply, "If you were a thief, would you leave any of the gold behind?"

Clements didn't bother to answer. He knew the other man was right. "So if they didn't kill all those people over money," he asked, "what did they kill them for?"

Beresford didn't know.

Not yet at least.

Clements's cell phone rang. The conversation was short and when he got off the phone Beresford could see by the expression on his face that something had just changed with regard to the case.

"Tell me we've been reassigned and I'll buy your lunch for the next month."

Clements grinned, but his heart wasn't in it. "Sorry. We're stuck with this one it seems."

"Bloody hell!" Beresford said. "Give me a good shoe bomber any day." He turned serious and asked his partner what the call had been about.

"We've got two more bodies," Clements said with a twinkle in his eye. "And this time it looks like we've got a couple of the bad guys."

HALF AN HOUR later Beresford was standing by the side of the road, looking down at the bodies of the two men in the roadside ditch below. One of the local detectives was just climbing back up the hill toward them.

Beresford flashed his badge and asked the other man to fill him in.

"Bodies were found by one of the patrol cars. Both male, both in their late forties or so. No IDs in the wallets and nothing in their pockets, either."

The officer pointed back up the embankment at an angle. "There's a pretty big bloodstain on the road over there, which is how our guy knew to take a look. Seems like whoever did it killed them up there, then kicked the bodies over the side. They rolled down the hill and ended up where you see them now."

Beresford pictured it all in his mind and decided the other man was probably right.

"Coroner been notified?"

"Came and went. We're just waiting on the wagon to come pick them up at this point."

Beresford nodded. "You finished up down there, then? Mind if I take a look for myself?"

"Go right ahead," the officer said, and then wandered back toward his patrol car to have a smoke.

Beresford made his way down the embankment to where the bodies lay, Clements on his heels. He crouched down next to the first body and directed his flashlight beam over it. Right away he noted two things; the pockets of the man's pants were turned out and the man's head rested at an unnatural angle.

The first was probably a result of the work of the cop who'd just left, but the latter certainly wasn't. At least they wouldn't have to wait long for the cause of death to be determined, he thought. A broken neck was a broken neck, unless, of course, the injury had occurred postmortem. The coroner would certainly be able to tell them that at least.

He moved to the second man, while behind him Clements began his own examination of the first. Two sets of eyes were always better than one, Beresford thought, and he'd made it clear to his new partner that he was to always look for himself and form his own conclusions in such situations. One of these days, it would probably save their lives.

The second man was smaller than the first, though not by much. A massive bloodstain colored the front of the man's shirt, however. Beresford took a pen out of the pocket of his sports coat and used the tip to push back a piece of material that was covering something on his chest.

Doing so allowed him to see the massive stab wound that had been previously hidden.

What the hell kind of blade would it take to do that? he wondered, then shook the thought away. He'd know soon enough; the autopsy would at least help him narrow it down. But still, it looked like the man had been stabbed with Excalibur, for heaven's sake….

"Hey!" Clements called. "You need to see this!"

Beresford stepped back to the first body. Clements had done the same thing he had, pushing a piece of clothing aside to reveal what was underneath, but in this case it had been the open collar of the first man's shirt.

On the man's shoulder was the tattoo of a red hand, fingers held together, palm facing out.

Both men recognized the mark.

You couldn't work terrorism in the United Kingdom, particularly close to Ireland, and not do so.

It signified the dead man had been a member of one of the last few remaining terrorists groups in Northern Ireland.

A quick check revealed that it wasn't just blind luck that the dead man had such a tattoo, either.

The other man had one in the same place.

"I guess they needed CT, after all," Clements said.

16

Shaw was confident that the torc would soon be his; he was certain the problems Trevor Jackson was experiencing were only temporary and so he continued with his preparations for both the auction and what he planned for the torc after that.

He'd already selected an appropriate recipient, so he moved on to the next piece of the puzzle, arranging the specific delivery method.

He decided to use the Russian, Ivan Perchenko, to make the necessary arrangements. Perchenko had a good supply of product and could be counted on to maintain the strictest level of security with regard to his operations. Of course, anything he told the Russian would be a complete fabrication. That way, if word of what he was up to surfaced somewhere, he'd know exactly where the story originated and could take the necessary measures to ensure that it never happened again.

He would hate to kill the man, as he'd found the

Russian and the materials he could lay his hands on rather useful so far, but he wouldn't hesitate to do so if it proved necessary.

Shaw opened his safe and removed a military-grade scrambling device from inside. The scrambler had been taken off a patrol unit of the Royal Irish Regiment a year before. It was slightly dated, but it still worked quite well for his purposes. With it, both the location of the call and its contents would be untraceable.

He plugged the scrambler into the telephone and waited for the two devices to shake hands with each other. When they were set, he dialed the Russian's number.

"Da?" came the man's scratchy voice. Perchenko had once served on the outskirts of Chernobyl and his scarred face and vocal chords were a constant reminder of how life can depend on the simplest of things, such as a shift in the wind at a critical moment.

"Hello, my friend," Shaw replied, knowing the other man would recognize his voice immediately. "I've decided that I'll take that consignment offer you made last week, after all."

"The price has gone up ten percent. I have another interested buyer."

Shaw laughed aloud, though inside his blood began to boil. "I was told it was an exclusive offer," he said, trying to see if the man was just giving him a hard time.

"It was," the Russian replied. "Now it is not."

"I should take my business elsewhere," Shaw replied, letting a hint of his anger show in his voice.

"Go ahead," Perchenko said easily. "I will sell it to the Libyans for twice what you are offering."

Shaw knew he was not going to get the man to budge from his position. The Russian was useful, but he was also stubborn. Once he'd made up his mind to charge Shaw an extra ten percent, he'd prefer not to make the deal at all if he didn't get what he was looking for.

The Libyans had no use for the package, Shaw knew, but he wouldn't put it past them to purchase it if the price was right and then store it away until they *could* make use of it. That might be never, but then again, it might be next week, given the state of unrest in the world and the potential availability of the other pieces they needed to utilize the package. Shaw was the type of man who approved of violence in order to achieve a desired end. He certainly didn't object to a few civilian casualties if that would help the cause. But the idea of the package being in the hands of the Libyans was something that made even a man of his dubious ethical standards think twice.

No, it would be best if he simply accepted the additional ten percent penalty for not completing the deal a week earlier and take the package off the market.

"All right," he told the former Russian commando. "Four million, plus another ten percent for your willingness to cut out the competition."

"Done."

"I will contact you in a day or two with delivery instructions."

"*Da,* I will be here," Perchenko said.

With that, the two men hung up.

17

It was almost noon by the time Annja awoke. She lay there in bed, blinking the fuzziness from her thoughts and trying to get a handle on everything that had happened. In the past thirty-six hours, she'd witnessed the murder of a good friend, she'd been shot at, knocked unconscious, dumped in a bog and left for dead. She'd had a Mercedes with armed gunmen try to drive her off the road and then had been forced into a showdown on a backcountry road where she showed them that trying to kill her wasn't going to be as easy as they thought. And to add insult to injury, she'd been forced to walk the last few miles when the car she'd "borrowed" finally gave up the ghost.

On the plus side of the equation she was still alive and reasonably unscathed. But she still possessed the ancient necklace that seemed to be the root cause of this whole mess. She was going to need it in order to get to the bottom of things.

It was clear that she couldn't turn to the police for help. The gunman's presence on the team that had responded to her distress call made that evident enough. She had no idea what role he played in the investigation or what his place in the police hierarchy might be. If she went to the authorities with what she knew, she might find herself in an interrogation room with the very man who had ordered the deaths of her colleagues. And if that happened, there seemed little doubt that she'd become the victim of a convenient "accident" as a result.

No, she was going to have to figure this one out on her own, it seemed.

She slipped out of bed, took a quick shower and dressed in the same set of clothes she'd been wearing when she'd arrived late the night before.

As she dried her hair with a towel, she turned on the battered old television set that sat atop the dresser and was startled to see her own face appear on the screen.

It was an old photo, one taken several years ago at a symposium in Brussels, where she'd been forced by circumstances to defend the possible existence of the abominable snowman thanks to the machinations of her producer, Doug Morrell. The photo might be old, but it still did a decent job of showing her face and it wouldn't be hard for anyone who saw it to recognize her on the street as a result. But it was the headline below the picture—Cable TV Host Missing, Presumed Dead—that really caught her eye.

Annja tossed the towel aside and turned up the volume, catching the announcer in midsentence. "...as more officers are called in to deal with this horrific tragedy. Among the dead are Oxford professor Craig Stevens, as well as Paolo Novick, a visiting professor from the University of Turin. Noticeably absent is the body of renowned archaeologist Annja Creed, who is thought to have arrived on-site just a few days before the devastating attack. Creed, who also serves as the cohost of the cable television program *Chasing History's Monsters,* has been missing in action before, most notably in the wake of the tsunami that devastated the Kanyakumari region of India early last year."

The image shifted back to the announcer, a blonde woman who would have been quite striking if it hadn't been for her unfortunately large teeth. "As we stated earlier, authorities are uncertain as to Creed's whereabouts. Searchers are combing the woods and the boggy areas surrounding the dig site, in the hope of finding some clue as to her condition. For now, let's go to our sister station in New York, WTXC, for a few words with the producer of *Chasing History's Monsters,* Doug Morrell."

The anchor desk was replaced by a live shot outside of the network studios in New York, where a reporter had caught Doug as he was trying to enter the building earlier that morning.

"What was Annja Creed doing in England, Mr. Morrell? Do you think she had any involvement in what happened at the site of the massacre?" the reporter asked, shoving the microphone in front of Doug's face as he drew closer to the entrance.

Despite his relative youth, Doug was the consummate professional when dealing with the media. He smiled easily at the reporter, his tone light and unconcerned.

"The idea that Annja had anything to do with what happened at the dig site is simply preposterous, as I'm sure you realize. She was there on assignment for *Chasing History's Monsters.* The entire staff and I are praying that she's all right." He turned and faced the camera directly, "And if she is, I'm sure she'll be in touch soon with answers to all of our questions."

Annja let out the breath she hadn't known she was holding. While Doug was a great guy, Annja was also too well aware that he'd do anything to promote the show. Like that time she'd been forced to go into hiding after that tsunami in India. A local website had run a story that she'd perished in the natural disaster and Doug had jumped to capitalize on the situation, creating the *Best of Annja Creed* memorial DVD with clips of all her fan-favorite moments from the cable show. He'd even tried to get her to stay in hiding when he saw how well the DVD sales were doing. At least this time around he was giving her a chance to get in touch before doing something crazy; his last line had been directed at her, after all.

She'd been too tired to check in with him when she'd reached the hotel last night, but there was no reason to put it off any longer. Doing so would only give Doug more time to wreak potential havoc.

Annja glanced at the clock. It was just after one, London time, which made it around 8:00 a.m. in New York, so Doug was probably on his way into the office. She didn't have her BlackBerry or laptop anymore, so she couldn't simply text or email him. Nor did she want to call him directly from the hotel phone, as she had no idea who might be listening in and didn't know how extensive the police investigation had gotten while she'd been out of touch for the past several hours.

Rather than risking the possibility of giving away her location, Annja went in search of a pay phone.

Thankfully it didn't take long. She found one outside the tube station just a couple of blocks down the street from her hotel and used her company-issued calling card to try and reach Doug's cell phone. When she couldn't reach him there, or on his office line, she left a message on the latter.

"Doug, it's Annja. I'm all right, but I'm going to need your help getting to the bottom of this craziness. I'm calling from a pay phone because my BlackBerry is busted. Until I can get a new one, you can't call me so I'll plan on calling you back just before lunch instead."

That should be enough to keep him from doing anything crazy, she thought as she hung up the phone.

At least I hope so.

She caught a cab over to a local shopping district and spent the next hour or so replacing some of the things she'd lost at the dig site. A surplus store offered up two pairs of cargo pants in her size, while a nearby fashion boutique gave her fresh T-shirts, socks and underwear. She snagged a prepaid cell phone from a tobacco shop and activated it while standing on the sidewalk outside, feeling slightly less isolated once she'd done so.

Her last stop was at an electronics shop, where she bought a secondhand laptop to replace the one she'd lost and then requested that the files on her old hard drive, which she'd rescued from the dig site, be transferred to a DVD so she could access them on the new one.

The kid behind the counter wasn't thrilled with the idea of having to actually do some work, it seemed, for he winced at the request. "Yeah, ya know, we're pretty busy in here today. It's gonna be a few hours before I can get to it," he said, shaking his head at the very thought.

Annja waved a twenty-pound note in front of him. "How about half an hour, instead?"

The money disappeared in a flash and the kid got to work.

While she waited, she grabbed some lunch from a fish and chips shop down the street and used her new cell phone to call Doug.

"Doug Morrell."

"It's me," she said, not wanting to identify herself in case anyone in the restaurant overheard her.

Doug, however, wasn't paying attention apparently.

"Me, who?" he asked.

"Me," she insisted.

"Look, me, I don't know who you are, but I'm waiting for an important call. You're just going to have to…"

Annja counted to three. There was no way she was getting to five, never mind ten.

"Doug, if you don't shut up and listen to me, I'm going to fly back to Brooklyn and—"

"Annja! Why didn't you say it was you?"

She used her free hand to rub her temples. Talking to Doug usually gave her a headache and this was turning out to be no different than usual.

"Did you get my message earlier?"

She could practically see him nodding. "Yeah. What the heck is going on over there?"

There were only a couple of other patrons in the place, but Annja figured it was better to be safe than sorry. "Hang on a sec," she said. She wrapped up the remains of her meal in the newsprint it had come in and then threw the trash into the bin by the door on her way out. Once on the street she felt better about not being overheard.

"Okay, listen up." She gave him a quick rundown on the events of the past two days, including the appearance of the armed gunmen at the dig site and their later attempt to run her off the road.

"Gunmen?" Doug said. "That sucks."

"I know, tell me about it," Annja replied, but Doug went on as if he hadn't even heard her.

"We can't use gunmen in the show. Way too boring, never mind overdone. Bog mummies on the other hand…"

Annja scowled. "Don't even start, Doug."

"But surely you can see that…"

She felt her head starting to throb. "Doug!" she snapped.

He was silent for a moment.

"You know, you could be a little nicer to me sometimes. All I'm trying to do is help you with your career."

"I don't need help with my career. I want you to help me get out of this mess and find out who's behind it all."

Doug sighed. "Okay, okay. What do you need?"

She described both the torc and the tattoos she'd seen on the arms of the gunmen as best she was able. "Use the research team and see if you can come up with any information on either of them, okay?"

"Yeah, okay. What do you want me to tell the police?"

She didn't want him to tell them anything, but she knew that wasn't a realistic option. As her employer, they were probably already sniffing around him, waiting to see if he had any information on her whereabouts. She might not be a formal suspect yet, but she knew that status wouldn't last too long the minute they found out she was alive and well.

"I don't care what you tell them. Stall them any way

you can. I need some time to run down these leads so I have a better idea of what's going on."

Doug perked up considerably at her reply. "Don't worry about it, Annja. I'll handle things on this end. Call me later—maybe the research team will have something by then."

Before she could say anything more, he hung up.

18

D.I. Beresford was in the midst of his lunch in the cramped little room that served as his office when his phone rang with a call from the desk sergeant downstairs.

"I've got a guy down here claiming he's got information for you on that Midlands thing."

Beresford glanced at the half-eaten meal on his desk. "He look legit?"

Ever since the news had broken the night before, the tip line had been flooded by hundreds of calls. Each and every one of them had to be investigated, no matter how unlikely or even ridiculous they might sound. Beresford couldn't afford to get sidetracked with wild-goose chases and he'd had more than his fair share of meetings with well-meaning but mistaken citizens convinced that the neighbor they don't really care for down the street was up to no good.

"The guy's a priest," the sergeant replied.

From the tone of the man's voice, Beresford wasn't sure if that meant the sergeant felt the witness was completely trustworthy or exactly the opposite. Nor could he find a way to ask without insulting the man.

"Send him up," he said with a longing glance at the lunch he knew he'd never get the chance to finish.

A few minutes later a uniformed officer led a harried-looking young man into his office. He was of average height and build, with sandy hair cropped comfortably short but not too much so, and he was wearing the official uniform of the Catholic church—black clerical shirt and pants.

Beresford knew that if he'd passed him on the street, he wouldn't have looked twice.

The detective inspector introduced himself, learning the newcomer's name in the process.

"What can I do for you, Father Anderson?" he asked, waving the other man into the seat before his desk.

Anderson eyed the chair like it might bite, frowning all the while. "I've never done this kind of thing before," he said, looking around the room as if searching for some hint as to how to do what he'd come here to do.

The inspector smiled, trying to put the man at ease. "Why don't you just tell me what happened?" he suggested as the other man finally sat down. "The desk sergeant said you have some information about the events that occurred recently near Arkholme, is that correct?"

The priest nodded, opened his mouth to say something and then changed his mind about whatever it was. Instead, he asked, "What if what I have to tell you can get me in trouble?"

Beresford's expression didn't change, but his level of

interest did. Perhaps this wasn't going to be the typically useless interview, after all.

"Do you mean with the diocese or with the law?" he asked.

Anderson winced, perhaps to hear it put so plainly, but answered nonetheless.

"The law."

Beresford shrugged. "That would depend on what happened and exactly which laws were broken. Would you like to have an attorney present before we go any further?"

The question was one he didn't like asking, as the suggestion of having an attorney present often derailed a witness's level of cooperation, but it was one that had to be asked, if only to be sure everything that was said during the rest of the conversation could be used as evidence if it ever came to that.

Anderson surprised him, however, by waving the suggestion aside.

"No, no, that's all right. It's in God's hands at this point, anyway."

Beresford nodded. He didn't quite believe that himself, but he certainly wasn't going to argue with the man. If he didn't want a lawyer present, that was his business.

He waited for the other man to continue.

Anderson hesitated, trying to figure out what to say, and then seemed to make up his mind to just let it all out in a rush.

"I picked up a hitchhiker yesterday. I think it was the American that's gone missing, this Annja Creed woman."

Beresford wasn't surprised; he'd heard something similar, if not those exact words, at least half a dozen times already that morning. Never mind the three-hundred-some odd sighting reports that had come in over the anonymous tip line in the past twelve hours. People were seeing the missing television host everywhere.

"Where were you when this happened, Father?"

"About fifteen miles south of Arkholme, on the M6," was the reply.

Beresford's interest perked a little. That was in the right place at the right time at least.

"Did she introduce herself to you as Annja Creed?"

Anderson shook his head. "No, she just said her name was Amy."

Amy, Annja. Both started with *A*. Easy to remember, too.

"Can you describe her to me?"

Anderson did so, noting the hazel eyes and the ponytail of dark hair. It was a good description, the kind with just enough details to make it believable, to make it seem that the priest had indeed seen someone who at least looked a lot like Creed, but Beresford wasn't quite convinced. After all, the woman's photograph had been featured in just about every major newspaper and popular magazine in the London area for at least the past twelve hours. Perhaps he'd just seen it there.

"Sounds like it could be her, but then again it sounds like it could be a hundred other American tourists, too," Beresford said. "Are you a fan of her show?"

"Me? Oh, heaven's no. I don't watch that kind of thing."

"So why do you think it was her?"

"Well, it wasn't so much her as it was the two men in the other car trying to kill us."

He said it so bluntly, so matter-of-factly, that for a

moment Beresford wasn't certain if he'd heard him correctly. When he realized he had, he sat up straighter in his chair.

"Someone tried to kill you?"

The priest nodded. "I know it sounds crazy, but I can't come up with any other explanation. Why else would they try to run us off the road?"

Why else indeed? Beresford thought, his pulse pounding as his instincts told him they were about to get a break in the case.

"Tell me what happened," Beresford commanded and, this time, Anderson did.

He described how he'd seen a woman walking alone on the side of the road and how he'd stopped to see if she needed any help. She'd told him she'd had some trouble with her boyfriend and that the lout had kicked her out of the car. Anderson had offered to give her a lift back into the city as he was headed that way, as well.

Shortly after she'd gotten into the car, a dark-colored Mercedes raced up behind them and rammed the rear of his vehicle.

By now Beresford was taking notes, capturing his first impressions of the individual who'd entered Anderson's car. At the top of his list he wrote "Already being pursued?" After that he put "Who/Why?"

"You're sure it was a Mercedes?" he asked, his pencil poised over his legal pad.

Anderson nodded. "The hood ornament was clearly visible."

"You said dark-colored. Can you be more specific?"

"I think it was black, though it might have been dark blue."

"License number?"

The priest shook his head. "Sorry."

"You're doing fine, Father. Keep going."

Anderson explained how "Amy" had used the hymnals he'd had in the backseat as makeshift weapons, forcing the other vehicle to keep its distance by throwing them at the windshield of the Mercedes.

"Stays calm under pressure," Beresford wrote.

"That seemed to work for a time. They kept their distance and I was starting to hope that we'd be okay if we could just find somewhere less isolated. I assumed they wouldn't continue attacking us in front of witnesses, you know?"

Beresford had been a police officer long enough to know that the presence of witnesses very rarely kept anyone from violence. After all, show the same scene to five different people and you got five different versions of it. Eyewitness testimony was horribly inaccurate.

He didn't, however, say anything of the sort to Father Anderson.

"That's a reasonable assumption," he said instead. "Is that how you managed to escape? By finding someplace a bit more lively?"

For the first time since sitting down, Anderson actually smiled, though it was still a sad, bitter smile. "Heck, no," he said. "That's when they started shooting at us."

"Shooting at you?" Beresford was starting to feel like a broken record, dumbly repeating what was said to him. But as crazy as the story sounded, he found himself believing the young priest. What did he have to gain by lying, after all?

"So what did you do at that point?"

"Do?" Anderson asked, apparently surprised by the question. "I didn't do anything, unless you count quaking in fear as an action. I was terrified. It was all I could do to hold the wheel steady as the maniac behind me tried to run me off the road while his partner in the passenger seat was turning my car into a lead pincushion."

"But you obviously got away, so something must have happened to allow that, right?"

Anderson tensed. "You asked me what *I* did. *I* didn't do anything."

Based on his reaction, Beresford knew that they had arrived at that part of the story that had prompted the priest to ask about the possibility of prosecution earlier for whatever happened next. It was a delicate moment and one that could just as easily have ended up with Anderson clamming up as much as it could with him relaying the rest of the tale.

Not wanting to lose what was turning out to be a star witness, Beresford said, "So far everything you've told me fits squarely into the category of self-defense. They attacked you on the road and, being afraid for your life, you defended yourself. Pretty cut-and-dry to me."

The best part about his statement was that it was true; it did sound like self-defense. Of course, depending on what happened next, that could quickly change, but he hadn't lied to the man. If that kept him talking…

Anderson considered that for a moment, nodded as if he'd realized the wisdom of the detective's statement and then continued.

As Beresford listened closely, Anderson went on to describe how "Amy" had convinced him to let the other car catch up and then, at the last minute, he slammed on the brakes. He and his hitchhiking passenger had been prepared for it—all buckled up and expecting the collision—but the men in the Mercedes had not.

The two vehicles collided with steel-shattering force, bringing them both to a shuttering halt.

"That's when she pulled out a sword, climbed through the shattered rear window and attacked the men in the Mercedes!"

"A sword?" Beresford asked, not certain he'd heard correctly. "I thought you said you didn't have any weapons?"

"I didn't think we did. But suddenly this woman is waving a sword that's longer than my arm and rushing off to do battle with the people who'd just been shooting at us moments before!"

Beresford was about to ask where on earth she could have gotten a sword, but then realized he knew the answer already. If it was Annja Creed, and his gut was telling him that it was, then she had probably taken it from the dig site. Her possession of it might also explain why she was being pursued, if the simple fact that she was a potential witness to a multiple homicide, and therefore needed silencing, wasn't reason enough. He couldn't imagine what a group like the Red Hand Defenders would want with an Iron Age sword, but that didn't mean they didn't have a reason. Perhaps it had a certain financial value and they intended to sell it on the black market in order to finance other projects. Or maybe its value was in its historical significance, something that would support the RHD's fight for Irish autonomy and independence.

The fact was, he didn't know.

Yet.

But he would.

He turned his attention back to his guest. "What happened after Amy charged the other vehicle?"

Anderson glanced away, unable, or perhaps just

unwilling, to meet Beresford's gaze. A long moment passed before he sighed and said, "She killed them."

The detective wouldn't let it go at that. "How?" he asked.

A look of distaste crossed the priest's face, but he answered nonetheless. "She stabbed them, I think."

Remembering the massive puncture wound he'd seen on one of the bodies they'd found in the roadside ditch, Beresford wasn't all that surprised to hear it. "Did you see her actually kill them?" he asked.

This time the priest shook his head.

"No, it happened so fast that I was still in my car for most of it. By the time I got out, the men were dead and she was staring at them through the open door of their car."

Beresford sat back and considered things for a moment. The way he saw it, there were two possible scenarios. One, Creed witnessed the massacre at the dig site, escaped the killers somehow and was now running for her life. Or two, she had been working with the killers, had double-crossed them at the last minute and was now running for her life with whatever it was she had stolen from them.

A sword, perhaps?

If Creed was on the run from those who'd murdered her colleagues, why hadn't she contacted the police? Half a day had passed since the confrontation on the highway. There'd certainly been ample time for her to get to a phone and report what happened to the authorities and yet she'd chosen not to. That made it seem like she was intentionally avoiding the police, which lent some credence to the second scenario. Yet nothing he'd read in the thin file they'd managed to put together since learning she'd been present at the dig site and was now missing gave any indication that she was involved in illegal activities of any kind. In fact, on more than one occasion, she'd personally disrupted the activities of international artifact smugglers and black marketeers.

It just wasn't adding up.

"Did she threaten you at all, Father?" Beresford asked.

"No."

"Even after you found her with the two dead men?"

"No, not even then. Though I have to admit that I didn't wait around for an explanation either. Seeing her with that sword in hand, I decided prudence was the better part of valor and got myself, and my car, out of there as quickly as possible."

"And she didn't try to stop you?"

He shook his head.

Now that makes things a bit more interesting, Beresford thought. Clearly she hadn't been worried about being seen or recognized by Anderson, nor had she moved to cover up her actions in any way.

Given the file and the fact that she hadn't sought to silence Anderson, Beresford was beginning to think that perhaps Anja Creed was on the side of the angels, after all.

He spent another ten minutes with Anderson, but didn't get anything more of importance from him. He thanked him for coming in, reiterated that he'd done the right thing and said that he'd be in touch.

19

Already regretting giving Doug a free hand to talk to the police, Annja headed back to her hotel. The clerk barely gave her a glance as she crossed the lobby and climbed the stairs to her room.

Once inside, she used the hotel's Wi-Fi service to log onto the internet. She'd had to put a deposit on the bed-sheets when she'd rented the room, and the beat-up old color television on the dresser nearby was bolted down to keep it from being stolen, but the hotel's wireless service was better than most at airports. Shows where their priorities are, she thought humorlessly. Given the amount of research she had to do, she reminded herself she couldn't complain.

It was time to learn more about this mysterious torc.

Celtic jewelry had exploded in popularity over the past few years and a simple Google search for "Celtic torc" turned up more than half a million sites, the majority of them selling replicas of one type or another. Mixed throughout, however, were articles discussing the history, manufacturing methods and significance of this type of jewelry, and Annja spent several hours digging through them for anything that might help her in identifying the importance of this particular torc.

She learned quite a bit in the process, such as the fact that the word *torc* was derived from the Latin *torques* which meant twisted bar. She discovered that one of the earliest images depicting Celtic gods and warriors wearing a torc around their necks could be found on the side of a silver cauldron from the first century unearthed at Gundestrup in Denmark. While it was interesting reading, it was all general in nature and not particularly helpful with identifying the one she had in her possession.

Annja turned her attention next to the carvings of the eagles that adorned the clasps on the torc. She knew that in many cultures the eagle represented the sun and, by extension, the ruler or monarch of the age. The eagle was also the symbol of the Roman Empire, a rather ironic fact given that the man who'd been wearing the torc had been buried with the remains of four sacrificed Roman prisoners. A bit more research told her that for the Celts, the eagle was traditionally seen as one of the oldest of creatures, ancient and wise. They were considered harbingers of good luck and success.

A couple of hours of research and that was all she could come up with.

There has to be a better way of doing this, she thought.

In the hope of getting even the smallest of leads, Annja posted messages to two of her favorite newsgroups, alt.archaeology and alt.archaeology.esoterica.

I'm looking for information regarding a black torc
and any ties it might have to Celtic culture or mythology. Just about anything would be helpful at
this point.

Signing it Curious Celt, she fired it off with a touch
of the enter key.

She knew that doing so brought with it a little bit of
risk. Data mining tools such as Google Alerts made it
easy for anyone to track conversations going on around
the web and if anyone was watching for mention of a
black torc her message would act like a big red flag, letting them know that someone else was interested in the
same thing. But right now she didn't have much choice.
So far, she'd gotten exactly nowhere with her research
and the trail got colder with every hour that passed.

Her back was stiff from sitting hunched over the
laptop for hours, so she got up and paced around the
room, trying to work out the kinks in her muscles. As
she passed the television, she turned it on, wanting the
sound of something other than silence in the quiet of
her hotel room.

To her surprise, a familiar voice came from the
speakers.

"I repeat, Annja Creed is alive and well. I spoke to
her a few hours ago from her safe house in London."

Annja stared in horror at the screen where Doug Morrell was holding a press conference in front of the cable
station's studios in New York. He stood in front of the
big glass doors to the studio, with a gaggle of reporters
gathered in front of him.

"Did Ms. Creed tell you who was responsible for
the brutal attack?" one shouted, while another wanted

to know how she'd been able to survive when everyone else had been killed.

Doug handled the questions with the skill of a veteran politician. Yes, Annja Creed had told him who was responsible for the attack. No, he wasn't going to share that information with them at this time, for it was still very much a police matter.

"But rest assured," he told them with a smile that stretched from ear to ear. "*Chasing History's Monsters* will be airing an exclusive two-part special on its co-host's harrowing ordeal just as soon as we're able. We'll tell you everything, including exactly what role the bog mummies played in the deadly attack!"

Annja clicked to the next channel.

"...what role the bog mummies played in the deadly attack."

Another click.

"...airing an exclusive two-part special..."

The press conference was being carried live or nearly so, on more than a dozen different stations. Annja stared at Doug's smiling face and wanted nothing more than to reach through the television set and strangle him where he stood.

Things were bad enough already. Did he really have to go and kick the hornet's nest like that? If the killers saw the broadcast—and chances were that they would, given how widely it was being carried on the various networks—they were going to think that Annja had either recognized them or had uncovered their identities in the time since the attack. Either way, they'd be worried she'd turn that information over to the police and the need to silence the witness would suddenly become a much bigger priority.

Doug had just painted a big red bull's-eye on her back.

In fact, he'd practically told them where to find her as well. Safe house in London? Why not just give out the address while you were at it, Doug? Maybe even roll out the red carpet?

"I'm going to kill him," she said to the empty room around her.

But not until he told her what she needed to know.

She had to have that information if she was going to stay out of jail long enough so she could kill him.

Annja gave herself fifteen minutes to calm down, which wasn't anywhere near long enough, and then used her cell phone to call him again.

"Doug Morrell."

"It's me again."

"Annja! I was just—"

She couldn't hold back.

"Are you out of your freaking mind?" she hollered into the phone.

There was a moment of silence, and then Doug said, "You sound upset, Annja. Has something happened?"

"Has something happ…" She sputtered, unable to even complete the sentence. Didn't he have any idea what he'd done?

Apparently not, as his next few words confirmed. Taking her silence for permission to continue, he said, "Now that the killers know that you are on to them, they'll have to leave you alone. Taking a shot at you would only land them in more hot water. I pretty much single-handedly saved your life." He sounded positively proud of himself.

"The only thing you've done," she shouted at him, "is to convince them that killing me is the only choice they have left. I can't believe that you are this naive! If I'm dead, then there isn't a witness to testify. No witness, no case. No case, no conviction and life sentence."

It took him a moment to realize the magnitude of his error. When he did, he gushed with apologies.

"Oh, jeez, Annja! I'm sorry! God, how could I have been so stupid? I just didn't stop to think!"

Unfortunately, that was a problem he had all too often. Still, his intentions had been good, she knew.

She pointedly ignored the voice in the back of her mind that was saying something about good intentions and the road to hell. She just didn't need to hear it right now.

"Fine, Doug, fine. I'll deal with it," she said into the phone in a clipped voice, cutting off any further discussion on the topic. "Just get me that information I need."

Far more subdued than when the conversation started, Doug agreed that he would and told her to call him in the morning her time. He should have something by then, he said.

Still irritated, Annja hung up the phone and tried to figure out just how much of a problem Doug's impromptu press conference was going to cause for her. The police were certainly going to want to talk to her now that Doug had made it clear that she'd been at the site during the attack. Of course they'd have to find her first and that wasn't going to be easy. London was a big place and the hotel she was staying in was so far off the grid for even a quasi-celebrity like herself that no one would ever think to look there. If she kept her head low, and didn't do anything outrageous that might call attention to herself, she should be good to go.

Doug, on the other hand, was probably fending off phone calls from Scotland Yard that very moment.

Serves him right, she thought.

At the same time, whoever was hunting her was going to have to face the same problems that the police were and with less resources on their side. If she could avoid the police, she could probably avoid her hunters, as well, giving her the time she needed to figure this whole mess out and put the responsible parties behind bars.

Okay, maybe so things weren't as bad as she'd initially thought.

Or rather, no worse than they were last night, she told herself.

Feeling a little bit better now that she knew Doug's machinations weren't immediately going to cause a whole new set of problems for her, Annja was able to focus her attention back on her research. A check of her email showed that she'd already received three messages in response to her newsgroup posting.

The first was from Lordofthesword@dungeons.net.

Sounds like a cool quest. I'm a forty-seventh level fighter with bracers of glory. I'll offer you my services for fifteen percent of the treasure. What do you say?

I say get a life, Annja thought, and then immediately felt bad about doing so. After all, she spent her days chasing legends and digging up ancient artifacts. Who was she to judge?

The next one, from Celticqueen@druidhome.com, was more to the point but wasn't very helpful, either.

Sounds like you've got your work cut out for you.
I'm not an expert in Celtic culture or mythology,
by any means, but I've never heard of a black torc
before. Most of the ones I've seen were made
from gold or at least gold plate. You might check
the legends associated with either Cúchulain
or Finn McCool—they're both Irish heroes who
got around a lot and there might be mention of
your black torc in one of their adventures. Best
of luck!

The third message showed some promise, however.
It was from HistoryBuff@oxfordarchives.edu, which
she took to be a good sign.

Several years ago I heard a presentation given
by an American professor working in Paris on
mystical artifacts that appeared in various Celtic
legends. I think the speaker's name was de
Chance. The talk focused mainly on weapons,
like the Gáe Bolg, Cúchulainn's spear, and the
Claiomh Solais, the sword of Nuada, leader of
the Tuatha De Danann, but he did mention a few
other objects. If I remember correctly, one of
them was a black necklace. I don't know if that's
the necklace you are seeking, but it might be
worth looking into. Last I'd heard de Chance was
still working in Paris.

Now that sounds more like what I'm looking for,
Annja thought. She did a quick Google search for a
Professor de Chance and came up empty, but there was
a Dr. Harry de Chance listed on the staff at the Natural

History Museum in Paris. In the Staff pages of the museum's website, she found a telephone number for him.

She called, got an answering machine and decided it was worth the risk to leave a message.

"Hello Dr. de Chance, my name is Annja Creed and I'd like to speak to you privately about a black torc that was recently unearthed in England. If you could call me at your convenience, that would be great." She rattled off her phone number, then disconnected.

Thinking of Paris made her think of her sometime mentor Roux. She'd resisted calling him to this point, thinking she could puzzle it out on her own, but given the circles he moved in he might just know Dr. de Chance and that was too good an opportunity for her to pass up.

Besides, she had to admit she kind of missed him. She'd never say that to his face outright, but it was true nonetheless.

She'd first met him in the mountains of Cévennes, France. She'd been hunting the Beast of Gévaudan, a legendary creature—some said a werewolf—that had supposedly terrorized the region in the late 1700s. Roux had been looking for the final pieces of a sword that had shattered almost six hundred years before, a sword once borne by Joan of Arc herself. It was only much later, when the sword was reborn in her hand, that Annja learned that Roux had been there on that fateful day when the sword had been shattered and a young woman martyred for her faith.

The breaking of the sword and the death of its bearer had caused Roux, and his young charge, Garin Braden, to be pushed outside the boundaries of time. They had lived through the ages, untouched by the passage of the years, amassing huge fortunes and watching history play out around them, spectators to a world that changed faster than they ever thought possible. For years Roux had sought the pieces of the sword, believing that he would be released from his fate once the sword had been forged anew. His one-time protégé, Garin, on the other hand, opposed his efforts, not wanting his long life to be cut short by the machinations of the remorseful old fool he'd once treated as his father.

For years the two men had alternately worked together and tried to kill each other with equal vigor. Annja's selection as the next bearer, something neither man ever expected, had thrown them into a kind of uneasy truce as they sought to discover what this new dynamic would mean for the sword and for them.

Annja was attracted to the dangerous sensuality that Garin exuded, which was probably why Roux had become her sometime partner, sometime benefactor in her search to protect and preserve the world's priceless artifacts rather than Garin. At the same time, Roux helped her identify and deal with her destiny as bearer of the sword, something she believed he'd done for his original charge, Joan of Arc, as well.

He was an irascible, ill-tempered, egotistical pompous ass who tried to tell her what to do all the time, but to Annja, who'd grown up in an orphanage, he was the closest thing she'd ever had to a family.

And when you needed help, that's who you turned to.

Family.

The phone rang several times before Roux's voice mail clicked in. She left a quick message, telling him she was all right in case he'd seen the earlier newscast and asking him to call her when he could.

With her thoughts still wrapped up in the stupid press conference Doug had held, she didn't realize that she'd forgotten to give Roux her new number.

With Roux unavailable, Annja considered calling Garin but finally dismissed the idea. Garin had a way of confronting situations head-on, which was all well and good when you wanted to make a statement but this situation called for a bit more finesse for the time being. She'd hold off for now; she could always give him a call if things began to spin out of control.

20

In another part of London, miles away from where Annja was hiding out, the head of the Red Hand Defenders and his senior captain were watching Doug Morrell's press conference.

"I thought you said you'd taken care of her," David said, his voice dangerously soft, while on the screen Morrell insisted that his beautiful star was alive and well.

"I did. Apparently I was mistaken."

Trevor Jackson waited for his employer to explode in anger but the other man somehow managed to retain control of himself. In Jackson's opinion, this was clearly a first, and it made him nervous.

"Could she be responsible for the deaths of our two operatives?" Shaw asked.

His subordinate gave it some thought. The two men in question had been found dead at the side of the road some distance from the dig site, but that didn't rule

out the possibility. After all, if this Creed woman had
survived being shot and then managed to cut cross-
country after escaping from the bog, she could easily
have crossed the motorway in that area. O'Donnell had
been an independent sort of cuss; if he'd seen the earliest
reports that had suggested the Creed woman was among
the dead and then saw her by the side of the road, he
might have tried to bring her in on his own. He'd been
spoiling for Jackson's job for some time; embarrassing
him in front of Shaw after he'd claimed the woman was
dead would have been right up O'Donnell's alley. Apparently he'd bitten off more than he could chew this
time around, though. Who'd have ever imagined that
some television personality could be so ruthless?

He kept his thoughts to himself, however, saying instead, "Yes, it's possible. We're still working to locate
their missing car, but if Morrell is telling the truth, and
she is indeed here in London, it's quite possible she
simply stole the vehicle after killing our men and then
used it to make the journey here."

"She must have the torc," Shaw said.

"It's certainly possible, yes."

As much as he hated to admit it, Jackson thought his
employer could be right. She must have hidden the torc
before attacking his people that night and then retrieved
it when she escaped from the bog. The thought got his
anger up. How she'd managed to survive that gunshot to
the skull, never mind the cloying grip of the bog afterward, was something he intended to ask her, right after
he beat her mercilessly for putting him in this position
in the first place.

On the screen, Morrell was still babbling on about
bog mummies or some other equally stupid subject for
his television show. Shaw watched him for a moment

and then tapped the glass, like a young kid knocking on the outer side of the pens in the pet store, expecting the canine, or in this case, the walking dead man, to notice him.

As the press conference began to wind down, Shaw said over his shoulder, "We still have people in New York, yes?"

Jackson nodded. "Of course."

"Put them on Morrell. I want his phone tapped, his house and office watched. If he's telling the truth, this Creed woman has been in touch and will likely reach out to him again. When she does, I want to know about it."

"I'm on it."

Shaw turned to face him. "The auction ends in thirty-six hours," he said. "You have that long to get me that torc. No excuses and no more screwups!"

Jackson told him he'd handle it and then took his leave before things could get ugly.

He was out of chances, he knew. If he didn't find the torc in time, there wasn't any place that he could hide. Shaw would hunt him to the ends of the earth.

Failure was not an option.

21

At just after four that afternoon, a man got off the elevator outside the offices of the *Chasing History's Monsters* production office in New York City. He was dressed in dark pants and a white shirt, with a tie that was intentionally tied an inch shorter than it should be. His hair, a little longer than the average corporate wage slave's, was slicked back without much regard for style or flair. He wore an unattractive pair of glasses and an ID badge—showing his picture and the name Newman in large letters—was hanging from a lanyard around his neck. In his left hand he carried a scuffed leather computer bag that sprouted a few inches of Ethernet cable and the end of a flowmeter out of its partially opened mouth.

The operative had been hired by a local fixer, who in turn had been contacted by an acquaintance overseas, who himself was a secondary cut out from the man who actually wanted the work done. The operative liked it that way; if things went sour and he ended up across the table from a couple of cops looking to send him up-river for a few years, he really didn't know squat, which meant that there was only so much crap they could hang around his neck and make stick.

He was always the type to face things head-on. None of this sneaking about in the middle of the night garbage for him—no, sir. At night, you had to deal with alarm systems and security cameras, never mind the guards themselves. You couldn't finesse technology—at least, not easily, the operative told himself.

But people? People you could finesse.

And that's what he specialized in. Finessing people. As he marched over to the reception desk, the woman behind it took one look at him and dismissed him as anyone interesting before he'd even opened his mouth. The operative knew that people saw what they wanted to see and very rarely ever looked any deeper than that. To the receptionist, he was just another computer geek from the IT department downstairs; she was probably hoping that if she ignored him, he wouldn't mumble something about how rad his latest massively multi-player online role-playing game was and ask her out, like the last tech who'd been sent up to fix a problem with the firewall. The operative used this tendency to his advantage. Act like you were supposed to be there, dress the part, and nine times out of ten they just sent you on through without a word.

The switchboard phone rang just as he got ready to give his spiel and the receptionist simply hit the buzzer and waved him on through, like he'd been there a hundred times before.

It was exactly what he'd expected to happen.

Once past the reception area, the operative wandered through the warren of cubicles until he found the office he wanted. He knocked and then opened the door without waiting for a reply.

His target, a producer named Doug Morrell, looked up from behind his desk.

"Yeah?"

The operative held his ID card away from his chest for Morrell to see and then let it flop back again.

"IT department," he said with that tone of bored indifference tech guys cultivated the world over. "I'm supposed to check the phone jacks as prep for the fiber optic install next week."

How you said it was far more important than what you said, the operative knew. Just the right amount of arrogance, that little bit of superiority that said, "You need me far more than I need you, Jack," and that was often all it took to get them to do just what you wanted them to do.

Which, in this case, was to leave the room.

"How long are we talking about?" Morrell asked with a glance at his watch.

The operative shrugged. "Ten, maybe fifteen minutes? I gotta pull out the wall plate, test the circuits, make sure you've got room for when they lay the dual cabling next week…."

Morrell's eyes were already glazing over. "Okay, fine. Fine. Do your thing. I'm going to go get a cup of coffee and I'll be back in fifteen minutes."

"Sure, man, whatever," he replied, already dumping his bag on the small conference table near the desk and pretending to dig through it for the right set of tools. By the time he looked up again, Morrell was nowhere in sight.

Works every time, he thought.

He leaned over the desk and took a look at the handset

for Morrell's telephone. It was like a thousand others he'd seen in offices the world over; two pieces of dark-colored plastic glued together around the internal components. Easy to produce and cheap as hell, too. He'd seen factories in Malaysia that churned out a couple of thousand of them a day for pennies each, only to sell them to business execs back in the States for $64.95 or something equally ridiculous.

Shaking his head at the craziness of it all, the operative opened his bag and dug around inside it for a moment, until at last he found the receiver he was looking for. It was a near-perfect copy of the one attached to Morrell's phone, with one major exception.

This one had a listening device already installed in the midst of the internal wiring.

Rather than trying to crack open Morrell's handset and implant a bug before he got back from his coffee jaunt, all the operative had to do was calmly unplug the existing handset, toss it in the bag and plug in the new one in its place.

Just minutes after arriving, the job was done.

To keep up appearances, the operative actually removed the phone jack's wall plate and pulled the wires out of the recessed box behind the plate, pretending to be sorting through the various pieces until he heard Morrell coming back down the hall, talking on his cell phone.

By the time the young producer came back through the office door, the operative had just finished screwing the wall plate back into place.

"All set?" Morrell asked.

"All set," the operative said with a smile.

It took him less than ten minutes to exit the building and disappear into the crowd outside, with no one the wiser. When he was a few blocks away, he pulled out his cell phone and dialed his partner's number.

"You're good," he said simply, and then ended the call. Even if Morrell left the office that very instant, his partner would still have plenty of time to get inside the man's apartment, bug the telephones there and get out again long before Morrell could make the trip over to the other borough.

Everything had gone according to plan, which was just how the operative liked it.

22

Annja waited as long as she could stand it the next morning, then called Doug. She could tell from the fuzziness of his voice that she'd woken him up.

"What did you find out about the torc?" she asked.

"Huh? Find out about the what? What time is—"

"Focus, Doug," she said sharply, not wanting to give him a chance to start complaining about the early hour. Once he got going, it would take a steamroller to stop him. "You were going to get me information on the torc, remember?"

"Yeah, the torc. Right. Okay, hang…agh!"

His unexpected shout made her jump in surprise.

"Doug? Are you all right?" she asked with some apprehension, visions of New York police detectives busting down his door to take him into custody were floating in the forefront of her mind.

"It's still dark out, Annja!" Doug said.

He didn't sound happy about it either.

Annja smiled, glancing at the clock on the desk beside her. It was 9:00 a.m. London time so it was just about 4:00 a.m in New York. Revenge can be so sweet.

"I know it is, Doug. After all, the sun still hasn't come up on your side of the world, but over here it's getting busy and I need to get going. So quit whining about the hour and tell me about the torc."

"Fine. But don't think I won't remember this."

"I'm shaking in my boots. The torc, Doug."

There was a pause and then he said, "The research team struck out. They tried the usual sources, but didn't find anything to match what you were looking for. The best they could come up with was to recommend that you talk with a guy by the name of de Chance, at the National History Museum in Paris. He's supposed to be the resident expert on Celtic culture, now that your friend Craig has been, uh, passed away."

Being reminded of Craig's murder took some of the wind out of her sails. But at least she had some confirmation that de Chance was someone worth talking to, so that was good news.

"And the tattoo?" she asked wearily, not expecting much more success than the team had had with the necklace.

Doug surprised her, though.

"Well, the research team did dig up some information on that, but I'm not sure you're going to like it. And I have to say, I don't see how it's even relevant."

"Tell me," she said.

He hemmed and hawed for a minute, then did what she asked, sounding as if he was reading directly out of the research team's report, which he probably was.

"The Red Hand of Ulster, also sometimes known as the Red Hand of O'Neill or the Red Hand of Ireland, is an Irish Gaelic symbol that originated in pagan times. It is often associated with a legendary figure known by several different names, including Labraid Lámh Dhearg, Labraid Lámderg and Labraid of the Red Hand."

"Go on," she said.

"There are two stories associated with the symbol. The first states that at one time the kingdom of Ulster had no rightful heir, so a boat race was staged to see who would be king. The first man to lay his hand on the soil of Ulster would take the prize. One competitor, a man from the Uí Néill clan, loved Ulster so much that he couldn't let the crown go to anyone else. When it looked like one of the other competitors might win the race, this man cut off his hand and threw it ahead of the other boat. Since his severed hand reached the soil of Ulster before anyone else's, the Ui Neill kinsman was named king."

"Gross. What's the other story?" she asked.

Doug snorted. "Two giants were engaged in battle on the shores of Ulster. One of them cut his hand and left a bloody handprint on the rocks along the shore. The men of Ulster took it as their standard to show how powerful they were."

Annja frowned. Giants? The Ui Neill clan? Ulster? What did any of that have to do with Big Red or the black torc?

"Is that it?" she asked him, her anger momentarily forgotten as she tried to see the connections between everything.

"Yeah, except for the terrorist thing. Personally, I think—"

"Wait! What terrorist thing?"

"Didn't I tell you about that already?"

The urge to hit something reared its head, but she took a deep breath and simply said, "No, Doug, you didn't mention that."

"Oh. Okay, then, hang on a sec." She heard him flipping the pages of the report in his hands.

"The red hand, specifically a tattoo of a red hand, has also been used in recent years as a symbol of the Red Hand Defenders, or RHD, a loyalist paramilitary terrorist group linked to the Ulster Volunteer Force in Northern Ireland."

She stared at the wall of her hotel room, lost in thought. What on earth would Irish terrorists want with a two-thousand-year-old necklace? It just didn't make much sense, from a practical standpoint. Sure, there was a burgeoning black market for rare archaeological pieces, but an unknown piece like this one wouldn't command big dollar amounts by any stretch of the imagination. And if wasn't about the money, why else would they want it?

Doug's voice brought her out of her reverie. "I wouldn't concentrate on that if I were you, though. Even the police seem to think that the RHD doesn't really exist. There's a quote here from a senior Irish official that says, 'The title Red Hand Defenders has been used to claim murders on all sides and is not thought to represent any real organization.' I'd think they'd be the ones to know."

"Could be," she answered, but she had a feeling they were finally on the right track. After all, if she'd run into just one gunman wearing the tattoo, she wouldn't have given it a second thought. But the two men in the Mercedes had also had the same mark. That made it more than a coincidence for her.

There was something there. She was just going to have to figure out what.

She thanked Doug for the help and told him she'd be in touch. He started complaining again that the sun hadn't even come up yet when she hung up the phone.

THREE BLOCKS AWAY from Doug Morrell's apartment, two men sat in the back of a van parked at the side of the street. They'd been there since early the night before and the air inside the vehicle was thick with the smell of body odor, stale coffee and the various cartons of take-out food that were piled in one corner of the cargo space in back.

As soon as Doug had picked up the phone in his apartment, the two men in the van had gone to work. Sophisticated computer equipment had begun the process of tracking where the call had originated. One man listened to the actual conversation, looking for clues to the caller's location in what was said, just in case the call didn't last long enough for the trace to go through. From the time references, it was clear that the caller was somewhere other than North America and the listener made a note to that effect on the yellow legal pad in front of him. As he worked to glean something from the conversation itself, his partner monitored the computer tracking program. It pinpointed the continent first, which turned out to be Europe, and then, a few minutes later, narrowed that down to the country, England. The man and the woman on the phone continued speaking and so the computer continued working, pinpointing the city the call was coming from as London. Finally, in the very last few seconds of the conversation, the computer was able to pinpoint the location right down to the building the call originated from.

By the time Annja hung up the phone, not only did the two men in the van know she was calling from a hotel on the outskirts of London, but they even knew the floor she was calling from.

The two men compared notes, agreed that they had reliable data to pass on to their employer and then sent a copy of the trace as well as a written report of the call to their employer.

Though neither one of them said it aloud, they were both thinking how funny it was that the woman their employer was searching for was right under his nose.

HALF AN HOUR LATER, Annja was sitting in a shadowy pub a few blocks from her hotel, staring at the greasy menu and trying to decide if she really trusted a place like this to cook something that wouldn't give her food poisoning, when her cell phone rang.

She glanced at the caller ID.

Museum d'histoire naturelle…it said.

Annja answered it before it could ring a third time. "Hello?"

"Is this Annja Creed?" asked a rich, warm voice.

"Yes, it is. Thank you for getting back to me so quickly, Dr. de Chance."

For a moment, he was confused. "How did you…oh, I see. Caller ID, correct?"

Annja smiled. "Yes, that's correct. I don't know anyone else at the Paris Museum of Natural History, so…"

De Chance chuckled. "Quite right, quite right. Silly me. Now what can I do for you, Miss Creed? Your voice mail mentioned something about a black torc?"

Relieved at both his receptiveness as well as the fact that he apparently hadn't heard the authorities were looking for her in conjunction with the events at the dig site in Arkholme, Annja explained that she'd recently been involved in an excavation that had uncovered an unusual specimen of torc that seemed to have come from the early Iron Age and that she was looking for any information relative to such a find that might help her pinpoint its origin and purpose.

It wasn't exactly why she wanted the information, but it was close enough to the truth that he shouldn't question her motives.

He didn't.

"Well, I'd certainly be willing to see what I could do to help you. Are you here in Paris? Could you make a three o'clock appointment tomorrow? I've had a cancellation and could fit you in then."

"Three tomorrow would be fine, Dr. de Chance. Thank you."

He told her he'd have a security pass waiting for her at the museum's information desk and gave her directions from there to his office.

When she hung up the phone, Annja felt hopeful for the first time in days. She had several leads now and that, more than anything else, told her that she was making headway. She would get to the bottom of this, no matter what it took.

23

Trevor Jackson reviewed the report of Annja Creed's whereabouts. It had taken several hours to pass from the two men in the van in New York, through three successive layers of cutouts, before it reached his ear. That was fine with him; he'd rather sacrifice a little time in the interests of security than have men knocking down his door at night and arresting him for actions against the Crown.

Treason wasn't something the authorities took lightly.

Shaw had made it clear that he didn't care what happened to the woman; it was the torc that mattered. Recover that and everything else was just a bump in the road that would either be smoothed over, or hammered flat, depending on the issue, once the torc was in their hands.

With that in mind, Jackson selected three men from the RHD's roster, good solid men with experience in this kind of thing. All of them had seen action before, both on behalf of the RHD and elsewhere, but he still wasn't totally convinced that they could handle the Creed woman.

He turned and picked up the file lying nearby, the one he'd assembled as soon as they realized who it was that had taken the torc. He'd read it thoroughly several times and still didn't understand how this woman had managed to escape from him and his men, not once but twice now. The two men who'd reported seeing her on the road had been professionals, men who'd been active during the Troubles, who's seen action against armed soldiers every bit as trained as they were. Somehow she'd beaten them.

Not just beaten them, he thought with chagrin, but made them look like total fools, their bodies left lying in a ditch beside the road for the police to find.

Never mind the fact that they still hadn't found the car the two men had been driving.

It pissed him off just thinking about it.

Still, he didn't have anyone better available, so these three would have to do.

He pulled the photo of Annja out of the file and stared at it for the hundredth time, as if it might contain some hidden clue to the woman's success, but there was nothing there he hadn't seen before.

And yet...

His instinct told him he was missing something.

Something important.

But what?

He considered what he'd read in the file. The many adventures the woman had been involved in. The many times she'd escaped at the last minute, slipping away from death's bony grasp. It didn't matter if the threat was a natural disaster, like the tsunami in India she'd miraculously survived—or man himself, like the Albanian terrorists she'd supposedly tangled with in Nepal recently; every single time she'd been able to snatch success at the last second from the yawning jaws of defeat. If he was a different kind of man, he'd almost believe she had a guardian angel watching over her.

He dropped the photo on his desk in disgust.

Enough of this nonsense. Guardian angel or not, this time Annja Creed will not escape. By sunrise, she'll be dead and the torc will be mine, he thought.

Jackson picked up his phone and made a call to the men he had standing by.

24

Annja had some planning to do before she'd be able to get herself to Paris—no easy feat when the police and a few killers were looking for her. She tried to concentrate but no matter how hard she tried, she couldn't get her mind to focus. It kept coming back to the events of the past few days, worrying at them like a dog with a bone. She knew she was missing something, something that tied all this together somehow, but she just couldn't figure out what it was. And until she did, it seemed her subconscious just wasn't going to leave her in peace.

Maybe some exercise will help, she thought.

The idea of a run through the city streets appealed to her. She dressed quickly, throwing on a loose pair of pants and a sweatshirt to ward off the morning chill. She did a few stretches to get the blood flowing and then took the stairs down to the ground floor. With a nod at the sleepy clerk behind the counter, she stepped out the lobby door and headed off down the street.

The air was crisp and cool enough that she could see her breath each time she exhaled. She'd run in worse conditions, however, far worse, and she knew a little bite in the air wouldn't slow her down any. It might, in fact, help her feel more calm once she got back to the warmth of her hotel room.

She took it easy at first, warming up the muscles and getting into a rhythm, then began to push herself harder, her feet slapping the pavement as she forced a faster pace. She could feel the frustration and tension of the past few days pouring out of her, burning away in the rush of endorphins the exercise pushed into her system. After the first mile she felt good. After the second, great. By the time she had the third one behind her, she began to feel a little tired and that was her signal to head back to the hotel.

Maybe now, with that gentle ache running through her bones, she could sit down and make some plans.

The clerk wasn't at the desk when she came in, but she didn't think much of it.

He's probably in the back room somewhere, she thought.

As she neared the top of the fifth flight of steps, her thoughts on the warm shower that awaited her above, she heard the floor of the hallway above her creak as someone shifted their weight.

It was a small, furtive sound, and that was what caught her attention.

People, ordinary people, don't try to avoid making noise when they walk down a hallway, Annja knew. They trundle along like a herd of elephants, completely unaware of how much noise they generate in their passing.

What she'd heard was someone doing their best not to give themselves away.

Thankfully their best wasn't good enough.

Annja immediately stopped moving. She stood where she was, her gaze fixed on the landing still several steps above her. When no one appeared after a long moment, she lifted her left foot and, very carefully, took a lateral step toward the wall. She knew the floor would be less worn there, less apt to creak and groan, and right now she didn't know how many were waiting up there for her and even the smallest advantage might be important.

She was three steps from the top of the stairwell and she kept her gaze fixed firmly on the landing above her, waiting. If the sound had, in fact, simply been the innocent result of someone coming down the hallway toward the stairwell, they'd appear above her any second now.

One, one thousand.

Two, one thousand.

Three, one thousand.

No one was coming.

Yet she knew someone was there. She could sense them waiting above her.

The landing at the top of the steps was a few feet wide, just enough space for a person to take a step or two before intersecting the end of the corridor that stretched away at a ninety-degree angle to the left. Since she couldn't see anyone standing on the landing, the sound must have come from the corridor itself. Perhaps, like her, whoever was waiting for her was pressed up against the wall on the other side of the corner, ready to jump out at her when she came around it.

She glanced back down the staircase behind her and saw that it was still empty.

That was good; it meant they weren't trying to box her in. They weren't professionals, then, she thought with an inward sigh of relief, knowing that increased her chances of coming through this without serious injury by a considerable margin.

It probably wasn't the cops, either, for they would have been waiting for her in the lobby, reducing the potential threat to the hotel's other patrons and giving the cops more room to maneuver if the need presented itself.

That left only the people who'd tried to kill her twice already. The Red Hand Defenders.

If that's even what they were really called.

The sound of another scuff reached her ears.

He's nervous, she realized. He doesn't know where I went or what I'm doing. All he knows is that I should have reached the top of the steps by now. Since I didn't, he's wondering what I'm up to, wondering whether I'm standing here waiting for him to show himself or if I've turned around and gone back down the stairs already.

She intended to take advantage of that.

Annja summoned her sword to hand, thankful for what felt like the ten thousandth time since she'd become its bearer that it could just appear and disappear at will. Very carefully, so as to not make any noise that might give her away, Annja lifted one foot, placed it on the step above her and then slowly settled her weight on it. When it didn't make any noise, she shifted her weight, lifting her other foot and bringing it up next to the first. Now she was one step closer to whoever was waiting for her above.

She paused, listening, and when she didn't hear a response she repeated the procedure, then did it again, until she stood on the landing. She kept her back away from the wall, not wanting to brush against it, and moved right up to the very edge of the corner.

For a second or two there was nothing, but then she heard him, very close on the other side of the corridor, breathing sharply through his nose as he mentally pumped himself up for what was to come.

She imagined what they must look like, both of them pressed up against opposite sides of the same corner, each of them waiting for the other to make a move, doing their best not to give anything away in the process.

Annja had no intention of letting him go first.

Switching the sword to her left hand, she suddenly reached around the corner, grabbed the man waiting there by the front of his shirt and yanked him around the corner.

She caught a glimpse of the surprise on his face and the gun in his hand as he went stumbling past her and then the forward momentum she'd imparted to him carried him headfirst down the stairs she'd just ascended.

There was a short, sharp cry that was cut off abruptly with a sickening thud.

Annja barely heard it; she'd already dismissed him as a threat. Instead, she was focused on whoever else might be waiting for her. Knowing that most gunmen were trained to shoot for the center mass, Annja spun around the corner in a low crouch, intending to buy herself an extra second or two should there be anyone else waiting to attack her.

The hall was empty.

It was only when she rose out of her crouch and moved forward a few steps that she could see the door to the room she had rented was open slightly, the light from inside spilling out into the corridor like an arrow directing her path.

She quietly moved to the other side of the hallway, so that she would be on the same side as her room, and then approached at a slow and careful pace. She held her sword before her like a talisman, prepared to deal with anyone who emerged from her room, but she reached it before anyone did so.

With the tip of her sword, she slowly pushed the door open.

There was a man standing on the far side of her hotel room, his back to the door. The contents of her backpack were strewn on the bed in front of him and he was slicing up what little clothing she had with a knife, to see if she had hidden anything inside the seams.

Annja's gaze flicked to the baseboard where she'd hidden the torc and, seeing that it appeared undistributed, thanked her lucky stars that she'd taken the time to find a hiding place for the necklace when she'd first arrived.

"Well? Anyone out there?" the intruder asked in a gruff voice, looking up as he did so.

Their gazes met across the room.

He went for the gun lying on the bed in front of him, scooping it up and bringing his arm up in Annja's direction.

She'd been expecting him to do something along those lines though, and she moved a split second faster than he did. Even as her brain registered the threat— *Gun!*—she was already turning sideways to present a smaller target and whipping her arm forward in a throw that would have made Sister Margaret, the nun in charge of physical education at the orphanage in New Orleans where she'd grown up, proud.

The sword left her hand, tumbled end over end twice and then embedded itself point first in the intruder's chest. The force of the throw allowed the sword blade to cut through skin and muscle like it wasn't even there, until, at last, the point of the weapon emerged from the man's back between his second and third ribs and slammed into the wall behind him, pinning him in place like a butterfly to a specimen board.

The shot he had been preparing to fire at her went wild, the bullet slamming into the wall a good two feet to her left, the sound of the shot itself muffled from the silencer attached to the end of the weapon's barrel.

The man hung there, his eyes wide with surprise, blood pooling at the edge of his mouth as his strength rushed away from him and the gun fell to the floor at his feet.

From across the room Annja willed the sword to disappear, and as it did, it released the man from its grip. He slid slowly to the floor, blood pulsing from the wound in his chest with every beat of his heart.

Annja crossed the room and kicked the gun away, then stuck her head in the bathroom to assure herself that it was empty.

Satisfied they were alone, Annja knelt in front of the dying man. He was already staring off into the distance, and Annja knew he didn't have long. Still, she had to try.

"Who sent you?" she asked. "What do you want?"

The sound of her voice seemed to bring him back to the here and now, but it wasn't enough. He looked in her direction, opened his mouth to say something and then died.

Annja watched it happen, not feeling anything. These people had tried to kill her several times now and she had no sympathy for them. It didn't matter if they were just following orders; that wasn't an excuse in her book.

They'd come after her and her own; there was no way she was going to let that just slide. If she had to take out every single one of them to remain safe, that's exactly what she planned to do.

Unfortunately, she didn't know anything more now than she did earlier.

The sound of a door opening and closing again in the hallway outside her room brought back her sense of urgency.

The gunshot might have been muffled, but eventually someone was going to use that stairwell and they'd find what was left of her first assailant.

She couldn't be there when that happened.

But first she had to know.

She reached forward and tore open the man's shirt enough that she could pull it down over his right shoulder.

The tattoo of a red hand stared back at her.

25

A quick check didn't turn up any ID, but it did produce a thick wad of bills held together by a gold clip. Knowing how limited her current funds were, Annja quickly stuffed them in her pocket. Next she grabbed her backpack, stuffed her computer and cell phone inside it, along with the few clothes her intruder hadn't already destroyed. After that she retrieved the torc from its hiding place behind the baseboard and then slipped out of the room, hanging a do-not-disturb sign on the door and closing it gently behind her.

The hallway was empty.

She strode over to the landing and glanced down the stairs. The body of her first assailant was still there, his legs on the last few steps and his chest stretched out across the landing. His head was bent at an unnatural angle and his eyes were open and staring back in her direction.

Annja hurried down the steps past the corpse and headed for the ground floor as quickly as she could.

She hailed a cab outside the hotel and had it take her into the heart of London. Right now she wanted to lose herself amid the crowds.

The route the cab driver took followed the Thames into the city and as they came up Cannon Street, Annja saw the familiar logo of a Federal Express office.

Inspiration struck at the sight.

"Can you pull over and wait a few moments?" she asked the driver, who was all too happy to oblige.

She went inside and approached the desk, asking for help in locating the address of the Hotel Apollinaire in the Montparnasse section of Paris. She'd stayed there before; she remembered it as a nice hotel on a quiet street and most definitely a step up from the kind of place she'd just left behind. With the address in hand, Annja retired to a table in the corner and, with the help of some materials she'd purchased from the clerk, packed up the torc and got it ready for shipping.

As she was getting ready to fill out the label, she called the hotel on her cell phone.

"Registration please," she said when it was answered.

She was on hold for only a minute or two before a clerk at the front desk answered.

"Hotel Apollinaire, how can I help you?"

"I'd like to speak to Stephan Marcineaux. Is he in today?"

"One moment, please."

This time the wait was considerably longer, but when the phone was picked up again she heard Stephan's deep voice on the other end of the line.

"This is Stephan. How may I help you?"

"Stephan, it's Annja. Annja Creed."

This was the tricky part. Stephan was the manager of the Apollinaire. A few years before two men had tried to rob the place, one of them holding Stephan and one of the desk clerks at gunpoint while the other worked to clean out the hotel safe. Annja had come in from a late night out and walked right into the situation, but rather than being cowed by the presence of the gun as the robbers clearly expected her to be, Annja had gone on the offensive, disarming the first man and getting his captives to safety before anything could happen to them. The police had caught the other man a few blocks away. A potentially terrible situation been averted and Stephan had promised his undying support if there was anything he could do for her. Annja needed help; she was going to call in that favor.

There was a moment of hesitation and then Stephan said, "Just a moment, please, ma'am."

She heard the receiver being placed on the desk and then the sound of a door closing somewhere on the other side. A second later Stephan was back on the line with her.

"Annja! I saw you on the news! Are you all right?"

Just as she feared, word of the attack had gone international, thanks in no small part, she was sure, to Doug's impromptu press conference. Now came the real test….

"I'm fine, Stephan, but I need some help."

It was the moment of truth. Stephan had seemed like the law-and-order type. If he had any qualms about helping someone currently wanted for questioning by the police, he would say so now.

"Anything. Name it."

"I'm on my way to Paris and need a place to stay for a few days while I sort all this out."

"Say no more," he replied. "When do you expect to arrive?"

"Tomorrow afternoon."

She could hear him punching something into a keyboard for a few minutes and then he said, "I've got a room reserved for you under the name Allison Smith. Ask for Suzette when you get here, as I'll be off duty then. I'll have everything taken care of—all you have to do is see Suzette and pick up your key, understand?"

"Thank you so much, Stephan."

She could practically hear him smile on the other end of the phone. "After what you did? Think nothing of it."

She told him she'd see him soon and they hung up. She finished filling out the paperwork for the package, and addressing it to Allison Smith at the Hotel Apollinaire. She put a Hold for Guest note on it, as well. When she was done, she dropped it into the slot designated for such parcels and that was that.

For the time being, the torc was safe.

If the RHD discovered that she'd fled England for the Continent, they'd most likely look for her first in the same hole-in-the-wall kind of place she'd stayed in London, so upgrading a few levels above that could throw them off the scent for a little while. Hopefully she'd have completed her business in Paris by the time they figured out what she'd done.

She knew that having some help on the ground in Paris would certainly make things easier, so she tried Roux's number again. As before, all she reached was his voice mail.

"I need your help," she said into the recording. "Please call me as soon as possible."

As she headed for the door she spotted a do-it-your-self photo-printing kiosk across the room. Making a split second decision, she detoured over to it and used the SD card from her digital camera to print out several of the pictures she'd taken of the torc after it had been cleaned. It seemed a prudent thing to do, given her planned meeting with Dr. de Chance the next day.

Returning to the cab, she quizzed the driver for a few moments about the various means of crossing the English Channel. Without a car of her own, she couldn't use the Tunnel and she soon discovered that the only other alternatives, short of flying, were to take either a train or a ferry.

"The train is faster," the driver told her, "and much more comfortable. The fare is reasonable, as well."

"The ferry isn't?"

The driver shrugged. "Reasonable, yes. Fast or comfortable, no."

Anyone following her would expect her to take the fastest route possible. In order to throw them off the track, she decided to do the opposite.

"Take me to the ferry, please," she told the driver.

"Which one?" was his laconic reply.

A discussion followed and Annja learned there were several different ferries making the crossing, the most popular ones being on the Dover to Calais route, and that the cost of each trip depended on just where you wanted to end up. In the end, she selected the ferry at Portsmouth. It would take her over to Cherbourg in just under four hours. From Cherbourg she could catch a train directly into Paris, which would tack on another three hours to her trip but would still get her into the city in plenty of time for her meeting with Dr. de Chance.

It would have to do.

With things now in the hands of the cabbie, Annja leaned back in her seat and stared out the window.

"Miss?"

Annja heard the voice as if from a long way off. She tried to ignore it at first, but it was persistent and after a moment she woke with a start.

She found herself staring into the cabbie's face as he leaned across the front seat trying to get her attention.

"We're here, miss," he said.

She glanced around, trying to remember where "here" actually was. It had been a long and exhausting few days. The smell of the sea and the sight of the ship at the dock nearby brought it all back to her.

She paid the cabbie with some of the money she'd taken from the dead operative and got out of the car, blinking in the sunlight.

The ferry was already loading as she approached, the long line of cars in front of the ramp moving slowly forward at the direction of the crew members who stood at the boat's stern. Despite this being one of the slower routes across the Channel, there were still plenty of cars being brought on board, as well as a decent crowd of pedestrians like her waiting to board at the gangplank.

The more the merrier, Annja thought. Less chance of anyone picking me out of the crowd.

With the brim of her hat pulled down low and her face pointed at the ground, Annja approached the ticket window.

"Round trip, please," she mumbled, sliding her cash through the slot below the window.

The clerk printed her ticket and slid that plus her change back in the other direction.

Annja joined the line waiting to board the boat. This was the most dangerous part of the process for her, when no one particularly had anything to do other than stand around and stare at their fellow passengers. She was using a fake passport she always kept with her as emergencies were frequent since she'd claimed the sword. She kept her eyes on the ground, didn't look at anyone else and made it onto the boat without anyone shouting out her name in surprise.

Once on board she made her way up several flights of stairs until she reached the upper deck. Here the passengers' seats were out in the open air and on a chilly day such as this the deck was far less occupied than any of the enclosed ones below. For Annja, it was the best place on the boat to keep the chance of being recognized to a minimum. She found a seat, settled down and waited for the ship to get under way.

26

She noticed the man watching her about half an hour after they left Portsmouth. He was dark-haired, dressed in blue jeans and a light jacket, with a backpack slung over one shoulder. She'd seen him on the deck with her, but didn't really pay attention until she'd gone down to the galley deck to get out of the wind for a few minutes and grab something to fill her empty stomach, only to have him show up there a few minutes later, as well.

She caught him giving her the eye several times as she waited in line.

So he thinks your attractive, she thought, is that such a big deal?

Normally it wouldn't be; having men find her attractive was something she dealt with on a regular basis. But right now, when it felt like half the world was looking for her, being followed made her distinctly uncomfortable.

How could they have found her again that quickly?

For that matter, how had they done so in the first place?

She didn't know, so she knew she couldn't ignore the man. Doing so could severely endanger her life.

Rather than return to the upper deck, Annja spent some time walking around one of the middecks, turning things over in her head, trying to find the pattern, the connection between recent events.

As she stood looking out the window, she glanced sideways and saw the man again. He was a short distance away and was studiously being certain not to look in her direction. In fact, it was his very stillness that had caught her eye; it was out of place among the other passengers who were laughing and talking, trying to pass the time.

Very casually, she continued turning, pretending to be looking for someone, a friend, a lover, but in truth she was scanning the rest of the passengers, trying to determine if the dark-haired man was alone.

As far as she could tell, he was.

Big mistake, she thought with a grim sense of satisfaction.

She stepped away from the window and headed for the exit, being sure to walk straight past where he was standing. He didn't turn and look at her as she went past, though his body went stiff with tension.

Amateur.

She stepped out into the passageway and immediately increased her pace, putting some distance between the two of them should he try to follow, so that she could be sure that she had time to spring her trap if she needed to. She passed several people going the other way and used the cover they provided to glance behind her.

Her pursuer was just coming out of the compartment

she'd vacated, pushing his way past several of those standing in the passageway as if afraid Annja would get so far ahead that he'd lose her.

Game on, she thought.

She led him down passageway after passageway and through compartment after compartment, always staying just a bit ahead of him, until she was certain that he was acting alone. If anyone had been working with him, they would have boxed her in long before now. Since no one had emerged from the crowds to hinder her, she had to conclude that he was flying solo.

Time to turn the tables.

She was half a corridor length ahead of him, and as he rounded the corner behind her she pulled open the door marked Crew Only and slipped inside.

If he was just an overzealous fan looking for an autograph, the sign would more than likely stop him. But if he was following her for other reasons—if he was a cop or, more likely, a member of the RHD, then he'd blow right through it like it wasn't there.

The room Annja found herself in was full of various pieces of machinery. She slipped into the shadows beside one, summoned her sword and waited.

A moment passed.

The sound of running feet reached her ears and then the door she'd just entered was opened, then closed quietly behind her pursuer.

Footsteps approached.

She waited, listening to them get closer, closer….

Her dark-haired pursuer stepped into view, his attention on the door on the opposite wall, and he didn't realize Annja was there until she reached out of the shadows, grabbed his arm and spun him around against the lump of machinery she'd been hiding behind. The point of her sword pressed up into the tender flesh beneath his chin.

"Who are you?" she asked with a snarl.

The man's eyes were wide with fear, his head straining upward as he tried to keep his neck as far from the edge of her blade as possible.

"Mike," he said, his voice shaking. "Mike Gilmore."

Annja started. She hadn't been expecting him to actually answer her....

"What the hell do you think you're doing?" she asked, putting a little more upward pressure on the sword.

Mike rose up on his toes, wincing. "Take it easy, lady! I'm not a rapist or anything, promise!"

"I asked you a question. If you don't want a back-alley tracheotomy, I suggest you answer me!"

Rather than send him into a panic, the notion that she might actually carry through with her threat and slit his throat seemed to steady him. When he answered her, his voice was calm and his pace steady.

"I'm a reporter for the *Minneapolis Sun-Times*," he said, staring directly at her, as if he might foresee her intent in her eyes. "I'm here on vacation and just happened to recognize you when I boarded the ferry. I thought I might have a chance at a story."

Annja snorted. "By following me?"

"I wanted to see what you were doing but didn't want to get too close." He raised his shoulders slightly in a shrug. "I guess I'm not too good at this kind of thing."

She studied him for a moment. "Got an ID to back up that story?"

He began to nod, then thought better of it when he felt the sword beneath his chin.

"Left pocket. You are Annja Creed, right? I mean I didn't get myself into this mess for nothing, did I?"

Ignoring his questions, and keeping the sword right where it was, Annja fished into the pocket of his coat and pulled out a lanyard that had an ID clipped to it. It was a standard press ID, with his name and photo over that of the newspaper.

Still, it paid to be certain.

"Take off your shirt," she commanded.

"What!" Mike exclaimed.

She gave the sword a little twist, watching a drop of blood well up under its tip. "Take off your shirt," she repeated.

As he moved to do as he was told, Annja took the sword away from his throat but kept it trained on his chest. One hard thrust would be all it would take.

Mike apparently recognized that, or else had concluded that he was dealing with a complete madwoman, for he made no move to escape. Instead, he let his jacket fall to the floor and then whipped his shirt over his head, exposing a decently muscled chest and a bare pair of shoulders.

No tattoo.

Satisfied, Annja stepped back, giving him a little more room.

"Okay, you can get dressed."

His shoulders slumped and he almost shut his eyes in relief, but then he remembered there was an angry woman with a sword in front of him and they snapped open again.

Annja found it almost comical.

Almost.

As she watched him pull his shirt back on, she considered the current situation. Not for the first time since she'd fled the dig site, she didn't know what to do. Clearly he was telling the truth, but rather than helping her out that fact created more problems for her.

He knew who she was and where she was. If she let him go, he would probably take that information right to the police. Heck, he didn't even need to wait that long. He could go to the ship's captain and have him radio ahead so that when they arrived in France, there would be law enforcement officers waiting there for her.

On the other hand, he was an innocent and she couldn't just get rid of him, convenient as that might be. Garin, and possibly even Roux, wouldn't think twice about it, but Annja just couldn't bring herself to do such a thing.

She was going to have to find a way to convince him not to turn her in.

When he was finished getting dressed, Annja asked, "What did you hope to get out of following me?"

He didn't hesitate to answer. "A story, of course," he said bluntly. "Ever since your producer gave that idiotic press conference, people have been wondering where you were and what, exactly, your involvement is in the Bog Mummy Case."

"Is that what they're calling it? The Bog Mummy Case?"

For the first time, Mike looked embarrassed. "Yeah. It kind of stuck after your producer made that wild-ass comment about bog mummies."

She was silent for several long minutes, trying to figure out her next move. Thankfully Mike had a solution.

"Look," he said, licking his lips a little nervously at her continued silence. "Despite the sword-in-the-throat thing, I don't think you're dangerous, nor do I believe that you had anything to do with the murders of those scientists. If you did, you already would have run me through with that pigsticker of yours, right?"

Annja just stared at him.

"So, uh, how about we do this? I'll keep my mouth shut about seeing you here if you give me an exclusive on the story."

With that, he shut up and didn't say anything more despite the fact that Annja let the silence grow.

He who talks first loses, Annja thought, an old sales saying she'd picked up from somewhere. She had to admit it was a truism if she'd ever heard one.

"Okay," she said.

Mike stared at her. "Okay? Really?"

She nodded. "Really. You allow me to get off this ship without informing the authorities and I promise to give you an exclusive interview when it is all said and done."

"Why not now?" he asked.

"Because I'm still trying to put it all together."

"But you promise to give me the full story before you speak to anyone else? A total exclusive? You'll tell me everything?"

Certainly not everything, she thought, looking at the sword in hand, but enough at least for you to get what you are looking for. Aloud, she said, "Of course."

"How do I know you're telling the truth?" he asked.

Annja frowned. "Are you suggesting I'd lie to you?"

You could see he was about to answer yes, but then he caught sight of the sword she still held in one hand and apparently changed his mind. "No, not at all," he said with a forced smile. "I just wanted to be clear."

Annja understood his predicament. If he walked away and she never made good on her promise, he'd be missing out on a huge story. On the other hand, she had to trust him as much as he had to trust her.

She said as much to him.

"Yeah, but you're the one holding the sword, not me. You can make me agree to anything, just by sticking me with that thing again."

"Fair enough," she replied. "Give me your notebook and a pen."

Frowning, he did what he was told, passing over a black notebook that he had in the back pocket of his jeans.

Annja took it, turned to a clean page and wrote out a short note to Doug telling him to draw up a contract giving the *Minneapolis Sun-Times* and its reporter, Michael Gilmore, an exclusive interview with her on the Bog Mummy Case when she was freely able to do so. She instructed him to sign it on behalf of both her and the studio and to keep a copy for their own records. When she was finished she read it over a second time, but decided against changing anything. Short and to the point, that was the best way of dealing with Doug.

When she was finished, she handed the pad and pen back to Gilmore and said, "Send that to my producer, Doug Morrell, at the corporate offices in Manhattan. He'll draw you up a proper contract to see that you get what's coming to you."

Mike read the note, looked back at her for a moment and then shrugged. "I can live with that," he said, then grimaced when he realized the double meaning behind his words.

Annja simply smiled.

27

At the same time that Annja was cutting a deal with her wannabe paparazzo, Detective Inspector Beresford was entering the morgue at New Scotland Yard, intent on checking the results of the autopsies that had been done that morning on the bodies of the two men recovered from the roadside ditch south of the dig site.

Clements had prepared a preliminary report after returning to the office earlier and Beresford had read it on the way over. Fingerprint analysis had identified the two men as Brian O'Donnell and Sean MacGuire. Both of them had records; they'd been in and out of prison several times over the past fifteen years. At first it was just small stuff—petty larceny, possession of stolen goods, assault and battery—but it wasn't long before they graduated to more serious crimes. The last time they'd been pinched they ended up doing five years together in Swansea on an armed robbery charge. It was there, according to the file, that they'd been recruited into the Ulster Volunteer Force.

Beresford wasn't surprised to see the notes to that effect. The UVF had been in need of men who didn't shy away from violence, and O'Donnell and MacGuire had equally needed the protection and standing that membership in the UVF would have given them. It was practically a match made in heaven. The two men had kept their noses out of trouble and had been released within a month of each other in 2005. There were rumors that they were involved in the slaying of a Catholic alderman in the summer of 2007 and again in an attempted car bombing in London in 2009, but that's all they were—rumors. CT Command didn't have enough to haul them in as accomplices, never mind pin the jobs on them. The two men had dropped off the radar and that had been that.

Until they were found cast aside like so much trash on the side of the road south of the dig site.

It wasn't a coincidence; that much was obvious. But how they fit into the bigger picture and what their roles had been in the massacre, Beresford didn't know.

It seemed clear that they had met their end in a confrontation with the now-infamous Annja Creed. Beresford had watched the sideshow of a press conference that her producer had orchestrated the other day and while it primarily raised more questions than it answered, it did seem to confirm his reasoning with regard to her behavior. If she had been a witness to the events at the dig site, as her producer had indicated, then it would be natural for her to go into hiding, especially if she had already fought off a second attempt on her life. Twice was usually two times too many for most people; he didn't blame her for wanting to avoid a third.

It still didn't explain why she hadn't come forward since then, and that bothered him.

What was he missing?

His musing ended, his question still unanswered, when he reached the guard posted outside the doors of the morgue. Given the importance of the evidence that passed through the morgue, access to the facility was carefully monitored and documented. Beresford had to show his identification and sign the log book before the guard would let him in for his appointment with the coroner, Jack Gibbons.

Gibbons had held the post for the past ten years and Beresford had worked with him on a number of cases. He found the man to be both highly dedicated and extremely skilled when it came to his job. He was also a very affable fellow, once you got through his carefully cultivated curmudgeonlike exterior. Beresford honestly liked the man and, as a result, it made this aspect of his job a little less upsetting than it might otherwise be.

"How are you, Jack?" Beresford asked as he stepped into the room and caught sight of the other man working at a nearby station.

Gibbons was in his early sixties, just a few years short of "put-him-out-to-pasture age," as he liked to call it. He was a large man, but moved with a grace and surety of motion. He had a full head of gleaming white hair and often wore it in a ponytail to annoy those younger, but less fortunate, members of the staff who were already losing their hair at half his age.

"I'm just fine," the other man replied, "but him," he said, indicating the man on the table in front of him, "not so much."

"What happened?" Beresford asked as he stepped up beside him and looked down at the body of a middle-aged man that looked both oddly crushed and bloated at the same time.

"Idiot decided to test the law of gravity while drunk by taking a high dive off the Tower Bridge. He must have sobered up on the way down, though, because witnesses claim he started screaming about halfway to the bottom."

Gibbons finished making notes on a chart that hung at the bottom of the vivisection table and then gave the detective his full attention.

"What can I do for you on this bleak and baleful day?" he asked with a smile.

"I heard you'd finished the postmortem on O'Donnell and MacGuire. Figured I'd get a jump on things by coming to see you rather than waiting for the official report."

Gibbons had pulled the sheet up over the body in front of them and was already moving across the room toward the refrigerated drawers before Beresford had gotten half his sentence out. That was one of the things the detective liked about the man; he was good at anticipating a detective's needs on a major case and didn't mind going around the official paperwork to give a guy a head start when necessary.

The rear wall held three rows of refrigeration units, or storage drawers, with four to a row. The coroner moved directly to two drawers in the second row, pulling them open simultaneously.

Standing between them, he asked, "What do you need to know?"

Beresford looked down at the bodies before him, figured out who was who and pointed at O'Donnell first. "Cause of death?"

"Severance of the third and fourth vertebrae."

In other words, a broken neck, just as he'd suspected at the crime scene, Beresford thought. "Any idea what might have caused it?"

"From the force of the impact and the damage to the vertebrae that resulted, I'd say it was an automobile accident. Probably wasn't buckled in."

"That's consistent with the scenario I'm putting together," Beresford said. "Anything unusual I should know about?"

"You saw the tattoo?"

"Yeah, that's why I caught the case."

Gibbons shrugged. "That's it for this one, then."

Beresford moved over to the other drawer. "And him?"

"That's where things get interesting. Timing wise, he was killed right around the same time as O'Donnell, give or take half an hour. In his case, though, death was the result of massive trauma associated with a sharp force injury that consisted of a severe stab wound in the upper left chest area."

Gibbons pulled the sheet down farther to show the wound in the corpse's chest. "The blade was close to three inches in width at its widest point and at least two and a half feet long."

He rolled the body up on one shoulder so Beresford could see the exit wound in the man's back.

"I suspect it might have even been longer," he said as he let the body fall back into place on the gurney, "but I've got no way of confirming it at the moment."

The detective did what he could to ignore the uncomfortable sound of the body slapping back against the steel table. "So what are we talking about? A combat knife, a machete, something like that?"

"A sword would be more likely, as the wound clearly shows that the weapon had a double edge."

So far, Gary Anderson's story was holding up. The first of the two victims had been killed in the crash, the second when the woman had rushed the other vehicle, weapon in hand.

Curiouser and curiouser, Beresford thought.

"A sword, huh? Old or new?" he asked.

Gibbons shrugged again. "No way to say for sure. Some older weapons will leave bits of particulate matter in the wound, tiny slivers of metal that break free of the blade when it strikes a hard surface like a bone, maybe flakes of rust if the weapon hasn't been cared for all that much, but I didn't find anything like that here."

That wasn't anything Beresford was happy to hear. It meant he'd have a hard time tying the weapon to the crime itself, even if he caught the Creed woman with the sword in hand. Gibbons would be able to say that a weapon of "similar make and style" had been used in the attack, but without additional forensic evidence like finding the blade stained with the blood of the victims, he couldn't make a more definitive statement.

But Gibbons wasn't finished.

"I recovered several different fibers from the exit wound, though. The first few matched the fabric from the shirt our victim had been wearing—the removal of the sword must have pulled them back into the wound. But there were also several slivers of a dark blue fabric that I couldn't match and I sent those over to the lab for further analysis."

"Want to hazard a guess?"

Gibbons didn't hesitate. "The angle of the entry and exit wounds suggest that the weapon entered the body at a slight downward angle, so I'm guessing our victim was sitting down when it happened. I'd say the fabric is from the upholstery of whatever chair he was sitting in at the time."

Wouldn't that be nice, Beresford thought. Anderson's testimony tied Creed to the vehicle and the deaths that occurred inside it, at least circumstantially. If the fabric turned out to be automobile upholstery, and he could match that to the vehicle itself, then he could put the body in the vehicle that was involved in the pursuit of Anderson's car, thereby tying the bodies discovered at the side of the road with the events described by Anderson.

It wasn't enough to secure a conviction, but it was a start. Successful investigations were like walls; they were built one brick at a time.

"Anything else?"

"Just that he was a member of the RHD, just like his partner there, but you probably already knew that."

"Yep."

"Looks like you've got a problem on your hands," Gibbons said as he covered up the bodies again.

"Tell me about it. Losing two of their men is going to make the RHD bloody difficult to deal with."

"Two? Try four."

Beresford gave him a quizzical look. "Four?"

"You mean you haven't heard?" Gibbons shook his head, as if he couldn't believe it. "Follow me."

He led Beresford back across the room to where two bodies were resting on wheeled stretchers under crisp blue sheets. He pulled the sheets back on both of them, exposing them from the shoulders up.

The detective barely noticed their faces for he was too busy staring at the tattoos that were visible on each man's shoulder.

Tattoos of a red hand.

"Bloody hell," he said under his breath. Then, louder so that Gibbons could hear, "Where'd you get these two?"

"Hotel over in Peckham," the other man answered. "Forensic Science Services just brought them in, after the responding detectives released the scene."

Oh, for the love of... Beresford couldn't believe that they'd cleared the scene without notifying him. Given that there was already an active investigation involving members of the RHD, standard protocol demanded that the bodies remain in place until the officers involved in the primary investigation, namely he and Clements, were given a chance to view the scene as it was found.

Losing four of their soldiers in less than forty-eight hours was not going to sit well with those in command of the RHD. There were sure to be reprisals. The trouble was there were far too many soft targets the RHD could take advantage of and there was no way for CT Command to cover them all.

It looked like things were going to get bloody very quickly unless he could get to the bottom of it.

"You happen to have the address of that hotel?" he asked.

28

Annja and Mike returned to the upper deck, where, by unspoken agreement, they stayed in eyesight of each other until the boat docked in Cherbourg. Gilmore's word had been good, for there wasn't a horde of police officers waiting to arrest her on the other side.

She used her fake passport to slip through customs without being stopped. Half an hour after arriving in France, she was on board a train bound for Paris.

She slept as soon as she was settled on the train, trying to catch up on what she had missed the nights before. It was an uneasy sleep, however, full of phantom figures chasing her through the streets and she felt no more rested when she awoke. Grabbing a cup of coffee at a café in the train station, she decided she'd be safest staying at the train station until it was time to head for the museum.

A GLANCE AT her watch as she climbed the steps told her she was right on time. A badge was waiting for her at the information desk, as promised, and a well-dressed young woman of Asian descent led her through the maze of hallways in the restricted part of the museum until they reached Dr. de Chance's office.

Annja knocked, then opened the door at the muffled, "Come in," from the other side.

Dr. de Chance was tall and thin, reminding Annja of a scarecrow that climbed down off his pole and learned to walk. He had a narrow, lined face that gave his mouth a pinched look, but his eyes were sparkling and full of life. She put his age at somewhere around sixty-five.

"Ah, you must be Miss Creed," he said with a smile, coming around his desk to shake Annja's hand. "Please come in, sit down."

He indicated the chair in front of his desk with the wave of a hand and returned to his chair.

"Thank you for taking the time to see me," Annja began, but de Chance waved the social chitchat aside.

"Skip the formalities, please. I'm too old to waste time on such nonsense. Let's talk one colleague to another. Tell me about this black torc you found," he suggested.

Surprised by his abruptness, but interested in learning what he knew nonetheless, Annja did so, explaining about the recent dig in the West Midlands. She kept waiting for him to interrupt and tell her he knew all of this from the newscasts but he did not; apparently Dr. de Chance was one of the few people who had not heard about the recent tragedy. She explained how the torc had been found around the neck of the Iceni chieftain they'd pulled from the bog's clutches, though she conveniently left out the part about how they'd known were to dig. When it came time to describe the torc, she simply handed over the copies of the photographs she'd had made the day before.

De Chance studied them for several minutes. Annja could feel the tension in the room rise as he did so, though she didn't understand why. When he was finished looking at the pictures, de Chance leaned forward in his seat, his gaze intense. "Do you have the torc with you, by chance?"

Annja shook her head. "No, I'm sorry. I wasn't able to obtain permission in time to remove it from the site."

There was something about the way de Chance had asked the question that made Annja a little uneasy and she didn't think twice about lying to him.

"Well, that's too bad," he said, putting the photos on his desk for the moment. "It would have been interesting to see it."

A frown crossed his face for a second, there and gone so quickly Annja wasn't even certain she'd seen it.

"So, how can I help you?"

"Well," she began, "you didn't sound surprised to hear there was a torc like this out there, so I'm assuming you've heard of it?"

He nodded. "Yes. There are one or two stories that mention a black torc, but they generally refer to it by its given name, the Tear of the Gods."

"The Tear of the Gods?" She hadn't come across that name in her research.

De Chance leaned back and got comfortable. "You've heard of Boudica and her rebellion against Rome?"

"Yes. Like most of those who tried to throw off the yoke of the empire, it failed."

"Quite right. But there are some who say that the failure was not due to her lack of intelligence or tactical know-how, but rather a result of the fact that she gave up her most prized possession."

"Let me guess. The Tear of the Gods?"

"The very same. According to the legend, a lowly blacksmith, his name now lost to history, was present when the Roman governor ordered his troops to rape Boudica and her daughters in punishment for the fact that her deceased husband, the previous ruler of the area, insulted the emperor by leaving the region to Boudica in his will. Enraged at the Roman treatment of his queen the blacksmith called upon the gods to help him fashion a weapon of mighty power, one that would overthrow the empire and keep this from ever happening again."

De Chance warmed to his subject. "Andraste, goddess of victory, heard his plea. But being a woman, and a beautiful one at that, she appeared to the blacksmith in a dream and convinced him to make a necklace instead of a sword. When the blacksmith agreed, Andraste wept bitter tears over the queen's plight. As her tears fell to earth, they were collected by the blacksmith and mixed with the other ingredients he had chosen at the goddess's suggestion. From that mixture the torc was formed."

De Chance paused, checking to be certain Annja was following the story, which she was.

"Some versions claim that the goddess was Agrona, goddess of war, instead of Andraste," he went on, "but that's not really all that important." He waved a hand to show his dismissal of the issue.

"The key here is that the Celts believed that the material used to make the torc had come from the gods themselves and was therefore imbued with mystical powers. Both Agrona and Andraste are gods associated with war, so a legend sprang up that anyone wearing the black torc would be invincible in combat, that they couldn't be defeated, by man or gods."

"Why haven't I heard of this legend before?" Annja asked. She considered herself pretty well informed when it came to the beliefs and mythology of ancient cultures.

De Chance shrugged. "Aside from the fact that Celtic mythology isn't the most likely cocktail party conversation?" he asked. "The legend is a very minor one and it died out fairly quickly given what happened to Boudica."

Annja could understand that. It was hard to claim that the necklace made the bearer unbeatable in battle when the Romans had crushed Boudica's rebellion so handily.

Of course, she might have given the torc to someone else before the big battle.

With thoughts of Big Red in the back of her mind, she suggested as much to de Chance, more to see what he would say than anything else.

"It's certainly possible," the professor replied, "but I tend to doubt it."

"Why's that?"

"If she had given it to another, say her most trusted lieutenant or someone like that, the legend would have lived on. We would have heard additional stories of the torc's existence. Instead, it disappears from history shortly after Boudica's death."

Unless the person to whom it was given was himself killed shortly thereafter and no one knew he carried it.

"In fact," he went on, "until your call the other day, I would have said that the black torc was nothing more than a myth. It would appear that you'll have the chance to prove me wrong."

He picked up one of the photos again, giving it a closer look. "This certainly isn't gold," he said, almost to himself. "Could it be iron?"

"I don't think so," Annja replied, "or, if it is, it's iron mixed with something else I don't recognize."

"It's not all that often that you stumble on the tears of a goddess, now is it?" de Chance joked.

"Hardly. One of my next steps is to have it analyzed."

De Chance put the photo back with the others and then handed the whole stack back to Annja. "I think that's an excellent idea. Do you have anyone in mind for the work?"

"Not yet, I'm afraid," Annja replied.

"Would you object to a suggestion?"

"Not at all."

"The best geologist in town is Sebastian Cartier. If I was in charge of the torc, he's the one I'd take it to. The trouble is that with all the work he does for the oil and mineral companies, he's usually booked for months in advance." De Chance gave a wolfish smile. "Thankfully he owes me a favor. A big one. Would you like me to give him a call?"

Annja smiled back at him. "I'd appreciate that very much."

De Chance picked up the phone and dialed a number from memory.

"Sebastian? It's Harry. I need some help…"

A few minutes later it was all arranged. Annja was to drop by Cartier's office at nine the next morning, supposedly after having the torc sent via overnight courier to her address, after which the geologist would do a series of tests aimed at identifying exactly what the torc was made of and how old it might actually be. In return, Annja promised to have a copy of the results sent over to de Chance's office and to arrange for him to view the piece at a later date.

Given the hoops she would have been forced to jump through to accomplish that on her own, Annja felt very lucky indeed to have made the trip to Paris to meet de Chance.

After a few more minutes of polite discussion, Annja thanked the professor one more time and then took her leave, anxious to get to her hotel and to be certain the torc had arrived without incident.

No SOONER HAD the American woman left his office than de Chance picked up his phone again and dialed another number. To de Chance's surprise, it was answered after only a few rings by Shaw himself.

"She just left," de Chance told his sometime partner.

The two men had met years earlier at a conference and recognized in each other a certain mutual interest in seeing the occasional archaeological artifact get rerouted into the hands of a private individual from time to time. The association had made de Chance a very rich man, and the opportunity before him at this moment made all the other transactions they'd conducted pale in comparison.

He had no intention of missing it.

"Does she have the torc?" Shaw asked.

"No, not yet. But she is having it sent to her via overnight courier so that she can have it dated and chemically analyzed tomorrow," de Chance said, and then proceeded to tell Shaw exactly where the elusive Miss Creed would be at nine the next morning.

It was a piece of information he knew Shaw would be more than happy to compensate him for at a later date.

29

The hotel wasn't much to look at from the outside and the interior didn't do much to dispel the initial impression, either. It wasn't the kind of place he'd expect an American television star like Annja Creed to stay in. Then again, he wouldn't have expected a woman like Creed to be wrapped up in a multiple homicide, either.

Shows you just never know, Beresford thought.

A nervous-looking young man in his mid-twenties with a bad case of acne watched him from the front desk, one hand held out of sight beneath the counter.

Beresford didn't blame the kid for his caution; if he was stuck working the late shift all alone in a place where two men had been murdered without anyone noticing until hours later, he'd have his hand on a weapon, too. To keep the clerk from getting nervous and blasting away with whatever he had hidden under there, the detective held up his ID as he approached the desk.

"Police," he said.

The clerk relaxed. Anticipating Beresford's next request, he took out a keycard and passed it across the counter to the detective.

"Fifth floor," the clerk said with disinterest. "Room 511. You'll have to walk, though, the elevator's out."

Of course it is, Beresford thought, because that's the kind of day I'm having.

He trooped up five flights of stairs and moved down the hall to where a ribbon of police tape stretched across a doorway.

He went inside and had a look around. It was your typical fleabag hotel room—a narrow bed, a dresser that had certainly seen better days and a nightstand with a television bolted to it. The bloodstain near the bed had dried hours before but the thick scent of it still filled the room. A fine black powder coated many of the room's surfaces, evidence that the forensics team had already been there looking for prints.

Good luck with that, he thought. It looked like the rooms were cleaned once a month; the place would have dozens, if not hundreds, of fingerprints all over it.

He didn't envy the poor tech who would have to go through and match them all.

He crossed the room, glanced into the adjoining bathroom, then squatted down near the bloodstain. From the way it spread across the floor Beresford surmised that the man had been in a seated position when he'd died, his back to the wall. They still didn't have an ID on either of the victims, but Gibbons had told him that the pattern had been repeated; one had died from a broken neck and the other had bled to death after being stabbed in the chest with a long-bladed weapon.

It seemed that anyone who got in Miss Creed's way ended up dead and he made a mental note to himself to be extra careful when he was ready to take her into custody.

After staring at the bloodstain for a few minutes without learning anything more, Beresford got up and turned to leave.

That's when he saw it.

A section of the baseboard near the dresser had been pulled free of the wall.

By getting down on his hands and knees, he could see that there was a small, recessed space at the bottom of the wall that normally would have been covered by the baseboard. He took out his key chain and used the penlight he kept clipped to it to peer inside the hole.

The light revealed a cavity that was about three inches deep and six inches long. It was the perfect place to hide something small and, in fact, he could see that the dust inside the space had recently been disturbed.

The space itself was empty.

The detective got up and dusted himself off, his thoughts churning.

He'd originally thought that the Creed woman might have been in on the attack at the dig site. The more he learned about her, however, the more unlikely that theory seemed to be. While everyone had their price, a fact that had been proven in his line of work again and again, what he'd been able to dig up on her showed that she was a staunch defender of those who couldn't fight for themselves. She was also well-liked and respected in the archaeological community; she seemed to have friends everywhere. So the idea that she would turn on the very people who supported and welcomed her into their midst was just too far-fetched for even a cynic like him.

Given that assessment, he'd been forced to revise his

theory over the past twenty-four hours to one that put her on the run from those who'd slain her companions, rather than a willing accomplice. Now it looked like she was intentionally hiding something from them, as well. The space behind the baseboard wasn't all that big. That meant the sword she'd apparently been using on those who came after her wasn't the item in question. She might have taken it from the dig site, as he suspected, but it wasn't what the RHD thugs were after.

No, it was more likely that it was something far more damaging to those involved, such as photographs, or possibly even video footage, of the attack on the dig site. Otherwise, why else would they be pursuing her?

Satisfied that he'd gotten everything possible from the scene, Beresford locked the room behind him and returned to the lobby.

"Are you Jeremy Hanscomb?" he asked the desk clerk as he returned the key.

The youth glared at him. "I didn't have anything to do with it."

"To do with what?" Beresford asked.

"Whatever you're here to ask me 'bout. I didn't have nothing to do with it."

Beresford considered that response for a long moment and then decided that explaining the concept of a double negative to the youth would definitely be a waste of time. It was simpler just to ignore the remark and push on.

"I don't care what you did or didn't do. I just want to talk to you about what happened last night."

The clerk glanced away, already bored with the line of inquiry. "I already told the other cops everything."

Beresford stamped on the irritation he felt at the kid's remark. What he'd told the first responders had been bull, plain and simple. Two men had died, one of them rather violently, and he hadn't seen or heard a thing?

Give me a break.

Rather than getting in the kid's face, he decided to try a different method. You caught more flies with honey than vinegar, as his mother always used to say. Pulling a twenty-pound note out of his pocket, he laid it down on the counter but didn't take his hand all the way off it.

The clerk glanced at it and then licked his lips, his tongue flicking out and then disappearing again, like a snake.

"I've got a few questions that the other guys probably forgot to ask. Help me out and I'll make it worth your while," Beresford said reasonably.

The kid looked at the money again and then nodded.

"The report said you were working the front desk when this happened, that right?"

Another sullen nod.

Beresford wasn't going to put up with talking to a bobble-head doll. The kid was going to talk, one way or the other. If he wanted to play hardball, Beresford could do that just as well as the next guy.

He slid the money back off the counter.

"Hey, it's no skin off my back whether or not you want to earn some extra cash. Either you talk here, where things are nice and comfortable, or I can haul your ass down to New Scotland Yard, let you sweat for a while in a small little room and keep my finder's fee. Which is it?"

Hanscomb glared at him for a minute, but couldn't keep it up. Breaking eye contact, he said, "Yeah, I was on duty."

Beresford smiled, a friendly kind of grin. He put the cash back on the countertop as a little positive reinforcement.

"And you always stay right here at the desk during your shift?"

"Where else would I be?"

Beresford kept smiling. "Where else would you be indeed? So then you saw the two guys come in, right?"

Hanscomb suddenly looked uncomfortable.

"I don't remember," he said.

"You don't remember? But I thought you said you were right here for your whole shift. How could you have missed them?"

"I don't know. Maybe I was helping another guest."

More likely you were goofing around out back, Beresford thought, but he let it go. He already confirmed the kid hadn't seen the assailants, so there was no sense embarrassing him further.

"Tell me about the woman who rented the room," he asked instead.

Hanscomb shrugged, though Beresford could see the relief in his eyes.

"Good-looking bird," Hanscomb said. "Nice arse, ya know?"

Now that's helpful, Beresford thought with disdain, but outwardly nodded as if he knew exactly what the clerk was talking about.

The things I do for this job.

"What else do you remember?" he asked. "Was she tall? Short? Blonde, brunette or redhead?"

He walked him through a physical description, checking it against the one he'd already given to the responding officers. It held up pretty well. More importantly, it matched the one Father Anderson had given of Amy, the woman he'd picked up on the side of the road.

Beresford pulled a publicity photo of Annja Creed that he'd printed off the web out from his pocket and put it down on the counter.

"This her?" he asked.

Hanscomb glanced at it, trying to play it cool, but then his eyes widened as he looked again and saw the caption identifying her as the star of *Chasing History's Monsters* underneath.

"Yeah!" Hanscomb said, surprise in his voice. "Yeah, that's her! I checked her in."

"Did she come in alone?"

"As far as I know."

"What do you mean?"

"A lot of guests check in alone. Doesn't mean they stay that way. Sometimes, people don't want other people to know their business, if you catch my drift, so they have the other person wait outside until the coast is clear or they let them in through the back."

Miss Creed didn't seem like the type to be setting up illicit trysts in a fleabag hotel, so Beresford let the comment pass.

"Do you remember what time she checked in?"

Hanscomb shrugged again, a habit that was starting to annoy Beresford.

"Late at night," he said. "Two, maybe 3:00 a.m."

Beresford nodded, doing a quick mental calculation to be certain that she would've had enough time to get there if she had, in fact, been involved in the events that occurred on the road near the dig site.

Turns out she could have made it here with time to spare, actually.

"Did she have anything with her when she came in? A wrapped package? A long box? Anything like that?"

"No. Just a backpack."

"You're sure?" While he couldn't see her just walking into the hotel sword in hand, it didn't feel right that she'd just leave it outside, either.

However, he wasn't about to solve that puzzle.

"Hell, yeah, I'm sure," Hanscomb said. "I gave her a good long look, if you know what I mean."

Unfortunately, Beresford did, and it really was too bad he couldn't just arrest the guy for being a creep.

He'd been operating on the idea that the RHD soldiers had followed Creed from the dig site, but it occurred to him that perhaps she'd just stumbled on them by accident.

Just to be certain that the hotel wasn't being used as a base of operations by the terrorist group, he pulled out photos of O'Donnell and MacGuire and showed them to Hanscomb. If the four men had met there previously, perhaps he'd seen them before.

No such luck, however.

"Anything else you can remember?" Beresford asked.

The clerk thought about it for a minute, and then nodded, much to Beresford's surprise.

"She had something all over the front of her shirt. A big reddish stain. At first I thought it was blood, but then I figured it had to be paint or something since she'd have had to kill someone to have that much…"

His voice trailed off and he visibly paled as he realized the possible connection between the two events.

The expression on Hanscomb's face actually brought a chuckle out of Beresford; it surprised him, given the day he'd had. There hadn't been many opportunities to laugh since he'd caught this case.

"Did she appear hurt or injured in any way?"

Hanscomb shook his head.

Okay, then, so it wasn't her blood. Best guess was that it was MacGuire's and she'd probably gotten it on herself when she dragged his body out of the car. If he could find the clothes, he'd have a direct link between her and MacGuire. That would be a big step in the right direction.

He thanked Hanscomb, left the twenty-pound note on the counter in front of him and headed back to his car, pulling out his cell phone as he went. Figuring Creed would have ditched her bloodstained clothing the first chance she got, he called Clements and instructed him to get half a dozen uniforms out into the neighborhood searching for that shirt as soon as possible.

With that done he sat back and stared out the windshield into the night, wondering just where in creation Annja Creed had disappeared to this time.

30

After leaving the museum Annja made her way across the city intent on checking into the Hotel Apollinaire. As planned, she'd asked for Suzette when she arrived at the registration desk and was quickly shuffled over to the cute, blond-haired woman who was now waiting on her under the name Stephan had picked out: Allison Smith.

"Ah," the woman said, a twinkle in her eye. "Stephan's 'special guest.' A pleasure to have you with us, Miss Smith, and if there is anything I can do during your stay, please do not hesitate to ask."

It took Annja a moment to read between the lines; Suzette thought she was sleeping with Stephan and was here for a wild weekend of illicit romance. Hence, the "special guest" comment. Annja thought about correcting her but swiftly decided against it. Stephan, she knew, had a reputation as a bit of a player and if the staff wanted to think he was trying to impress his latest conquest with a suite at the hotel, so be it. Leaving that impression with the staff might make things easier for her while she was there, as their desire to stay on Stephan's good side would keep them from looking too closely into the situation.

"Do you have a package waiting for me?" Annja asked, and then spent an anxious moment as Suzette spent several minutes pecking away at the keys and staring at the computer screen, as if the presence or lack thereof of a package for her was an issue of national security. In the end, though, the package was right where it was expected to be and it took only a few more minutes for the bellhop to bring it to her while she waited at the desk.

Annja felt a definite sense of relief once the torc was back in her hands. The chances of the package having been intercepted by her pursuers were so miniscule as to be astronomical, especially when you factored in her use of the name Stephan had chosen for her on the mailing label, but that hadn't stopped her from worrying about it. Her thoughts had run through a gamut of problems, from a simple error in delivery to a catastrophic accident involving the delivery truck in which the package itself was destroyed in a fiery conflagration.

Thankfully nothing out of the ordinary had happened.

Her room turned out to be a gorgeous suite on the second floor of the hotel. From the balcony outside her bedroom she could see the Montparnasse Cemetery. She knew a number of important historical figures were buried there, including Frédéric Bartholdi, the sculptor of the Statue of Liberty, and Paul Deschanel, a former president of France.

She ordered room service, ate a leisurely meal for the

first time in what felt like weeks and then drew herself a hot bath. Soaking in the warm water, she tried to make sense of everything that had happened in the past few days.

When the Red Hand Defenders, if that was indeed who they were, had first attacked her on the road south of Arkholme, she'd assumed that they'd done so in an attempt to eliminate her as a possible witness to the slaughter at the dig site. She'd gotten a good look at several of the men who had participated in the attack, so getting rid of her made sense; after all, a dead woman would have a rather difficult time testifying against them, now wouldn't she?

But the men who had broken into her hotel room in London seemed to have been looking for something— the torc?—as much as they were looking for her.

The question was why? What would an avowed terrorist group want with a two-thousand-year-old necklace?

Her meeting with de Chance might have provided her with the answer to that very question.

De Chance had scoffed at the legend surrounding the torc, that whoever wore it in battle would never suffer defeat at the hands of his or her enemies. After all, magic wasn't real, right? The idea that the torc had some kind of mystical power was simply absurd.

At an earlier point in her life, Annja might have agreed, but no longer. After all, she carried a sword that once belonged to Joan of Arc and that could appear and disappear at will. Never mind the fact that one of the primary missions in the life of her friend and part-time mentor, Roux, was hunting down such artifacts and safeguarding them from falling into the wrong hands.

Sure, she'd debunked more than her fair share of

myths and legends, but she couldn't dispute that there was often a core of truth behind even the most outrageous beliefs and that every now and then she stumbled upon something so extraordinary that she had a hard time explaining it away with conventional means.

What if this was one of those times? What if the legends surrounding the torc were true?

It might help to explain why a terrorist group like the Red Hand Defenders was interested in it, to start. The truth was there wasn't much that could be done with a two-thousand-year-old necklace, aside from selling it on the black market. Sure, the money obtained by doing so might finance a number of operations to support the group's cause, but there were easier ways of obtaining money, Annja knew.

Like robbing a bank, for one.

Attacking the dig site in the fashion they had just didn't make sense if the necklace was just a necklace. The baggage that came along with murdering a few dozen people in the process would practically outweigh any benefit they could gain. It would make selling the artifact that much more difficult, for law enforcement agencies the world over would be on the lookout for it.

But if that same necklace gave you power over your enemies?

Then it became a far more valuable prize.

One a group like the RHD would have no qualms about killing over, as they'd so clearly shown.

It explained so much. The blatant disregard for the lives of the archaeologists at the dig site. The relentless nature of their pursuit. The lack of concern shown by attacking her in a public place like the hotel.

Clearly the RHD was playing for keeps.

Annja realized that she knew nothing about the

organization itself. Doug had explained that it was an Irish terrorist group, but that was about it. If she was going to have to defend the torc from their repeated attempts to gain control of it, it would probably make sense to learn as much as she could about who they were and what their particular ideology might be. Knowledge that would help her understand what they might use the torc for, which in turn would help her keep it from falling into their hands.

With a renewed sense of purpose, Annja climbed out of the tub, wrapped herself in the big terry-cloth robe provided by the hotel and headed for her computer.

Know your enemy and know yourself and your victory will never be in doubt, the great Sun Tzu had once said.

Annja fully intended to put that strategy to work for her.

31

As Annja was digging into the beliefs and goals of the Red Hand Defenders, Roux was activating the video-conferencing program on his computer that would connect him to Shaw and the other members of the artifact group. The seventy-two hours were up. It was time for the auction to end.

Shaw wasted no time in getting to business.

"Seventy-two hours ago I placed the Tear of the Gods, a one-of-a-kind Celtic torc once worn by Queen Boudica herself, up for auction among you," Shaw said with a smile that looked to Roux to be as phony as a three-franc note.

"Despite some furious bidding, we have a winner."

Having submitted his final bid just moments before, Roux leaned forward in anticipation while on the screen Shaw's smile grew wider and phonier, if that was at all possible.

"The final bid was for six million dollars and…"

Roux turned away, no longer interested in hearing the rest. His bid had not been that high, which meant the torc was going to one of the other five. He'd have to have Henshaw look into it, see if he could ferret out who had been the final bidder. With that information in hand, he could decide how he wanted to proceed. There were, after all, other ways of acquiring the artifact.

As had become his habit, Roux listened to Shaw prattle on for ten more minutes and then remained on the line after the others disconnected, clandestinely listening in on the events taking place in Shaw's office, hoping to hear something useful.

This time, his diligence paid off.

When dealing with Vanguard business Shaw would normally have his secretary initiate his calls, so when Roux heard him dialing the phone himself it perked his attention.

"Da?"

The voice that answered was male, with a thick Russian accent.

"Is the package ready?" Shaw asked.

"Of course. You may take delivery whenever you like."

To Roux, it sounded like Shaw was obviously preparing to take control of the torc from whatever third-party agents he'd hired to seize it.

"Tonight, then. There is a park just south of the Pont Louis-Philippe on the Quai de Bourbon."

"I know it," the Russian said.

"Ten o'clock. Use the signal from our previous meeting."

"Da."

The conversation over, the two men hung up.

Roux felt his adrenaline rise. By intercepting the

delivery he'd have a chance to secure the torc for himself without having to pay the six-million-dollar price tag currently attached to it.

Never mind that he'd be screwing Shaw over in the process. That alone made it worth his while.

Sanctimonious little cockroach, he thought.

His mood soaring at the idea, Roux was about to break the connection when he heard Shaw address someone in the room with him.

"You heard?"

"Yes."

"Then you understand how important it is that you finish this now."

"Yes, sir. I'll take care of it personally."

"You'd better," Shaw said, and there was no mistaking the threat in his voice. "She'll be at this address in the morning."

The rustle of a piece of paper let Roux know that something had changed hands.

"Recover my property and then get rid of her."

"What about the geologist?" the other man asked.

"Get rid of him, too."

"Consider it done."

Shaw snorted in derision, but didn't say anything more. After another few seconds the connection went dead, indicating that Shaw had powered down his computer.

Roux didn't know who they were talking about, but it was clear that good things were not in store for whoever it was.

No matter, he thought, he had other things to worry about. Like how to steal the Tear of the Gods right out from under Shaw's nose.

He pressed the intercom on his desk.

"Henshaw, a word, please," he said.

A minute passed, maybe two, and then his major-domo stepped into the room. The former SAS officer had a strained look on his face and he moved directly to the television set in the corner.

As he turned it on, Henshaw said, "I think you should have a look at this, sir."

On the screen a short man in an ill-fitting suit stood on the steps of New Scotland Yard, an array of television reporters and their ever-present microphones thrust in front of him. Roux was reminded of vultures, waiting for their kill to finally fall over and die before moving in to feast.

Unfortunately for them, this particular police detective still had plenty of fight left in him. He stood there, staring them down, until silence fell and he could hear himself speak without shouting over the clamor.

"I'll make a statement and answer a few questions," he told them in a calm and controlled tone of voice. Roux recognized it; it was the voice of command.

Here is a man who is used to getting what he wants, he thought to himself, even as he wondered why on earth Henshaw had him watching a London newscast.

A moment later he didn't have to wonder any longer.

"The whereabouts of Annja Creed are still uncertain," the detective said, and hearing his protégé's name, Roux immediately gave the man his full attention.

"The investigation into what happened in the West Midlands continues. We have several leads, though I am not at liberty to discuss those with you at this time. Suffice to say that we now believe we understand the motives for the attack and intend on bringing the perpetrators to justice as swiftly as possible."

Attack? Just what on earth had Annja gotten herself into this time?

"Is Miss Creed still a suspect, Inspector?" a reporter at the back of the pack cried out.

"Not at this time," the man replied curtly, delivering the line along with a blistering glare of displeasure at being interrupted. "We are still very much interested in speaking with Miss Creed, but as a witness, rather than a suspect. If anyone has information on her whereabouts, we urge you to call the hotline as her life may be at risk."

A telephone number appeared at the bottom of the screen and Roux absently memorized it.

Having her life in danger was nothing new for Annja, Roux knew, but it bothered him that she was in danger and he hadn't known anything about it until now.

"Do you know what's going on?" he asked Henshaw, but the man shook his head.

"Caught it while flipping channels, sir. I had no idea Miss Creed was in trouble or I would have brought it to your attention earlier."

Roux nodded. Henshaw had been with him for years; his loyalty was unquestionable. That didn't tell him what was going on, however.

"I wonder why she didn't call?" Roux said, more to himself than to Henshaw, but the other man heard it and answered, anyway.

"Perhaps she has, sir," he said, gently chastising his employer in the process.

Roux scowled. He'd lived for more than six hundred years. Was it really his fault that the petty concerns of the world held little interest for him? He'd seen it all, from the Crusades to the launching of the Apollo space program, and through it all he'd walked like a ghost, living out lifetimes in perfect health while those around him grew older and died. Was it any wonder that he could become absorbed in his own activities, as he'd done recently, and forgotten about the world passing by outside his window?

Realizing, as Henshaw knew he would, that he hadn't checked his cell phone for several days, perhaps even as long as a week, Roux fished it out of his desk and stared at the display.

The icon indicating that he had voice-mail messages stared back at him.

Swearing to himself in French, he tapped the keys and listened to the messages one at a time.

The first was inconsequential—a business matter from one of his many managers that didn't really need his immediate attention. He'd deal with it later. The second and third messages, however, were from Annja. In the first she sounded mildly harried but otherwise okay. It was the second call that disturbed him; she was clearly stressed and didn't sound like she was thinking too clearly. The log on his phone said the call had come in the previous day. She sounded…hunted.

His cell phone had failed to capture the number from which her calls had originated, so he called up his address book and tried to reach her. After several rings he received an automated message stating that her voice mail was full and would not accept any more messages.

Roux hung up and considered his next move. His gaze returned to the television screen, where the detective was once again asking those in the audience who had information on the crime to contact New Scotland Yard.

If he was going to help her, he needed to understand what was going on first.

"Get me everything you can on whatever incident it is he's talking about," Roux told Henshaw. "I want to know it all—who, what, where, when, you name it."

"Very good, sir."

"And while you're at it, figure out who this joker is, as well," he told him, pointing at the figure of Detective Inspector Beresford as he turned away from the mikes and the shouted questions left unanswered behind him. "He's looking for Annja; I want to know what he intends to do if he finds her."

Henshaw nodded and then slipped out of the room.

32

Henshaw and Roux arrived at the rendezvous more than an hour early, wanting to be in position long before the primary targets arrived at the scene. Henshaw parked the car several blocks away, in the heart of a local neighborhood, and exited the vehicle, carrying a long leather case in one hand. Roux waited a few minutes and then got out of the car himself, heading off in the other direction. The delay would minimize their chances of being seen and remembered by a nosy resident.

It was agreed that Henshaw would settle into the coffee house on the corner and wait a bit before taking up position on the bridge over the Seine. In the meantime, Roux would use the pedestrian walkway along the water's edge to approach the park itself and observe the exchange from there. The two men would stay in contact via radio.

The plan was simple enough: observe the exchange and then, when the chance presented itself, move in and take the torc from whichever party had it at that time. Adapt to the situation at hand and then use it your advantage. It was the kind of loose strategic thinking that had served Roux well for all these centuries and he had no intention of changing it now.

The walkway was dark, but the lights of the apartment buildings lining the river were reflected in its waters and he had no trouble making his way toward the park. As he walked, he glanced frequently at the waters beside him, his thoughts on another place and time. Local legend claimed that after she had been burned at the stake, Joan of Arc's ashes had been collected by a former supporter and cast into the Seine, bringing God's favor down upon both the river and the city through which it ran.

Roux knew this to be untrue. Her ashes had been collected, and by a former supporter no less. That much was a fact, for he had been the one to do it. But rather than cast them into the river, he'd secretly interred them on holy ground, allowing her to rest in the arms of the God in which she'd believed so fervently.

Perhaps he'd made a mistake, he mused as he neared his target. Perhaps his long life and continued existence today was due to the fact that the Almighty was angry with him for his irreverent act. After all, if heresy was a sin, then burying a heretic on holy ground was certainly worse, was it not?

He'd find out eventually, he supposed. For now, he had to concentrate on the issue at hand.

Reaching the steps that led up into the parking lot, he settled himself into place and began to wait.

After all these years, Roux was good at waiting.

DAVID SHAW ARRIVED at the designated meeting area shortly before ten that night. The park was empty; there were no other cars in sight. He pulled to the very end of the lot and turned his vehicle around, facing back toward the entrance in case he needed to make a quick departure.

He'd done business with Perchenko several times in the past and had no reason to suspect the man might double-cross him, but it never hurt to be prepared. The device itself was valuable, as were the codes to the accounts Shaw would be using to transfer the purchase price directly to Perchenko. And there were the Libyans to consider. If they had convinced Perchenko that their patronage was more important than his own...

It simply meant that Shaw hoped the handover would go smoothly, but if it did not, he was prepared to deal with it. After all, he hadn't reached his current position through brilliance alone. He'd done his time on the streets, had more than enough blood on his hands to hold his own, even against the former Russian commando.

Still, it would be better if the problem never arose and he simply took his package and left after the transfer.

His thoughts turned to Jackson and the events set to play out in the morning. The torc was the key. Without it, the package he was planning to pay Perchenko so handsomely for would be about as useful as a eunuch in a brothel. He didn't understand why Jackson was having such difficulty with the task. How formidable could the woman be, for heaven's sake? Perhaps she'd simply been lucky so far.

Well, no longer. He'd instructed Jackson to use as many resources as necessary to ensure that the operation went down without a problem. He didn't care how many men died in the process. All that mattered was taking control of the torc before that Creed woman disappeared with it again.

A car turned into the parking lot.

Shaw tensed, waiting for the signal, but it never came. The other car simply used the space to pull a U-turn, its lights washing over Shaw's vehicle at the back of the lot but not really seeing him at all. Seconds later the car was gone.

Relaxing once more, Shaw's thoughts turned to what would happen once he had both Perchenko's device and the torc in hand. The goals of the Red Hand Defenders were simple—to throw off the yoke of British rule and to set up a free Irish republic across the entire breadth of Ireland constituted under Irish rule. They were the same goals that the Provisional Irish Republican Army had fought to achieve, the same goals that had been swept aside for political expediency in the wake of the Belfast Agreement in 1998. Shaw, a young solider in the Cause at the time, had been appalled by the agreement and privately vowed that he would never accept such conditions. When the PIRA had announced an end to the armed conflict and had gone so far as to decommission their weapons in 2005, Shaw had made good on that vow.

He'd spent the years since the Belfast Agreement doing everything he could to be certain that any decision he made with regard to the cause would be well-funded. To that end he'd created the Vanguard Group and built it into a multi-million-dollar conglomerate of companies whose primary mission was to simply make money for the cause. By the time the decommissioning was announced, Shaw had both the connections and the funding to continue the fight on his own terms.

The Red Hand Defenders were born.

In the years since, his agency had been responsible for taking the fight to the enemy in a way that would have made his old mates proud. They'd been responsible for eight successful bombings, including the deaths of three high-profile targets, as well as two shooting sprees that had forced the British and Irish governments to sit up and take notice.

Still, all that was nothing compared to what he intended to carry out next. This time it wouldn't be just the British government that was paying attention. This time, he would capture the eye of the entire world.

And when he had it, he would make his demands.

The Red Hand Defenders would no longer be considered a second-class organization and the demands of the true loyalist amid the Irish people would finally be heard.

It was going to be a glorious day indeed!

His reverie was broken by the arrival of another vehicle. He watched as it stopped only a few feet into the parking lot, facing in his direction. The lights flashed twice, quickly, and then once more.

Shaw exhaled and repeated the signal.

Perchenko had arrived.

He waited as the other vehicle, a Land Rover, approached, watching it come to a stop just a few feet away. When it had, he got out of the car.

Across from him, the Russians did the same.

Perchenko had a bodyguard with him, which wasn't unexpected. He'd brought one along at the last meet, as well. Shaw remembered the Russian joking that the man's name was Insurance; after all, that was his purpose.

Shaw hadn't found it all that amusing.

This one seemed to have been cut from the same cloth. He stood several inches over six feet and had shoulders that would have made an American football player proud. His hair was cut short, military-style, and Shaw had no doubt that's where Perchenko had recruited him from.

He waited for the two men to join him.

"Good to see you again," Shaw began, a smile on his face.

Perchenko's expression was noncommittal. "You have the money?"

"Of course," he said smoothly, never letting the smile falter from his face despite the Russian's rudeness. "You have my package?"

Perchenko grunted and flicked a hand at his companion. As the other man led the way to the back of the vehicle, Perchenko and Shaw followed.

The bodyguard opened up the rear of the vehicle, revealing what was stored there.

It was a dark gray metallic case, about the size of a typical footlocker. The designation RA-115 was stamped on the top of the case in white letters. At a nod from Perchenko, the other man stepped forward, unlocked the two clasps that held the container closed and then lifted the lid before stepping back out of the way.

Shaw moved forward, looking at but not touching the device. What looked to him to be a large artillery shell rested in the center of the case, with two square objects on either side that he assumed were the neutron generators. A fourth item, a rectangular device about the size of a hardcover book, sat in the upper right-hand corner of the case and had several wires running out of it and over to the rear of the artillery shell.

"It is operational?" Shaw asked.

"Da," Perchenko replied.

Shaw knew the other man had to be lying. Smuggling the shell of a Soviet-era tactical nuclear device out of the

Ukraine was one thing. Doing so with an accompanying load of weapons-grade plutonium was something else entirely.

As far as he was concerned, the shell was good enough. He would get the necessary plutonium from a different source.

He gave no indication that he knew the truth about the device.

Instead, he said, "Very good. You have the account number?"

Perchenko handed him a slip of paper with an account number comprised of eighteen letters and numbers. Shaw knew without asking that it was the number of a Swiss bank account. With the other two men watching, Shaw took out his phone and used a mobile banking application to initiate a transfer of funds from an account he'd set up under a false name for just this purpose into the account Perchenko had given him.

The transfer took five minutes.

No one said anything while they waited.

When it was finished, Perchenko gave his companion another signal and the big man moved the tactical nuclear device Shaw had just purchased from the back of the Land Rover to the trunk of Shaw's Mercedes.

Just like that the exchange was done.

33

Roux watched the entire exchange from his concealed position on the stairs leading up to ground level. The pair of miniature binoculars he held in his hands had been designed by a high-tech firm to his exact specifications and were the best that money could buy. Thanks to the way the Russian had parked, they allowed him to see directly into the back of the vehicle.

One thing was for certain.

That case had not been built to house the Tear of the Gods.

While he couldn't see directly into it, it was clear from its weight alone that it couldn't be the torc. The big Russian's arm muscles had bulged when he'd lifted it and Roux estimated it probably weighed a good fifty to seventy-five pounds. The back of the Mercedes had dropped an inch closer to the ground when the case had been placed inside.

So if it wasn't the torc, what was it?

For a moment, he considered just walking away. His interest was in the torc and this clearly wasn't it, so why get involved? But something made him hesitate. While he didn't recognize the Russian, he'd seen his type before. The man was clearly a former soldier. You could see it in the way he held himself, in the way he would scan the surrounding area on a regular basis, searching for threats.

Which begged the question, what was someone like that doing with a guy like Shaw?

Something wasn't right here. Roux could feel it in his bones. Something told him he needed to find out what was in that case.

As he was mentally debating the situation, Shaw said some final comment to the Russian and then got into his car and drove off.

With his options dwindling, Roux made his move.

"Now!" he said into the microphone at his throat and then rushed up the stairs, heading directly for the two men standing near the Land Rover.

This was the dangerous part. There was no doubt that the two men in front of him were armed and they were likely to shoot first and ask questions later when they saw him charging across the parking lot toward them. If Henshaw was even a half second too late…

Roux had covered half the distance to the Land Rover when the leader of the duo caught sight of him. The man shouted something to his companion in what Roux presumed was Russian and then shoved a hand inside his jacket, no doubt going for his pistol.

That was as far as he got.

Something struck him in the side of the neck, knocking him backward against the vehicle, and the gun he was reaching for clattered to the ground beside him.

The leader's shout caught the other man by surprise, so he was slower off the mark than his boss had been. He was still reaching for the gun at his back when the second dart from Henshaw's rifle struck him in the shoulder. Roux was close enough by that time to see the red fletching on the end of the dart and he drew himself up short at the sight, expecting the other man to go down, just as his companion had.

Unfortunately, he didn't.

As the other man shook his head, trying to clear it, Roux realized what must have gone wrong. The darts were calibrated with enough tranquilizers to knock down your average human being, but this man's size must have diluted the dose.

Roux had hundreds of years of fighting experience at his disposal, and if there was one thing he had learned, it was never give your opponents the opportunity to do you harm. While he was confident that he would eventually prevail in a hand-to-hand fight against the bigger Russian, there was no sense in finding out if he was right. A protracted battle would call attention to them and that was the last thing they needed. Speed and silence were the key.

So as the big man shook himself and seemed to bring his attention back into focus, Roux stepped up and without pausing delivered a smashing kick to the man's groin.

The big Russian's eyes rolled back in his head and he toppled over like a sack of bricks.

Roux didn't waste any time. Working calmly and efficiently, he grabbed the now-unconscious bodyguard and hefted him into the back of the Land Rover, then did the same with the other man. When they were both inside the vehicle Roux closed the rear doors and then took a moment to look around. As far as he could tell, no one had seen what had just happened.

He keyed the mike again.

"I'm headed for the rendezvous point. See you there."

"Roger that," came Henshaw's reply a moment later.

The keys to the Land Rover were still in the ignition. Roux started the car and drove smoothly out of the parking lot.

From start to finish the entire assault had taken less than three minutes.

I've still got it, Roux thought to himself with a smile as he turned out of the park and headed into the Parisian traffic.

HALF AN HOUR later Roux was sitting in a chair in the living room of an isolated farmhouse in rural France, waiting for the man in the chair across from him to wake up.

The man's driver's license identified him as Ivan Perchenko. Roux didn't have any idea whether that was the man's real name or an alias, but, in truth, it really didn't matter. All Roux wanted from the man was some information and for that a name wasn't necessary.

The man's partner, name unknown since he hadn't carried any identification, was in the garage outside, tied securely with a thick piece of rope and being watched over by Henshaw. If they couldn't get what they wanted out of Perchenko, they'd turn their attention to the bodyguard. For now, though, they'd start at the top.

After sitting there for several minutes, Roux watched the man stir and then come to full consciousness. It was like watching a lizard wake up; one minute they were completely asleep, the next they were watching you with those cold, reptilian eyes, gauging just how much of a threat you might be.

Roux intended to pass the test. On the table next to him, in full view of his captive, was an assortment of devices designed to make Perchenko think twice about what lay ahead for him—a small sledgehammer, an electric drill, a hand drill, several different types of saws, a pair of metal snips, even a handheld blowtorch. Roux didn't have any immediate intention of using them; they were just there to provide Perchenko with the proper motivation to answer his questions.

If Perchenko refused to do so, Roux knew he'd have to reconsider their use, but for now, they would remain where they were.

Perchenko's gaze flicked across the table, taking in the objects arranged there, and then moved around the room, assessing his options.

Roux waited. He wasn't in any hurry.

When the man's attention returned to him, Roux said calmly, "I have a few questions—"

Perchenko cut him off with a stream of angry-sounding Russian that went on for several minutes.

When the Russian had apparently run out of steam, Roux tried again.

"I know you speak English, so you might as well stop the act. As I started to say, I have a few questions for you. It would be easier for you if you simply answered them."

Perchenko laughed. "You do not frighten me, old man."

Roux smiled. The Russian was talking. The hard part was already behind him. It didn't matter what he was talking about. The fact that he was doing so at all instantly put the advantage in Roux's hands.

"I wouldn't expect them to frighten you, Mr. Perchenko. I know your background: I know that you are capable of resisting for quite some time."

The truth was that Roux knew next to nothing about Perchenko's real background, but he could recognize a soldier when he saw one. Most modern soldiers were trained in anti-interrogation techniques and Roux had little doubt that at some point or another in his training Perchenko had undergone just such a course. Eventually he would talk, everyone did, but he was likely to resist Roux's efforts for several hours and that wasn't something Roux wanted to wait around for.

"But whether they frighten you or not is completely irrelevant to the pain they will cause," Roux continued, "and pain is never a pleasant experience."

He reached out, picked up the blowtorch and saw Perchenko flinch slightly from the corner of his eye.

Gotcha, Roux thought.

"So let's make this easy for both of us," he said, putting the tool back down on the tabletop. "I desire some information. I have no doubt that you have the information I'm looking for. So let's make this a business arrangement. I will ask my questions and I will pay you for your answers."

The Russian stared at him blankly for a moment, and then said, "Pay me?"

Roux smiled. Maybe this would be easier than he thought.

"For every question you answer to my satisfaction, I'll give you ten thousand dollars."

"Bah! Ten thousand dollars is nothing."

"Well that would depend on how many questions I ask, wouldn't it?"

With the Russian considering the offer, Roux sweetened the pot.

"I'm not interested in any of your other clients, nor am I looking for you to betray any confidences about them. All I want to know about is your meeting with Shaw."

Perchenko said something in Russian and spat on the ground. Roux guessed that he didn't much like Shaw, either.

"Do we have a deal?" he pressed.

"How do I know you will keep your word?"

Roux shrugged. "You don't. You can either take a chance and earn some money for your troubles or go back to the first alternative. Either way, I'll find out what I need to know."

Perchenko really didn't have much choice and he knew it, too. After another moment of thought, more to save face than anything else, he gave a sharp little nod.

Roux got right to it.

"What was in the case that you handed over to Shaw at the park?"

"A Soviet-era RA-115."

Roux wasn't familiar with that designation. It sounded like a weapon, but then again it really could have been anything. Rather than guess, he simply asked what it was.

Perchenko eyed him cautiously. "A man-portable tactical nuclear device. What you in the West used to call a suitcase nuke."

"You can't be serious."

"I don't joke when it comes to business. If the fool

had come up with another six million dollars, I would have been happy to sell him two."

Six million dollars. The same price that was paid for the torc. That couldn't be a coincidence. Just what on earth was Shaw up to?

Roux had long suspected that Shaw and his Vanguard Group were involved in some less-than-savory activities above and beyond the man's penchant for dealing in the black-market artifact trade. He didn't have any direct evidence, just hints that there was something else beneath the surface, like the way a shadow on the ocean floor might conceal the bulk of a sunken ship buried beneath the silt. Since laying eyes on the case in the back of the Russian's car, Roux had envisioned a lot of different items that might be inside but a tactical nuclear device certainly wasn't one of them. He was almost afraid to ask his next question.

"What does he intend to do with it?"

Perchenko laughed. "Blow something up, I'd guess. What else do you do with a bomb? I wish I could see his face when he realizes his plans don't really matter, though."

"Why is that?"

"Because the damn thing's inert. The Soviets took the plutonium out of it years ago. Six million dollars—for a piece of worthless junk!"

While the Russian arms dealer continued to laugh at the stupidity of his latest customer, Roux considered the implications of what he'd just learned. Clearly his hunch about Shaw was correct; the man *was* involved in something much more dangerous than artifact smuggling. Just what remained to be seen.

Several more questions without real answers let Roux know that he'd mined this particular well dry. He'd also racked up a bill close to one hundred thousand dollars with his questions.

It was a bill he had no intention of paying, of course. He was pretty sure Perchenko knew it, as well. The Russian had either answered his questions out of the simple desire to screw Shaw over or he figured that he was more likely to live through the experience if he appeared to be cooperating. For all he knew, Roux was going to shoot him in the head when all was said and done.

It was a simple solution to a thorny problem, and Roux had considered it, but in the end he'd decided that the Russian's cooperation was worth something. He held no ill will toward the man and gunning him down for no real reason just didn't seem sporting to Roux.

There was still the possibility that the man was lying to him, but Roux didn't believe that was the case. The Russian had been genuinely amused at the thought of his client paying such an inordinate amount of money for a nonoperational device and that wasn't the type of emotion that was easily faked. It was just as Roux had said to his captive earlier—he was going to have to trust that the Russian was telling the truth, for he had no real way of confirming otherwise at the moment.

But what was he was going to do with his two captives?

The house had been sanitized of anything that could help the Russian identify them. Everything had been bought secondhand by hired help who had themselves been hired through other cutouts. The deed was held by a private trust that went back generations and the ownership was so tangled that it would literally take years for anyone trying to track him that way to even come close. Aside from the private poker tournaments that he occasionally indulged in, Roux was not a very social man and so there was little chance that Perchenko would run into him in another setting. They certainly didn't operate in the same circles.

Given all that, Roux didn't feel that he would be in danger by letting Perchenko go free.

So why am I hesitating, he asked himself.

He didn't have to think too long to realize it was the RA-115 that was bothering him.

The Russian had sold Shaw a nuclear weapon. That it was inoperable didn't matter; the fact that he was willing to put a device like that, working or not, in the hands of a man like Shaw was clear evidence that he'd do it again if the opportunity arose. He'd said it himself; if Shaw had the money, he would have sold him two.

Roux wouldn't consider himself a crusader for the greater good, not by a long shot, but the idea of letting this guy back into general circulation just didn't sit well with him. He'd given his word that he wouldn't kill him, but that didn't mean that he had to just let him go with no thought at all to consequences.

Getting up, he checked Perchenko's bonds, making sure they were secure, and then joined Henshaw in the garage where he was watching over their other captive. Out of earshot of the other man, Roux explained what he wanted his majordomo to do.

Henshaw agreed with the plan and disappeared back into the house for the few minutes it took him to blindfold Perchenko and lead him down into the cellar where he wouldn't be heard if he started to call for help. When he was finished with Perchenko, he did the same with the bodyguard. Roux spent the time gathering the tools from the table in the living room and wiping down the surfaces they'd touched while in the house.

They made a final sweep through the property to be

certain they hadn't missed anything and then they were on their way.

Eventually, he knew, the Russians would free themselves, particularly if they worked together. It might take a little while—a day, maybe two at the most—but they certainly wouldn't starve to death before getting loose. In the meantime, Roux could give the situation a bit more thought and decide exactly what to do with them.

It was actually a decent solution to a rather thorny problem and as they drove off into the night Roux felt he had the situation under control.

34

Trevor Jackson gathered seven of his best men together in one of the conference rooms at the Vanguard offices in Paris just after dawn the next morning. Their quarry wasn't due to arrive at the target destination for hours yet, but Jackson wanted to be certain to brief his men thoroughly beforehand. That way there would be less chance of a screwup when the operation actually went down.

He was out of second chances and knew it. Shaw wouldn't accept another failure. If Jackson failed to produce the torc this time around, he might as well find the fastest route out of the country, for Shaw was not known for showing mercy to those he considered unable or unwilling to carry out the tasks he'd assigned to them. Jackson either returned with the torc in hand or he'd spend the rest of his life holed up in some third-world shantytown, constantly looking over his shoulder and wondering when Shaw's men were going to show up to put a bullet in his brain.

No doubt about it, he thought, this one had to go right.

To that end he'd selected men he'd worked with on various jobs in the past. Each and every one of them had been tested in the crucible of combat and wouldn't fall apart at the first sign of difficulty.

There had been some talk of moving in ahead of time and simply being in place when the Creed woman arrived at the offices of the geologist, but Shaw had vetoed that idea. He wanted the geologist to run the tests first; that way he wouldn't have to spend the time or expense to do them himself. Jackson and his men were to find positions where they could observe the activity going on in the lab and only move in to secure the torc once the tests had been completed.

Jackson felt it was an unnecessary risk to wait, for it increased the chances of his men being seen and identified before they could make the snatch, but he wasn't about to argue about it given his prior failures.

Focus on doing the job, he told himself, and worry about the rest later.

He used the conference room computer to connect to Google Maps, then pushed the image up onto the screen on the far wall. He zoomed down to street level and was able to give his men an accurate view of the target site. It was so much easier than sending a man out with a camera and hoping he got some decent shots of the surrounding area.

The screen showed a quiet street lined with old houses that had been converted into office space for lawyers, accountants and other professionals. Number 4522 was in the middle of the block, sandwiched between an import/export company and an architectural firm. There was parking on both sides of the street, which eased one of Jackson's concerns. A quick in and out was what they needed and this would allow for that without difficulty.

"All right," he told his men, "here's the drill."

He zoomed back slightly, so his team could see the entire building as well as those around it.

"We're going in as two units. I want Green and Danvers with me at the front door." He highlighted the location on the map.

"Connor, O'Brien and Driscoll, you've got the back door," he said, pointing it out with the mouse. "There's an alley that runs behind the buildings here—" another quick highlight "—and you can use that to gain access. When you give the signal that you're in place, we'll go in.

"Michaels and Baker will be our wheelmen. I want the vans positioned here and here," he said, indicating the two positions, one on either side of the road facing in opposite directions. "If necessary, we'll split up and rendezvous later at the usual location.

"Our best intelligence indicates there will be two people inside, though there may be more. The first, a geologist, is of no real consequence. I don't expect him to do anything but whimper and die," Jackson said, which elicited a few laughs from the grim-faced men sitting around the table with him. "The other is this woman."

He put a picture of Annja Creed up on the screen and then waited for the catcalls and whistles that followed to die down.

"Yes, she's a looker, I'll give you that. But she's also as deadly as a pit viper. She single-handedly defeated both of the teams we've sent after her, so I'm not taking any chances this time around. If you see her, put her down. It's that simple. I don't even care how many bullets it takes, just be sure she doesn't get up again."

Jackson looked directly at each man one at a time, making certain they understood his order.

"I've yet to see her use a firearm. She seems to prefer a sword, of all things. Don't laugh," he said to the chuckles that sounded from around the table. "That blade can kill you as quickly as a bullet. Just ask O'Donnell or MacGuire."

Hearing the names of their dead comrades quieted the laughter.

"We've been tasked with recovering an ancient Celtic necklace from the premises." He took a moment to describe the torc and even put the grainy photograph they'd received from Professor Novick up on the screen for them to see. He wanted everyone to be aware of what it looked like, just in case the geologist, Cartier, or Creed had a chance to hide it from view.

"We won't be claiming responsibility for this strike, the way we usually do, but it is an important mission nonetheless. In fact, it is absolutely crucial to a larger mission that will take place next week, so there isn't any room for failure."

It was going to be a typical smash-and-grab, something these men had all done multiple times, so he expected it to go smoothly. There was always the chance that they'd run into a roaming police patrol, but the chances were slight, particularly in that area, and he expected them to get in and out again before anyone even had a moment to figure out what was happening. Speed was the key, he knew, and he fully intended to implement it.

If things went well, he would be back in Shaw's good

graces, and his place in the RHD hierarchy would be secured for the foreseeable future.

Repaying the Creed woman for the embarrassment she caused him would just be one of the side benefits of the job.

AN HOUR LATER they were in position on the street outside Cartier's offices. Traffic was light, though there were enough vehicles parked in either direction that the vans they were using didn't look out of place or irregular. Jackson was seated in front, in the van driven by Michaels, the more experienced of the two wheelmen. They'd worked together on the bombing of a member of the Royal Irish Constabulary a few months before and Jackson knew Michaels would keep his head together if things went to hell, which was why he'd chosen to ride with him rather than Baker.

He expected the snatch to go off without a hitch, but it was always good to be prepared just in case.

35

Annja was a few minutes early for her appointment, so she had her cabdriver drop her off at a nearby coffee shop, intending to walk the rest of the way on foot. It was a cool, blustery day, which gave her an excuse to slip inside and order a hot chocolate to go.

Cup in hand, she continued on her way.

Before going to bed the night before, she'd caught the tail end of a press conference on the BBC run by a detective out of New Scotland Yard. Her name had been mentioned several times, along with the fact that the police were still hoping to speak to her in conjunction with the events at Arkholme. Clearly she had more than just her enemies looking for her now.

Paris was a world away from London and the chances of anyone recognizing her on the street were slim, but she'd still done what she could to disguise her appearance. Most of her publicity shots showed her with her hair down, so she'd bundled it up on top of her head and slapped a baseball cap down over it all. A thick sweater and a baggy pair of jeans hid her trim figure.

It wasn't perfect, but it would have to do.

Sipping her hot chocolate as she walked along, she admired the morning and the quaint French neighborhood.

Annja knocked on Cartier's door right at the appointed time.

She heard a voice call out, "Coming," and then the clatter of locks before the door opened to reveal Sebastian Cartier waiting on the other side.

There was only one problem.

He was gorgeous.

He had thick, dark hair that hung in lazy curls in front of his forehead. His eyes were piercing blue. His smile was like a one-hundred-watt lightbulb. Never mind the broad shoulders covered by a blue T-shirt or the trim waist and long legs encased in a pair of dark jeans.

Annja had been expecting some stuffy academic, someone a lot like Professor de Chance, actually, and so finding Cartier to be not only younger—in his mid-thirties was her guess—but so good-looking as well left her momentarily tongue-tied.

She opened her mouth to introduce herself and nothing came out.

Thankfully Cartier barely noticed. Or, if he did, he was enough of a gentleman not to let it show. He smiled upon seeing her standing on his stoop and said, "Miss Creed! What a delight to meet you in person. Please, come inside."

His accent threw her off as well; it was classic Chicago and not Parisian at all. Who was this guy?

She followed him through the small reception area and waiting room that was just inside the front door and through a door on the left into a well-appointed office that she knew was his sanctum sanctorum. The walls were lined with bookshelves and a desk with two soft leather chairs in front of it sat in the center of the room.

"Can I get you anything to drink?" he asked.

She shook her head. "I'm all set, but thanks," she said, holding up the remains of her hot chocolate to show that she wasn't just being polite.

Cartier flashed a smile that practically lit up the place and Annja felt some of her initial apprehension fading. She hadn't known what Cartier's response to her would be; after all, she was currently wanted by the police in conjunction with a multiple homicide and she wouldn't have put it past him, or anyone else for that matter, to make a few calls and have a few members of the local law enforcement division waiting to speak to her when she arrived.

Apparently she'd given him too little credit.

He waved her into a chair and took the one opposite for himself. "I'm sorry if I sound like a total fanboy, but I can't believe that I have *the* Annja Creed right here in my living room. I watch your show whenever I'm not out trooping around the field on behalf of one mining organization or another and really enjoy your mix of archaeology and historical insight. From one scientist to another, you're a credit to our profession."

Relaxing back into her chair, Annja said, "Thank you, Dr. Cartier. I really appreciate—"

"Sebastian. Please," he said, interrupting, and she found herself warming to that smile all over again.

"Sebastian," she replied. "And I'm Annja."

"Annja, it is!"

She found her thoughts straying from the torc to how

blue Sebastian's eyes were and brought herself back to the present with a quick bit of mental scolding.

Focus, girl, focus, she told herself.

"What can I do for you, Miss…sorry, Annja. Dr. de Chance mentioned that you needed to determine the composition of a particular object?"

"Right." She explained how they'd found the torc at the site of an Iron Age burial site in Britain, conveniently leaving out the actual location in case he'd been watching the news and just hadn't put two and two together yet. "More often than not, torcs like this are made of gold, occasionally silver. They were signs of nobility and high status, after all, so you'd expect them to be made of precious materials of one kind or another. But this one is different."

"How so?" Cartier asked.

"It's made of a type of metal I've never seen before. Maybe it's something mixed with iron, maybe it's a combination of other elements. I really don't know. Understanding what it is, however, can tell us a lot about the society that produced it."

Cartier was already nodding his head. He understood that archaeology was as much an adventure in guesswork as it was hard science and that sometimes a single piece of the puzzle, when viewed in the proper light, could make all the difference in piecing the rest of it together in coherent fashion.

"I'm assuming you brought the torc with you?"

Annja nodded. "I had it shipped in overnight," she said, remembering the lie she'd given Dr. de Chance and not wanting there to be any discrepancy should the two compare notes. She didn't owe either of them anything, but still…

"Well, get it out and let's get started."

He led her out of the office, back through the reception area and down a hallway leading deeper into the building until they came to what was obviously his working area and laboratory. It reminded her of a college chemistry lab more than anything else. There were several workstations standing like islands throughout the room and the counters were covered with a variety of equipment and racks of test tubes and various-size pipettes. There was an electron microscope along one wall and what she thought was a squat-looking spectroscope against the other.

Sebastian walked over to one of the workstations and spent some time examining the torc, first with his naked eye and then with a bank of high-powered lights and a series of magnifying glasses. Just as she'd done, he marveled at the intricacy in the strands of braided metal that made up the length of the torc and in the fine detail that went into fashioning the eagle-head clasps.

"You say you found this where?" he asked, after thinking about what he'd seen for several long minutes.

"A peat bog, in northern Britain."

"Any idea when it might have been fashioned?"

Annja considered for a moment, and then said, "Based on the artifacts discovered with it, we're guessing the burial site was established in the first century, somewhere in the neighborhood of 70 A.D., give or take a few years. I'd think the torc itself was fashioned in that general time frame as well, though I suppose it could be older. Why?"

"I'm surprised at the level of craftsmanship, that's all. Most of what I've seen from that time frame has been considerably rougher in nature—less refined, if you will. Metallurgy techniques were just growing out of their infancy and the ability to craft hard metal like this was beyond most of the societies I'm familiar with from that era."

"I'm listening," Annja told him.

"Well, take gold, for instance. It's what we call a soft metal. It's easily workable, even when cold, and extremely malleable. You can force it into pretty much any shape you want, especially when heated."

He pointed to the torc. "Now take this, whatever it is," he said. "It's very similar to iron, which means that it would require a very high heat to make it malleable and constant attention to get it to do just what you want. Creating a twisted braid with this much detail would be extremely difficult."

Annja was disappointed; she'd hoped for something much more unique. "So you think it's iron or some derivative thereof?" she asked, unable to keep some of that disappointment out of her voice.

But Sebastian surprised her. "Chin up, now," he said. "I didn't say it was iron, just that I was guessing it would act like iron. In fact, I don't know what it is. I've never seen anything like it before."

He paused, considering. "Is there anything else you can tell me? Items that might have been near it when it was found? Unusual stories or myths involving a torc like this?"

Annja hadn't thought it relevant at first, but since he'd asked she decided to share with him the legend that de Chance had told her the day before.

As the story unfolded, she could see Sebastian getting more and more excited.

"Why didn't I see it?" he exclaimed when she was finished. "That makes so much more sense! Damn, I'm an idiot!"

"Want to fill me in?" Annja asked, amused at the way he was talking to himself and smiling in response.

He nodded. "As an archaeologist, I'm sure I don't have to tell you that there's often a kernel of truth hidden in the myths and legends that have been passed down to us through history."

Annja nodded; that was certainly true. The ancient city of Troy was a perfect example. Until Schliemann found Troy in 1870, no one believed that Homer's Iliad was anything but fiction. The same could be said for legends from hundreds of cultures the world over.

"So how did the legend put it? The blacksmith fashioned the necklace with the tears of the goddess that he'd collected once they'd fallen to earth, right?"

"Right…"

Sebastian got up from his stool and began pacing back and forth, his excitement rising. "So, just for the sake of argument, let's say that the blacksmith actually did collect something that fell to earth and used it to make the torc. What could that have been?"

Something that fell to earth… Then she had it. "A meteorite!" she exclaimed.

"Maybe even more than one," he agreed. "That has to be it."

"But I thought meteorites were mostly just stone and nickel?" Annja said.

Sebastian waved his hand back and forth in a so-so gesture. "Meteorites fall into three basic categories— stony, stony iron and iron. They're your basic chondritic meteorites, the kind that were formed during the early days of the solar system and as such have the closest relationship to your average Earth rock. These kinds of meteorites are made up of mostly iron, with a little nickel and stone thrown in. The easiest way to tell if they are meteorites is to test for the amount of nickel in them. Earth rocks either have a lot of nickel or very little, while the amount of nickel found in a meteorite falls within a very specific range."

Frowning, Annja said, "But I thought we decided that the torc wasn't made from iron?"

"We did, and it's not," Sebastian replied. "I'm getting there, just bear with me. Along with chrondritic meteorites, we also have achondritic meteorites, the kind that were formed long before the solar system even existed."

He paused, to be certain she was following his explanation. "Achondritic meteorites are much more rare and sometimes fall so far out of the usual expectations that we have trouble even classifying them as meteorites. There was one found in Antarctica last year, nothing more than a speck of a rock really, but its chemical composition was so unique that they couldn't conclusively identify it."

Annja saw where he was going now. "So you're suggesting that the blacksmith in the legend found a meteorite, extracted the metal from it and used that to make the torc?"

"Yes!" he cried. "It makes sense, doesn't it? You've got this metallic substance that neither of us can immediately identify, which means it's pretty rare, and given the nature of the legend surrounding the necklace even makes sense."

"So how do we prove it?"

"Simple, really," he said. "We just run a sample of it through the spectrograph and look at the results." He turned to face her. "All I need is a small sample and with that I could probably tell you exactly what it is."

Annja winced. "How small is small?"

"Just a few grains, really, that's all."

A few grains? That she could handle.

"I say we do it, then!"

Sebastian brought the torc over to a weird-looking device that resembled an enclosed incubator of all things and put the torc inside it on a little shelf.

"I'm going to shave off a few grains from the outside of the torc with this laser," he said as he closed the lid and began to calibrate the device to get the smallest possible beam. "Once we have that, we'll take the resulting sample over to the spectrograph and see what we get."

"Good enough for me," Annja said with a smile.

36

Roux was enjoying a nice cup of Kenyan coffee the following morning when there was a knock at his door.

"Come," he called.

It was Henshaw, as he knew it would be.

"I have that information you asked for, sir," Henshaw said, crossing the room and laying a file on Roux's desk.

Roux glanced at it, noting its thickness. "Why don't you give me the highlights," he suggested.

"Very good, sir. With respect to the news conference last night. The man's name is Ian Beresford. Detective Inspector Ian Beresford. He's a twenty-year veteran of the force, primarily with the Specialist Crime Directorate, handling high-profile cases and working multijurisdictional task forces. A few years ago he was transferred to Special Operations, specifically the CTC."

Counter Terrorism Command? That's interesting,

Roux thought. Why would someone like that be looking for Annja?

"Several nights ago an archaeological dig site in the West Midlands just north of Arkholme was attacked by armed intruders. The local office of the regional police received a call from a woman identifying herself as Miss Creed. She informed them of the attack and asked for immediate assistance. When the officer in charge tried to obtain more information, the call was abruptly terminated.

"At first the call was considered a hoax. Why would armed insurgents attack an archaeological site? Then someone decided to check into the name and discovered Annja's background as a television personality and host. That prompted them to send out a patrol to look into the situation."

Roux frowned. "And by the time the patrol got there, the intruders were long gone, right?"

"Yes, sir. To make matters worse, when the patrol arrived they discovered the call hadn't been a hoax at all. The site personnel had been murdered and their bodies dumped in a nearby bog. An initial report incorrectly listed Miss Creed among the deceased and then later, when it was clear she was not, there was some speculation that she might have been in league with the perpetrators."

The very idea was preposterous, so Roux brushed it aside with barely a thought.

"Do we have any idea where she is now?"

Henshaw shook his head. "No, sir, though she is clearly alive. She contacted you twice, and she has apparently been in contact with her producer, Doug Morrell, as well. He held a press conference in New York recently claiming to have the inside story on exactly what happened at the Arkholme site."

Roux doubted that, doubted it highly. He'd met Annja's young acquaintance and hadn't been all that impressed.

"Suspects?"

"The police haven't released that information. Unofficially speculations are running rampant, from al Qaeda to resurrected bog mummies. The latest reports out of—"

Roux interrupted. "Did you say bog mummies?"

Henshaw colored slightly. "Yes, sir. Oddly enough, the suggestion came out of the press conference Mr. Morrell recently gave in New York. A few of the more liberal news organizations have apparently decided to run with that as their lead theory."

And to think he said that all with a straight face, Roux marveled. Aloud, he said, "I think we can dismiss that possibility, don't you?"

"Of course."

His majordomo took a moment to compose himself again, and then said, "The latest reports out of New Scotland Yard claim that they have several suspects in the case, but they aren't releasing any more information than that. Miss Creed is still wanted by the police, but as a witness rather than as a suspect."

Roux wondered how much of that was true and how much was simple posturing. If the Met really had a suspect, they wouldn't want to tip them off before they could take action. On the other hand, if they didn't have a suspect, perhaps claiming that they did would cause those responsible to panic and make a mistake, bringing them to the police's attention. It was impossible to know which was more accurate—which, he supposed, was the point of it all, anyway.

"There's something else," Henshaw began. "I'm not sure of its relevance, but it seems like too much of a coincidence to ignore."

Roux raised his eyebrows, indicating Henshaw should continue.

"In the first few days following the massacre at the Arkholme site, Detective Inspector Beresford was called out to look at two other homicide scenes, one on the highway south of Arkholme and the other in a run-down hotel on the outskirts of London.

"There were two bodies recovered from each crime scene, all men in their late twenties or early thirties, all with criminal records of one kind or another. In each case the men had been identified as alleged members of the Red Hand Defenders, an Irish terrorist group with the goal of freeing Ireland from British rule and oversight."

"Do the police consider the three events to be connected in any way?" Roux asked.

Henshaw shrugged. "I'm not entirely sure. My contact inside the MPS didn't want to dig too deeply and risk tipping his hand to anyone who might be watching. But he was able to tell me that at least one individual at each crime scene had been killed with some kind of bladed weapon, most likely a sword. There's also a report from a clergyman who claims to have been saved by a 'dark-haired angel wielding a holy sword' on the highway earlier that afternoon."

The combination of events made Roux sit up and take notice. The connection between them all was obvious, once you had the right cards in your hand. A quick shuffle put the cards into the proper order and let him see them the bigger picture.

An unknown group attacks the dig site at Arkholme. Annja witnesses the assault but is unable to do anything about it—hence the call to the regional police. Before she can finish the call she's interrupted, perhaps even discovered by the enemy. Despite this she manages to escape capture but ends up being confronted by her pursuers again on the highway not too long after that, this time in full view of the traveling clergyman.

Forced to defend herself, Annja uses the sword and leaves the two men dead on the road in her wake. Somehow she makes it to London, where she rents a room, believing she's escaped her pursuers. The latter turns out to be untrue, however, and she must flee for a second time, leaving even more bodies in her wake.

So if the Red Hand Defenders were after Annja, then it stood to reason that they were the ones who had attacked the archaeologists at Arkholme.

But what had they been after?

That was what was bothering him about this whole scenario. The idea that an Irish terrorist group would have an interest in something unearthed from a peat bog in the middle of...

All of a sudden the connections came together in his head.

He glanced at the calendar in his head, then turned to Henshaw. "When was the attack on the dig site?"

The other man told him.

Just as he'd suspected, it was the same night that Shaw had announced that he would be auctioning off a one-of-a-kind Celtic torc that he'd recently acquired. If it had been any more obvious it would have sat up and hit him in the face.

How could he have missed it?

The implications were staggering.

He needed to get in touch with Annja and he needed to do it quickly.

"Do we have a number for Mr. Morrell?"

Henshaw nodded.

"Let's get him on the phone. Perhaps he knows how to contact Annja."

The first two times they tried to reach Morrell the call went straight to voice mail, which irritated Roux to no end. It was only when Henshaw offhandedly reminded him that he'd inadvertently done the same thing to Annja that Roux was able to stifle his irritation and wait with a bit more patience.

Then, on the third try, almost an hour later, someone finally picked up.

"Morrell," a young man said.

Roux wondered if he'd ever sounded that young and decided that no, he never had. Even if he had, centuries of life had certainly burned the memory out of him.

"Hello, Mr. Morrell. My name is Roux."

"Roux? That's it? Just Roux? Like Prince or Madonna?"

Roux gritted his teeth. "No, Mr. Morrell, I am nothing like one of your so-called American pop stars. You might remember me as a friend of Annja's?"

"Yeah, I've heard the name before," the other man said cautiously, "but how am I supposed to know it's really you?"

Roux was taken aback for a moment. "Who else would it be?"

"There are a lot of people looking for Annja right now, Mr. Whoever-You-Are. If you think I'm just going to turn her over to the first person claiming to be a friend of hers, you've got another think coming."

"Do you have caller ID, Mr. Morrell?"

"Of course. Doesn't everyone?"

The know-it-all tone was starting to get to him. It must have shown, too, for Henshaw was now staring at him quizzically from the other side of the room. Roux ignored him, concentrating on keeping his temper, something he wasn't very good at.

"If you do, then you should see that I am calling you from Paris, France. Perhaps you might remember Annja mentioning that is where I live the last time we met?"

Morrell snorted. "That doesn't mean anything. You could be any Joe Blow calling me from France."

That did it. Roux finally lost his temper. Snarling into the phone, he said, "Why you little cur! When I get my hands on you I'll have you whipped and then tied to the back of my horse for an energetic ride around the estate until you'll wish that I'd simply gutted you on the spot! You will help me find Annja!"

There was a moment of silence and then Morrell said, "Hello, Roux. I thought that was you."

If he'd been in the same room with him, Roux probably would have killed him. As it was, he needed a moment to regain control.

"Roux? You still there, Roux?"

"I am," he said through still-gritted teeth. "It is urgent that I speak with Annja—her life may be in danger. Do you have a way of reaching her?"

"Did you try to call her cell phone?"

Roux paused again as he fought to keep from yelling a second time. When he was reasonably confident that he could do so without losing his cool, he answered, "Yes. It seems to be out of operation at the present time."

"Oh," Morrell said with a little laugh. "Not that cell phone, her other cell phone."

Dear Lord, granted me patience… "Her other cell phone?"

"Yeah. She lost the first one when the bog mummies attacked. Or, at least, that's what we're going to show on the episode. It's going to be incredible! I've already got special effects working out this fully articulated bog mummy replica that we can—"

"Morrell!" Roux said sharply, stopping the other man in midsentence. "The cell phone number?"

"Oh. Right. Hang on, I've got it right here."

Roux could hear some rustling in the background and then Morrell was back, reading off a phone number from the piece of paper that he must have been holding in his hand.

He was still chattering away about something or other when Roux hung up on him.

37

Shaving a few grains of material from the torc proved to be a simple task with the help of the laser. Sebastian collected the sample and moved over to the mass spectrometer that Annja had seen earlier upon entering the room.

Sebastian placed the sample inside the device and then fired up the computer that was a part of the unit. As he worked, he explained to Annja what was going to happen.

"The first thing we're going to do is vaporize the sample, producing a gas that includes all of its component elements. The gas will then be exposed to an electron beam, which will charge the molecules of the gas and convert them into ionized particles."

There was a brief flash of light from inside the spectrometer as the first step he'd mentioned was carried out. He barely acknowledged it, continuing his explanation while manipulating various controls through the computer.

"The ionized particles will be exposed to a series of magnetic fields that will sort the ions by their masses. The detector will then provide a quantitative analysis of the ions that are present."

Good-looking and intelligent, Annja thought as she watched him work.

"In the end, we should know exactly what our legendary blacksmith used to manufacture the torc."

He set a few more switches and then sat back to wait. They spent the time sharing a bit of background information about each other; Annja talked about some of the projects she'd been involved in while filming *Chasing History's Monsters* while Sebastian entertained her with tales of being a mineral scout in some of the most remote places on earth while working as a contractor for the big petroleum companies that were his bread and butter.

Finally, after almost an hour of waiting, though it only seemed like ten or fifteen minutes to Annja, the spectrometer churned out its results.

Sebastian picked up the report off the printer and began paging through it.

"Pretty consistent with an achondritic meteorite, just as we suspected. Iron, nickel in limited quantities, some silica formations and various assorted minerals."

He got quiet all of a sudden.

"Sebastian?" Annja asked.

He didn't seem to notice, his attention absorbed in whatever he'd found there on the page.

"Sebastian?" she said, a bit sharper that time. "What is it?"

He looked up from the paper, a dazed expression on his face.

"Plutonium."

"What?" she asked. She wasn't sure that she'd heard him correctly. *Couldn't* have heard him correctly.

"Did you say plutonium?" she repeated.

Sebastian nodded, his attention still on the report in front of him. He was tracing the lines of information with one finger, then double-checking the numbers against a reference volume he'd pulled from a nearby shelf. "No doubt about it. In fact, it is probably one of the purest samples I've ever seen outside of a nuclear laboratory."

"But plutonium is virtually nonexistent in nature," Annja protested. "You can sometimes find it in uranium, but only in the tiniest trace amounts."

"I know, Annja, I'm a geologist, remember. But I'm telling you, the torc has one hell of a lot of plutonium in it."

That just didn't make any sense to her. Bewildered, she sought an alternative solution. "Can the spectrometer be malfunctioning? Or calibrated incorrectly or something?"

"There's one way to find out."

Sebastian got up and began digging through the cabinets on a nearby wall. After a few minutes of searching he returned with a small handheld device about the size of a waffle iron. A small wand was attached to the device.

Annja immediately recognized it as a Geiger counter.

Stepping back over to the laser where the torc still rested, Sebastian turned on the counter and waved the wand over the torc.

A sudden series of clicks erupted into the room from the side of the Geiger counter.

Annja knew what that meant without having to be told.

The torc was radioactive.

Sebastian, and his spectrometer, was right. As crazy as it sounded, the torc had been fashioned from a meteorite that consisted primarily of naturally produced plutonium.

At that moment, a phone began ringing.

Annja looked at Sebastian, expecting him to answer his phone, but he shook his head.

"Not mine," he said.

Surprised, Annja realized it was her new phone. She hadn't heard it ring before and didn't recognize the sound.

She dug it out of her backpack and answered it, already expecting the caller to have hung up given the few frantic moments it had taken her to find it once she'd realized it was her own. "Hello?"

"If you expect me to call back," Roux said, "it is generally a good idea to actually leave me the number where I can reach you."

"Roux!" Annja exclaimed, surprised by the call but delighted to finally hear from him. She'd seriously started to worry that something had gone wrong on his end.

As it turned out, Roux was right. In all the craziness that was going on, she'd forgotten to leave her new cell phone number with him when she'd called. She endured a few minutes of scolding; as her mentor and friend, she figured he was entitled.

"I've been seeing your name all over the press,

Annja," he said. "Just what have you gotten yourself into this time?"

"Hang on," she told him, then turned to Sebastian. "I'm sorry, I've got to take this call."

He flashed his megawatt smile again. "Of course, why don't you use the reception area, where you'll have a little privacy? I'll continue working on these results."

A moment later she was sitting by a window in the front room, looking out over the street, and bringing Roux up-to-date on everything that had happened to her since finding the torc.

SEATED IN THE back of his limousine with Henshaw at the wheel, Roux listened to Annja's story and as he did the pieces of the puzzle he'd been struggling to understand finally fell into place.

It was Annja's dig team that had uncovered the torc. How Shaw had learned about it, Roux couldn't say, but somehow he had and had decided to acquire it and sell it to the highest bidder. He'd sent his thugs from the Red Hand Defenders to *acquire* the torc from those who had uncovered it.

Annja's presence at the dig site had prevented that from happening. When the intruders had shown a callous disregard for the lives of her associates, she'd hidden the torc and fought back.

Her explanation also revealed why she was so reluctant to go to the police to share what she knew; seeing one of her attackers wearing the uniform of a regional police officer would have caused Roux to question just who he could and could not trust, as well.

Learning of her escape, Shaw had sent some of his thugs after her, determined to recover the torc, while all along he'd been deceiving those he'd called together to bid on the object. He'd never had the torc in hand at all…

"Where are you now, Annja?"

"In Paris, at the offices of Dr. Sebastian Cartier, a geologist I've hired to analyze the chemical composition of the torc. And get this, we've just discovered that the torc was fashioned from a meteorite full of plutonium."

"Plutonium? Give me his address," Roux said, jotting it down on a piece of paper as she did so. Forget the meeting. This was too important. "Henshaw and I are going to…"

Roux trailed off in midsentence as the memory of the last conversation he'd overheard in Shaw's office replayed in his mind.

"She'll be at this address in the morning. Recover my property and then get rid of her."

"What about the geologist?"

"Get rid of him, too."

With a growing sense of horror, Roux realized Annja had the plutonium Shaw needed to turn his inoperable suitcase nuke into an operational one. Even worse, Shaw had known since sometime last night where Annja would be this morning and had already dispatched a team to eliminate her and recover the torc!

"You've got to get out of there, Annja!" Roux said urgently. "Drop everything but the torc and get out of there now!"

Annja didn't understand. "What's going on, Roux?"

"I don't have time to explain," he replied. "Shaw knows you're there and he's already sent his men to recover the torc. No matter what, you can't let that happen."

"Shaw? Who the hell is Shaw? And how do you know someone is after the torc?"

She was just about to demand that Roux explain himself whether he wanted to or not when she happened to glance out the front window. She was just in time to see a group of armed gunmen wearing black face masks exit the van parked across the street and head directly for the walkway leading to Sebastian's front door.

Into the phone, she said, "We're too late, Roux. Shaw's men are already here."

She then ran for the back room, calling her sword to her as she went.

38

Sebastian looked up as Annja burst into the room and she saw his eyes go wide at the fact that she was carrying a medieval sword in her right hand. With her pursuers only moments behind her, though, she didn't have time to explain. She pointed at a door on the other side of the room and shouted, "Run!"

She expected him to jump to and do as she said and had taken a few steps in that direction herself before realizing he hadn't moved. He just stood there, holding the test results in one hand and a pen in the other, staring at her in amazement.

"What's going on?" he asked as he watched her dash across the room and grab the torc from inside the cutting crib.

Before she could answer him there was a resounding crash from the front of the house.

How long is that door going to hold? Annja wondered.

Sebastian tore his gaze away from her and looked toward the front of the house, uncertain.

They were wasting precious time. "In another thirty seconds armed gunmen are going to come swarming through that door, looking for this," Annja said urgently, holding up the torc. "We need to be somewhere else when that happens."

A crash of glass was heard and quickly followed by shouts from the front of the house.

Apparently the door wasn't going to hold them for very long at all.

Sebastian glanced once more in that direction and then made up his mind. He turned and hurried over to the door on the far side of the room, Annja close at his heels.

"Is there a back way out?" she asked as they left the lab and its equipment behind and headed deeper into the building down another short corridor.

"Yes," he told her as they emerged into another big room like the one they'd just left. To her left was a spiral staircase leading upward to the next floor. On her right was a makeshift storage area, with shelves overloaded with discarded equipment and boxes piled high with records that had yet to go to long-term storage.

As Annja glanced around, Sebastian hurried forward to the rear exit, half-hidden in the shadows against the far wall.

"This will lead us out in the alley," Sebastian said, reaching for the knob.

Realizing what he was about to do, Annja cried, "Wait!" but she was too late.

Sebastian either didn't hear her or was too caught up in the excitement for it to register. She was a few steps behind when he grabbed the door and yanked it open.

She didn't know who was more startled, Sebastian or the gunman standing on the other side of the door, reaching for the knob from that side.

Unfortunately for Sebastian, the gunman was armed and he was not.

Sebastian shouted in surprise as the other man brought up his weapon and put two rounds right into Sebastian's chest at almost point-blank range.

The gunman only lived a few seconds longer than his victim however, for even as Sebastian's body toppled backward to the floor, Annja stepped over him and thrust her sword forward, skewering the intruder through the chest.

Automatic gunfire split the morning air and bullets chewed up the door frame around her. Looking past the man impaled on the end of her sword, Annja could see two other intruders just entering the small backyard from the alley behind the house, firing as they came.

Ignoring the flying splinters and the whine of bullets as they zipped past her, Annja released her sword, snatched the gun from the dying man's hand and then dove back inside the house. She dragged Sebastian's body clear of the doorway and then kicked the door shut.

Bullets slammed into the other side, but the door must have been reinforced with steel or something similar for it held up under the assault. Annja took one look at Sebastian and knew he was gone; his eyes stared blankly at the ceiling above, unseeing.

She looked around, frantically hoping for a way out. Her gaze fell upon the staircase leading to the second floor and for a moment she gave it serious consideration, but she didn't know what lay in that direction and the last thing she wanted to do was get cornered without a way out. Dismissing it, she chose instead to charge back in the direction from which she had come, thinking the gunmen wouldn't be expecting her to retreat that way.

As she ran she glanced at the gun in her hand. It was an MP-5, a weapon common with SWAT teams the world over, and thankfully one with which she was familiar. She hit the release and let the magazine fall into her other hand, noting its weight.

About half-full, she thought. Gotta make every shot count.

She slapped it back into place as she raced into the lab.

The door leading to the reception area was still open, giving her a clear view all the way to the front of the building. Several figures were coming in through the front door and she didn't have to see them closely to know they were up to no good. The guns in their hands and the ski masks over their faces kind of spoiled the surprise.

Annja dashed over to the workstation closest to the other door and took up position behind it. She pointed the gun in the direction of the intruders and sent a short burst their way before ducking down behind the counter.

Almost immediately a withering hail of answering fire came in her general direction, but most of the shots were inaccurate and she wasn't seriously threatened by it.

The room around her, however, took a beating, as did the hallway leading from the reception area as bullets chewed into the walls, floor and ceiling.

Annja waited for a lull and then popped her head around the side of the island. Two of the intruders were headed down the hallway in front of her, trying to gain ground while she kept her head down.

Oh, no, you don't.

She stuck the gun around the corner and held the trigger down.

When she looked again, the gunmen were on the ground, unmoving.

This angered their companions, for another blistering wave of bullets came in her direction. Annja simply hunkered down behind the workstation and rode it out.

Good thing she did, too, because as she rose to her knees to return fire, she glanced back the way she had come and saw three men crossing the storage area, headed for the door to the lab. The lead gunman saw her, as well, and snapped out a shot in her direction.

The bullet streaked past her ribs, coming so close as to tear the side of her shirt but missing her tender flesh.

Annja returned the favor by putting a bullet of her own right into the gunman's face.

As the dead man fell back against the others struggling to get by him, Annja used the time, and the confusion, to scramble over and behind a different workstation. This one would give her more protection from the gunfire coming from the front of the house while simultaneously bringing her within arm's distance of the door to the back hallway.

Once in place, she called her sword to hand.

As the first of the intruders moved cautiously forward into the room, his gun held out in front of him, Annja swung the sword downward, taking the hand holding the gun off at the wrist.

He started screaming, startling the man behind him, which gave Annja the split second she needed to step around the corner and fire past the injured man, taking out his companion in the process.

That should even up the odds a bit, she thought with satisfaction.

That was when she heard the clatter of something bouncing across the floor toward her.

Whirling, her eyes tracked the round egg-shaped object as it came to rest against one of the other workstations.

She was already moving as her mind registered what it was seeing, diving for the cabinets nearby, her only thought to get under cover as quickly as possible.

The grenade went off a moment later.

39

With his heart in his throat, Roux handed the address over the front seat to Henshaw, saying, "As fast as you can. Annja's life depends on it."

His majordomo needed no further urging. He stomped his foot down on the accelerator and with consummate skill began to weave the limo in and out of traffic as he sped through city streets, headed for Sebastian Cartier's office.

Roux had made a trip like this once before, rushing off to save a young woman in his charge, only then he'd arrived too late and she'd perished at the hands of her English captors.

This time will be different, he told himself.

This time his young protégé would not be left to perish alone.

As they approached the address, they saw two dark-colored vans pull away from the curb and speed off in opposite directions. For a moment Roux considered giving chase; if they were Shaw's men and they had the torc, this might be the only chance he would have to take them out. But his concern for Annja overrode his instincts and he watched them disappear down the street unhindered.

No sooner had Henshaw pulled to a stop in front of the house than Roux was out of the car and dashing toward the entrance, calling Annja's name as he went.

The house looked like it belonged in war-torn Baghdad than on a quiet Parisian street. The door was open and from the walkway Roux could see that the room just inside—a reception area of some kind—had been riddled with gunfire. As he stepped inside, shell casings rolled underfoot and the air stank of cordite.

"Annja?" he called, desperately hoping for an answer.

Silence was the only reply.

He took a few steps forward. There were two exits, one to his left that opened into an office and another dead ahead that looked like it would take him deeper into the building. He could see into the room on his left, a ransacked office that appeared empty, and so he chose the other way out of the reception area.

A narrow hallway stretched out ahead of him and it was there that he found the first two bodies. He hurried forward, concerned, but upon getting closer it was obvious that they were both male. He couldn't see their faces due to the ski masks they wore but that was fine; his interest in them immediately waned when he realized that neither of them was Annja.

The doors on either side of the hallway were locked, which left him only the direct route ahead.

Roux could hear sirens in the distance and knew he didn't have much time. He had to find Annja and get out of there before the authorities arrived or there was going to be trouble.

He stepped over the bodies, being careful not to put his feet into the widening pool of blood that was seeping out of them and onto the floor, and then pushed ahead.

The room at the end of the hall was in even worse shape than the reception area had been. Cabinets hung half on and half off the walls, their exteriors riddled with bullet holes. Water shot up from a shattered sink and flowed down onto the floor where it mixed with a pile of broken glass and other debris. The ceiling and part of the wall in the far corner had collapsed, burying the cabinets beneath in an avalanche of wood, plasterboard and ceiling tiles.

Sticking out of the pile of debris was the lower half of a woman's leg, wearing blue jeans and a familiar style of hiking boot.

Annja!

Roux rushed over and quickly dug her out. Her face was covered in blood, a mask of crimson obscuring her features, and for a moment he feared the worst, but then he noticed the steady rise and fall of her chest and knew that she was merely unconscious. The blood was from a sizable cut at her hairline, and she was clearly bruised and battered, but she was alive and for that he was thankful.

He scooped her up and headed back the way he had come.

The sirens were louder, probably only a few blocks away now, and a small crowd was gathering outside. Henshaw was holding them off with stern looks and his impressive size, but it was obvious that it wouldn't work for much longer. Several were already fondling their mobile phones, no doubt getting ready to take pictures of what they were seeing if they hadn't already done so. It was time to get out of there.

"Let's go!" Roux shouted as he rushed out of the house.

Henshaw had the back door open and the car running by the time Roux slid Annja into the backseat and climbed in after her. There were several shouts of concern from the crowd at that point, people openly wondering if they were witnessing a kidnapping, but Roux ignored them as Henshaw hit the gas and got them out of there just seconds before the police arrived at the scene.

Annja was still unconscious, but that was to be expected. Roux used the opportunity to give her a quick once-over, making certain he hadn't missed any more serious injuries.

"Home or the hospital?" Henshaw asked from up front.

"Hospital."

Definitely, a hospital. Just not one the public knew about.

As Henshaw drove, Roux picked up his cell phone again and made the call that he'd been putting off since earlier that morning.

"Detective Inspector Beresford, please," he said when his call was answered by the police operator at the other end of the line.

"Detective Inspector Beresford is on another line at the moment, sir. Would you like to leave a message?"

"No," Roux replied. "I'll hold. It's urgent that I speak with him. Please tell him it's about the Arkholme case."

Music played for a moment or two and then the line was answered a second time.

"Beresford," said a gruff and tired voice.

"My name is Roux, Inspector," he began. "And I believe it is time that you and I had a short chat."

40

Annja lurched upright in the hospital bed, her mind and body unaware of the time she'd spent unconscious so that they both thought she was still in the midst of the firefight, still in danger. Her hand curled around the nonexistent hilt of her great sword and suddenly it was there, swinging forward in an arc designed to disembowel her opponent.

Thankfully Roux had foreseen just such an occurrence and was standing off to one side, out of reach.

"Annja!" he called sharply.

His familiar voice brought her to full wakefulness and she glanced about, taking in her surroundings, noting Roux standing off to one side, prudently out of reach of her sword.

She was in a hospital; that much was obvious. An IV tube ran to her left arm, no doubt pumping glucose and other necessary fluids into her body in the wake of the battering she'd taken at the hands of the intruders who'd come for the torc. She also had a bandage around her head right at the hairline and another wrapped around her ribs. Her body beneath her hospital gown felt beaten and bruised, which was to be expected given what she'd been through, but her thoughts, now that she was awake, were surprisingly clear. She remembered the phone call from Roux, warning her to get out of the geologist's offices before Shaw's men arrived.

How had he known they were coming? she wondered, which then prompted another, perhaps more important, thought.

How deeply was he involved?

Annja kept her sword in hand, her gaze locked on Roux.

"What happened?" she asked.

Roux's eyes narrowed slightly as he realized she was not putting her weapon away, but he didn't say anything about it, simply answered her question instead.

"By the time Henshaw and I arrived, the mongrels who attacked you had fled, taking the torc with them. We managed to extricate you from the scene before the police arrived and brought you here."

"And that is?"

"A private hospital outside of Paris. The kind of place that caters to those who do not wish to have their business aired in public."

She hated to ask, but she had to know. "Sebastian?"

Roux shook his head.

Annja knew what that meant and vowed she'd take the time to properly grieve her new friend when all this was over.

For now, though, she still had to get to the bottom of things.

Watching Roux carefully, she said, "You knew they were coming."

It was more a statement than a question, but Roux answered it as if it were the latter.

"I was offered a chance to bid on an artifact, one that might have some unusual powers attributed to it. As I dug into the offering, it became clear that the man running the auction, David Shaw, was up to something untoward and I made it my mission to find out what that was. By the time I discovered the connection between you, the torc and Shaw's activities, it was almost too late. I warned you as quickly as I could and then did my best to extract you from the situation."

He was telling the truth. She could feel it in her bones, could sense his honest concern for her and what she'd been through. The fact that she'd doubted him at all now seemed ludicrous.

She released the sword, letting it disappear back into the otherwhere, to wait for her next time of need.

She seemed to be having them a lot lately.

Roux stepped forward, coming over to her bedside. "The doctor said you should drink this when you woke up," he said, handing her a glass.

"What is it?" she asked suspiciously, her discomfort with doctors and hospitals showing through.

Roux smiled. "It's just water, Annja. Nothing more sinister than that."

She smiled back at him, the initial awkwardness between them already forgotten. She took the glass and it was only when she held its cool surface in her hands that she realized how thirsty she was. The water soothed her parched throat and she drank two more before she was finished.

When she'd had enough, she said, "This guy, Shaw. Do you know how to find him?"

She asked the question in a casual tone, but Roux knew her extremely well. There was nothing casual in her desire to know the answer.

"At the moment, no, but I have people working on that. Unfortunately, we have a much bigger problem on our hands."

She raised an eyebrow at him. "And that is?"

Before he could answer, there was a knock at the door.

Annja glanced at Roux, her mind already halfway to calling the sword to her side, but he shook her off, gesturing that she cover herself up with the blanket.

As she did so, the door opened, revealing a short, stocky man with gray hair standing in the doorway. His shirt and suit had been well-pressed at the start of his shift, but since that was forty-eight hours ago, he was starting to look a bit worse for wear. Annja knew this because she'd seen him in the same suit the night before, giving a press conference regarding the events in Arkholme.

Detective Inspector Ian Beresford looked them over, then stepped into the room.

"It's good to see you still alive, Miss Creed," he said, his voice much deeper than it sounded on television. Without waiting for an answer, he turned to her companion and said, "You must be Roux."

To her surprise Roux stepped forward and shook the detective's hand. "Thank you for coming, Detective Inspector. I appreciate your willingness to meet with us on such short notice."

Beresford's face was a carefully controlled mask as

he said, "You made a persuasive argument for doing so, Mr. Roux."

Roux's smile didn't falter as he automatically corrected the other man. "It's Roux, just Roux."

"Indeed," Beresford replied. "How interesting."

"If you two are done fencing with each other," Annja said, "maybe one of you could tell me what the hell is going on?"

"I'd like to hear that, as well," Beresford said.

Roux pointed at the chair in the corner. "Why don't you have a seat, Inspector? I have a hunch that this will take a while."

IT TOOK MORE than an hour, as it turned out. Roux began the process, telling them how he'd been approached as a potential buyer for a rare Celtic artifact that had been unearthed by what he had been told was a private collector on private property. That wasn't exactly the truth, but ally or not, Roux had no intention of telling a police inspector that he'd been breaking the law right from the very start. That was one detail that he had no qualms about leaving out. Annja went next, describing the attack at the Arkholme dig site and the ruthless way in which her colleagues had been cut down with gunfire. She told them how she'd managed to survive when the others did not and then of the two subsequent attacks by armed men, all with the same peculiar tattoo that she'd seen on the intruders at the dig site.

Beresford joined the tale at that point, confirming Annja's guess that the gunmen were members of the armed insurgency group known as the Red Hand Defenders and then gave a little background information on the group's motives and membership.

That cleared a few things up in Roux's mind,

particularly what Shaw intended to do with the portable nuclear device he'd bought from Perchenko, and he filled the others in on his activities the night before and what he suspected they meant in the overall scheme of things.

Beresford listened carefully as the story unfolded, letting each of them speak and only occasionally interrupting to ask a question if he didn't understand something. It was only when Roux mentioned Perchenko by name that Beresford acted surprised.

"Ivan Perchenko? The arms dealer?"

Roux nodded. "Acting on some information I received, I followed Shaw last night and witnessed him buying a piece of what I took to be surplus military equipment from Perchenko."

"Do you have any idea what that equipment might be?" the detective asked.

Annja wasn't surprised when Roux said, "I do," but she was shocked to hear what he had to say next.

"Suspecting something was amiss, I decided to question Perchenko myself. After some conversation, he revealed to me that he sold Shaw a Cold War–era RA-115, which, in plain English, is a man-portable nuclear device, or suitcase nuke."

Roux's revelation stunned them into silence, but only for a moment.

"Is the device operational?" Beresford asked, leaning forward in his chair, practically vibrating with tension as he did so. "And is Perchenko still able to answer questions on the subject?"

"Perchenko thought he'd pulled a fast one over on Shaw. The device had been rendered inert by the Soviet military years before and he found it remarkably funny that Shaw had been willing to pay for a piece of equipment that was useless without the plutonium necessary to activate it."

Beresford visibly relaxed as Roux continued.

"Figuring the authorities might be interested in hearing what he had to say for themselves, I left Perchenko and his bodyguard securely locked in the basement of a facility outside of Paris late last night."

Annja couldn't believe what she was hearing! From what she'd put together, it looked like this guy Shaw was clearly a member of the Red Hand Defenders, possibly even their leader. She'd thought the torc's mystical properties were what made it so attractive to the organization, but now she understood that it was much more down to earth than that. Apparently it was the torc's plutonium base that was of interest to them and not its alleged mystical qualities!

"I'm not sure I want to know what it took to ring that admission out of him," Beresford told Roux, "but I guess I should thank you for your efforts. CT Command has been watching Perchenko closely for the past few years and hasn't been able to pin anything definitive on him. With your testimony, we should be able to put him away for a good number of years."

But Roux shook his head. "I'm afraid we don't have time for that, Detective Inspector." He turned. "Annja, would you be good enough to share what you learned about the torc before it was taken from you?"

Beresford turned to face her, a look of confusion on his face. Clearly he didn't understand where this was going.

It's only going to get worse, she thought.

She did as she was asked, telling him about the tests they'd run using the mass spectrometer in Cartier's office and how those tests had shown that the torc was mostly composed of a type of plutonium that did not exist naturally on earth. How Shaw had known about it, she didn't know, but it now seemed clear to her that it was the nature of the necklace that had attracted him to it in the first place.

Beresford's face got more and more pale as she spoke, until he looked like he'd seen a ghost. Perhaps, like Scrooge, he was seeing the ghosts of things to come. The idea that a working nuclear device had fallen into the hands of the Red Hand Defenders, an organization that hadn't shied away from targeting Catholic schoolteachers and postal workers, for heaven's sake, was nearly unthinkable.

It also raised another, vital question.

What were they going to do about it?

41

In the wake of Annja's announcement, silence filled the room as they all considered the implications of what had just been revealed. A group with a known hatred for British rule was in possession of what they considered to be a working nuclear device. The dangers that presented were staggering.

Even worse, however, was what Beresford said next.

"There's nothing we can do. We have no proof."

Annja, who'd pulled on a robe and gotten out of bed to pace back and forth with tired little strides of her aching body, whirled to face him.

"Nothing you can do?" she repeated. "Are you insane? Call out the freakin' army, for heaven's sake! Terrorists have a nuclear bomb and for all we know they're getting ready to use it against the city of London!"

Clearly agitated, Beresford rose and shouted at her in response. "It doesn't matter, Miss Creed. This is a country of laws! We don't bend them to suit our needs like your country tends to do! All I have right now are statements from the two of you, which, in a court of law, will be practically useless. Need I remind you that you're a potential suspect in a multiple homicide?

"Never mind that your companion here," he said, pointing at Roux with his thumb, "has all but admitted to kidnapping and holding the principal subject against his will. The magistrate will throw the case out of court before I can even get a word in edgewise!"

Roux's brow furrowed and Annja knew he was trying to reconcile his fifteenth-century ideas of right and wrong with the modern legal code. "Would it help if I gave you a written record of the discussion I had with Mr. Perchenko? Would that convince you?"

Beresford held up a hand, visibly trying to get his emotions under control. When he had, he turned to face them both. "You don't need to convince me, Roux. Nor you, Annja. I believe you both. Who would make up a story as crazy as this. It's so ludicrous that I've got no choice but to believe it. But that's not the problem."

Annja understood immediately and tried to explain it to Roux. "Detective Inspector Beresford also has to convince those above him in the chain of command that there is an urgent threat, and if the only proof he has at his disposal is our word, then he'll be hard-pressed to make anyone listen."

"Quite right, Miss Creed."

Annja had never wanted to be more wrong in her entire life. "There has to be something we can do," she insisted. "We can't let Shaw just disappear with a tactical weapon like that. We have to stop him!"

Beresford nodded his agreement. "I'll do what I can to sound the alarm. Someone, somewhere, has to listen to me. But at the moment my hands are tied until I get that official go-ahead. Shaw runs a multi-million-dollar corporation. The powers that be aren't going to take kindly to me accusing him of being the mastermind behind an Irish terrorist group, never mind one with a bomb that big and that scary."

"Perhaps there is something we can do in the meantime," Roux suggested.

Beresford shrugged. "Talk to me. As the Americans say, I'm all ears."

THEIR FIRST ORDER of business was to figure out where Shaw's henchmen had taken the torc. That, at least, was something Beresford could work on without waiting for approval from those higher up the food chain. He didn't waste any time getting in touch with the French authorities in charge of the crime scene at Cartier's office and suggesting, one detective to another, that they be on the lookout for two dark-colored vans that left the scene just before law enforcement officers arrived. When asked what he knew about the incident, Beresford said that it appeared to be related to a series of previous incidents under investigation by New Scotland Yard and promised he'd be in touch later with more information. That seemed to satisfy them and he was confident that they'd let him know if and when they found anything. He then called his partner, Clements, and ordered him to place Shaw's home and The Vanguard offices in London under a round-the-clock observation, citing a link to the Arkholme case as justification.

Given that no one expected Shaw to remain in France, they turned their attention to getting out of the country and back to England. Beresford suggested taking Annja into protective custody and bringing her across the Channel as an official "guest" of the Metropolitan Police Service, but doing so would require the cooperation of the French authorities, who might then want to question her in connection with the Cartier homicide. None of them were ready to let Annja's involvement in that situation become public knowledge yet, as doing so might tip Shaw to the fact that a witness to both the initial attack and the killing of Sebastian Cartier still lived. Right now Shaw wasn't looking for her, no doubt believing that she perished along with Cartier, but that would change rather quickly if he learned that she was alive and talking with the police.

While they were still debating their options, Annja's doctor arrived for his afternoon rounds. Dismissing the other men from the room, the doctor gave her a thorough examination, paying close attention to the cut on her head and the injury to her ribs. He removed the bandage from her head, cleaned the wound with some antiseptic gel and then covered it up again with a fresh bandage. When he was finished, he turned his attention to her ribs. Unwrapping the bandages let her know she was more sensitive that she'd realized.

"Tell me if this hurts," he told her, and then gently pressed against her rib cage with one hand.

Pain went off like a supernova in her head, blacking out the room and everything in it. When she came back to herself, she found him standing over her, a look of concern on his face.

"Definitely yes, that hurt you, I see."

She nodded weakly.

"You have several cracked ribs and some serious blunt-trauma damage to your torso," he said as he removed the IV line and taped a bandage over the slight puncture it left behind. "Unfortunately, other than wrapping it up again, there's not much we can do for it. It will heal, but it's going to take time. I'd suggest several weeks of nothing more strenuous than bed rest," he told her. "Though, based on your reputation, I'd say I'd be lucky if you stayed off your feet for a day."

Annja smiled weakly in his direction, not bothering to contradict him. She'd be lucky if she could get even another four hours, but she wasn't going to be the one to tell him that.

When the doctor left she hobbled into the bathroom and took a shower, wanting to be rid of the stink of blood, cordite and plaster dust that surrounded her.

When she emerged from the shower, she found a clean set of clothes laid out on the bed for her along with a note from Henshaw saying that he hoped he'd gotten her size right.

It was meant as a joke; he'd replaced her torn and bloodied clothing enough times that he probably knew her size better than she did.

She didn't want to think about what that said about her so-called social life.

She was standing beside the bed, pulling on the new pair of sweatpants she'd taken from the pile of clothes Henshaw had supplied, when Garin Braden suddenly strode into her hospital room.

As was typical, he didn't bother to knock.

"No need to get dressed on my account," he told her with a laugh as she stared at him in surprise. "In fact, I think I'd prefer that you didn't."

The thought of being undressed around Garin made her unexpectedly blush, which simply ticked her off. Thankfully the towel she was wearing covered the vast majority of her body.

"And I'd prefer that you learned to knock, you

ass," she told him. "Turn around while I finish getting dressed."

Smiling a boyish grin, he did so.

She dropped the towel, glaring at the back of his head and mentally daring him to turn around as she pulled on a dark blue t-shirt. She'd clobber him if he did.

The truth was that she found Garin Braden far too interesting for her own good. That he was devilishly handsome wasn't justification enough, particularly since she was well aware that a devil's heart beat in his breast. His black hair and perfectly groomed goatee gave him a suave, debonair appearance, but she knew he'd kill without a second thought if it served his purposes.

Garin was tied to her life in much the same way Roux was and she had the sword to thank for it. Like Roux, Garin had been there at Joan's death, apprenticed to the older man by his own father years before. Somehow he had been bound up along with Roux in whatever mystical force the sword had spawned when it had been shattered before them by the English who held Joan captive.

For centuries the two men had alternated between trying to kill each other and being grudging friends and occasional partners. Annja had somehow adopted them when the sword adopted her.

"You can turn around now," she said, wincing as she straightened again.

He must have seen her reaction, but he gave no sign of having done so, which she appreciated. He was a warrior and hated to show weakness, so by extension he thought she wouldn't want to, either. It was a thoughtful gesture, in its own, unique way, and it was those little things that made her wonder what else he hid beneath that decidedly deadly exterior.

"Can you walk or do I need to get a wheelchair?" he asked. His teasing tone was gone; he was back to being all business.

"Are we going somewhere?"

"Unless you'd prefer to spend the rest of your days in the hospital," he replied. He opened the door, checked to be sure the hallway was clear and then gestured that she follow him.

Crazy as it seemed, Annja did so.

She knew Garin wouldn't be here unless Roux had called him, she just didn't know why. She assumed it had something to do with getting them all out of France; as the head of a multi-million-dollar empire, Garin could call up all kinds of resources at a moment's notice, resources that neither Annja nor Roux had access to.

Her hunch was confirmed when Garin led her to the nearest stairwell and followed her slow but steady progress up to the roof.

A helicopter was waiting there for them, a sleek-looking thing painted black, with the logo of a golden dragon in flight emblazoned on the tail. The helicopter door stood open and inside Annja could see Roux and Beresford waiting for her.

Garin caught her arm gently in his and helped her across the rooftop. It was a good thing he did, for the four flights of stairs they'd climbed to get there played havoc on her energy levels.

They were met at the door by a medium-size black man with a shaved head and wraparound shades who greeted her with a smile. "A pleasure to see you again, Miss Creed," he said, in that lilting accent that always made Annja think of Jamaica.

She nodded. "And you, too, Griggs."

His full name, she knew, was Matthew Griggs, though

whether that was the one he had been born with or one he'd acquired over the years, she didn't know. Griggs was a senior commander in Garin's high-tech security firm, Dragontech Security, and had shown himself to be extremely capable whenever she'd encountered him.

She wasn't just being polite. It felt good to have a team of competent people around after being alone and on the run for the past few days.

She climbed into helicopter and got settled while Garin had a few words with Griggs and the pilot. Once Garin was aboard, the pilot fired up the rotors and took them up over the city, heading toward the English Channel.

42

They landed at a private airfield south of London. Beresford presented his ID to the customs official who came out to greet the helicopter. They had a short, whispered conversation, and then were all waved through without delay.

Two SUVs were waiting outside the terminal, courtesy of Dragontech. Garin got behind the wheel of the first, with Annja, Roux and Beresford joining him. Griggs and the other men from the helicopter got into the second. Once on the road, they headed for the security firm's London office.

They had just settled into the conference room on the third floor when Beresford took a call on his cell phone. It turned out to be Clements alerting them that Shaw and some of his men had just been observed walking into the Vanguard headquarters. Thirty seconds later, with the help of a computer loaned to them by Garin, they were watching the footage the police observers had captured at the scene.

The video showed Shaw and three other men arriving in a dark-colored Mercedes. Shaw headed for the steps, with one of the men in tow, while the other two took a large metal case out of the trunk before following.

"Him!" Annja exclaimed, pointing to the man with Shaw. "That's the bastard who shot Craig Stevens and Paolo Novick!"

Beresford froze the video for a closer look. "You're sure?" he asked.

Annja nodded. There was no way she was going to forget that face.

"His name's Trevor Jackson," Beresford told her. "He's Shaw's right-hand man and bodyguard. As a former member of the SAS, he's not a man to be trifled with."

Oh, I intend to do far more than trifle with him when I see him again, she thought.

"And is that the device?" the detective inspector asked Roux.

The Frenchman studied it for a moment, and then nodded. "Yes, that's it," he said, then turned to Garin. "How soon can your men be ready to go?"

His former apprentice smiled. "Would now suffice?"

Roux's answering smile was more than a bit wolfish.

Garin moved to his desk and tapped a few keys on his keyboard, activating the flat-screen monitor that hung on the wall nearby. A building schematic appeared on the screen.

"These are the latest blueprints I was able to obtain for the Vanguard building." He moved the trackball on the mouse, flipping through pages until he reached the one he wanted. "This is the eleventh floor, where Shaw has his office. It's the most likely place for him to take the device. There are three points of ingress, here, here and here…"

"Wait a minute!" Beresford said, his voice rising above Garin's. "What do you think you're doing? And where did you get those blueprints?"

Garin frowned, then turned to Annja. "Is he for real?"

Annja opened her mouth to say something to calm the situation, but Roux beat her to it.

"Inspector Beresford," he said politely, holding up a hand in Garin's direction in an unvoiced request for patience. "By your own admission you do not think you could mobilize a law enforcement response quickly enough to keep the device contained where it is. Is that still correct?"

"Yes, it's correct, but that doesn't mean I can allow you—"

He got no further.

"I'm afraid that's actually what it means," Roux said. "Right now we know where the device is. That might not be the case an hour from now, never mind tomorrow. We do not have time to wait for the bureaucratic red tape to untangle itself. If we are going to stop him, we have to strike and we have to do it now."

It was clear to Annja that Beresford didn't know what to say. He was frustrated by his official inability to do anything and yet the idea of having a private security force assault a public place of business must have been making his toes curl.

"You asked for an alternate plan," Roux said, not

unkindly. "This is it." His speech over, Roux turned back to Garin. "Go on."

Annja was still watching Beresford as Garin began laying out the tactical plan for invading the Vanguard offices. At first it looked like the detective wanted to continue protesting, his law-and-order view of reality not really having room for this kind of thing. Then Annja saw his shoulders droop and knew he had come to the same conclusion that she had.

Someone had to do something. Why not them?

Why not indeed?

After that, it was just a matter of deciding who would do what.

In the end, the plan was a simple one. Griggs would lead the first team through the front door as a diversion. If they could get to the eleventh floor, great, but if they tied up the Vanguard security forces somewhere lower, that was fine, too. Meanwhile, Garin would lead the second team out of the helicopter and in from the roof-top, coming down to the eleventh floor from above.

If possible, the two teams would meet and take Shaw's offices together. Once the device was located, it would be hustled up to the rooftop where the helicopter would be used to take it to safety.

As plans went, it was a good one. It was simple, with limited chance of confusion over what to do causing something to go wrong unexpectedly. As far as they knew, Shaw was unaware that he was being watched— never mind that anyone knew he had access to a po-tentially operable nuclear device. His success thus far would make him overconfident. They would use that to their advantage.

Garin had informed his men about the pending action while en route from France, anticipating that using his team would be the only real option at their disposal, and so it didn't take long for Griggs to brief them on the exact target and get them ready to roll.

While he did that, Garin armed himself from a selection of weapons from the safe in his office. Annja took the handgun he offered her, making certain that it was loaded properly and then stowing it at the small of her back.

Beresford had remained quiet throughout the planning and team briefing but spoke up, saying, "You realize we could all be arrested and thrown in jail for the rest of our lives for this?"

Roux laughed. "Trust me, Inspector, that's the least of our worries right now. Unless you missed it, there's a madman with a nuclear weapon hiding out in that building. Stopping him is far more important than worrying about getting arrested."

To Annja's surprise, Beresford laughed along with him. "I understand that completely, Roux. I just wanted to be sure everyone knew what they were getting themselves into."

He turned to Garin and pointed at a dark shadowed object inside the safe. "I'll take that Benelli, if you don't mind, Mr. Braden. Something with a little kick sounds rather good right about now."

Garin grinned, withdrew the combat shotgun and tossed it over.

TWENTY MINUTES LATER they were airborne in the same model helicopter they'd used to make the trip from France, but this time it was minus the logo and other identifying marks that might help the authorities track them down after the fact.

Below them, Annja could see the three black SUVs

containing Griggs's men pull out of the parking lot and head east, toward the target. She silently wished them luck, then turned to watch their passage through London's night skies.

It didn't take the chopper long to reach their target. They made one flyover of the building and in doing so discovered their first problem.

Initial reports had shown an empty helipad on the rooftop. Now, however, a helicopter occupied the space. The large white *V* of the Vanguard logo could be seen on its side.

There was no talk of aborting the mission, for they all knew they couldn't take the chance of losing track of the device if it was taken out of the building.

"Looks like we're going to have to use the ropes and rappel onto the roof," Garin said through the headset.

No one objected.

They made a great curving arc back toward the building and took up a position several hundred yards away and at an altitude where they wouldn't be noticed by the casual observer on the street.

Once there, they slipped into the rappelling harnesses they would need to make the descent and waited for Griggs's signal.

It didn't take long. About fifteen minutes after they had gotten into place, Griggs's voice came over the channel.

"We're inside," he said, shouting to be heard over the noise around him, "and taking fire. Mostly handguns, nothing heavy yet. We should be able to break through and reach the elevators in a few more minutes."

"Roger that," Garin said. "We're starting our run."

There was no need for Garin to signal the pilot; he'd been on the same radio channel as the rest of them.

Before Garin had even finished his last sentence, the pilot dipped the bird to the left and was taking them in sharply toward the Vanguard building.

As soon as the pilot had taken up position hovering over the rooftop, the door in back was thrown open by one of the Dragontech security team. Ropes were secured to the bar above the door and one by one they clipped the ropes into their harnesses and disappeared out the door, descending to the roof below.

By the time Annja reached the roof, the team leader had the door to the stairwell open and the group quickly descended into the building's interior.

They made their way down two flights of stairs and through a variety of corridors without difficulty, only to stumble directly into a group of Vanguard security men headed for the confrontation on the lower floors. The resulting firefight was short but deadly. When it was over, four of the Vanguard team were dead, with two wounded. Garin and his men stripped them of their weapons and radios, bound the wounded with quick ties and then continued on their way.

The clock was ticking now; there seemed little chance that Shaw wouldn't figure out that something was amiss and try to make his escape, so they had to get to him before he had the chance to do so.

After cutting down a short corridor, they emerged into the sales bullpen. Chin-high cubicles filled the area, turning it into a labyrinth of sorts, leading to the executive conference area on the other side.

Just beyond that was Shaw's office, where they hoped to find both him and the torc.

They were halfway across the room, intent on their destination, when the door on the far side of the bull-pen suddenly opened and a group consisting of Shaw,

Jackson and a half dozen armed men stepped through the door.

For a split second, everyone froze.

Then chaos ensued as both sides opened fire.

Not being as skilled with a firearm as the Dragontech personnel, Annja kept to the middle of the pack, close to Garin, which was how she ended up crouched behind a cubicle wall with him as bullets whipped through the air around them and chewed up everything they hit.

The noise was incredible, the snap of handgun fire punctuated by the snarl of the enemy's machine pistols and the booming voice of Beresford's combat shotgun. The cubicles proved to be poor protection, not being thick enough to stop a bullet entirely, and within minutes men on both sides were down and bleeding.

Annja did what she could for her side, popping up and around corners to fire at any moving targets before ducking back down and shifting to one side or the other, trying to keep them guessing.

Their opponents were doing the same, and it might have gone on like that a lot longer if Shaw hadn't decided to make a break for it.

43

"Look!"

Annja followed Garin's pointing finger. On the far side of the room she could see a red Exit sign. The door beneath it was sliding closed, but through the gap she caught a quick glimpse of Jackson and Shaw, and a metal case being carried by one of them, though she wasn't quite sure who.

Garin moved closer, so she could hear him over the noise of all the gunfire. "If we circle around," he said, "we should be able reach the stairs."

It was either that or let Shaw get away while they were pinned down by his security team. Nowhere near ready to admit defeat, Annja nodded in agreement.

She fired several shots at the other side, forcing them to keep their heads down. When she did, Garin slid out of position and disappeared amid the maze of cubicles behind them.

She waited a moment, joined the others in firing off

another blast and then followed suit, slipping into the cubicle behind her, then into the one after that, moving in a wide circle around the edge of the firefight until she could see the door.

Garin was about ten feet in front of her, peering out from beneath a nearby desk. In the cubicle just beyond him, Annja could see a Vanguard security officer standing and looking around, as if he'd heard something.

Annja watched the other man, and when he turned the opposite way she waved a hand signal at Garin.

Right on cue, he popped out from beneath the desk and put a bullet into the man from just a few feet away.

With the way clear, the two of them dashed the last few feet to the exit door and slipped through.

They found themselves in a stairwell identical to the one they'd used to gain access to their current floor, with the steps going both up and down.

"Which way?" Annja asked.

As if in answer, bullets came flying down at them from somewhere up above. The shots missed, though one bullet ricocheted off the nearby wall and carved a furrow in Garin's calf.

Annja waited for a lull in the shooting, then stepped out and fired off a few snap shots upward between the switchbacks of the staircase.

To her surprise, she heard a cry of pain and something came clattering down, bouncing off the railings to land a few steps below her.

A glance told her it was a pistol.

When no more fire came from above, they cautiously made their way up the stairs to the next floor.

Garin went through the door at a rush, Annja close behind, the two of them counting on the fact that Shaw and Jackson would be more concerned with getting away than lying in ambush. Thankfully their guess was right. They found themselves in a long corridor with doors to either side, but they were saved from having to check each one of them by the sight of Shaw disappearing through the door at the far end.

If Annja remembered correctly, that was the staircase they'd used to come down from the roof, which meant Shaw was going for the helicopter they'd seen on the helipad.

If he reached it before they did…

Garin must have come to the same conclusion, for he sprinted off down the corridor after Shaw.

Annja followed.

Halfway down the hall a figure stepped out of one of the side rooms and clotheslined her across the throat with his extended forearm.

44

The blow knocked Annja right off her feet. The impact with the floor sent her gun skittering from her hand. It disappeared through the open doorway of the room off to her right. She was left flat on her back, staring up at her attacker.

It was Jackson.

He glared at her with hatred in his eyes and drew a dangerous-looking combat knife from his belt. The blade was at least half a foot long and changed from a smooth to a serrated edge closer to the hilt.

As Annja scrambled to her feet, she saw past Jackson to where Garin was hesitating, trying to decide whether he should return to help her or continue after their man.

She made the decision for him.

"Go after Shaw!" she shouted, hoping he would listen to her for once, and then turned her attention back to the opponent in front of her without waiting to see if Garin complied.

Jackson was bleeding from a wound in one shoulder, she noted, and a smile stitched across her face when she realized that her shot in the stairwell had taken a bite out of him. It must have been his gun that fell, she thought, otherwise he would have shot us as we ran past.

"You again," Jackson said, his disgust evident. "What the hell does it take to kill you?"

"More than you've got, apparently," she replied.

He didn't care to be taunted. "We'll see about that, you bitch."

He stalked toward her, a look of expectation on his face.

Annja didn't flinch. She stood her ground, waiting.

"You should run, little girl," he told her, his voice growing rough with whatever twisted images he was seeing in his mind's eye—images of what he intended to do to her, she had no doubt.

But Annja was imagining an entirely different end to the confrontation and she let it show on her face, along with her hunger to pay him back for what he'd done to Craig and the rest of the crew at the dig site.

"I don't think so," she replied.

Maybe it was the look, or the tone of her voice. Either way it was enough to cause him to hesitate for a moment, uncertain.

She pressed her advantage, trying to enrage him and force him to do something stupid.

"What's the matter?" she asked. "Afraid of a little girl?"

That did it. He moved forward eagerly, waving the knife back and forth in front of him.

She considered drawing her sword. With it, she could

end the confrontation quickly and its length would keep her out of harm's reach, but she forced down the urge, trusting in her abilities to handle Jackson without it. She wanted to make him pay for what he'd done, to make him suffer for all the harm he'd caused.

The sword was there if she needed it; for now, though, she'd use just her hands and feet.

It will be more satisfying that way, she thought.

He rushed the last few steps, trying to overpower her with his size and a sudden jab of the knife.

Jackson telegraphed his attack with a quick glance before he struck and that was all Annja needed to evade it. She spun to her left, her right arm coming across the front of her body in a vicious strike to the inside of his forearm, stopping his attack cold. Then she let her momentum carry her around as she landed an elbow strike to the side of his face.

The blow staggered him, forcing him back a few steps, and Annja moved to close the distance, but he'd learned his lesson the first time and was ready for her. He parried the various strikes she threw in his direction and lashed out with the knife, carving a furrow along the outside of her right arm when she didn't pull it back quickly enough.

They moved along the corridor, trading blows, neither one managing to get the upper hand. Annja could feel herself slowing down, however—a result of what her body had recently been subjected to—and she knew she had to gain the advantage or things could spin out of control.

The next time Jackson jabbed at her with the knife, she stepped in close and trapped his arm in a vicious wrist lock. He yelped in pain as she forced his hand backward, the knife falling to clatter on the floor.

So intent was she on her success in disarming him that she didn't realize he'd allowed it to happen until it was too late.

The punch slammed into her injured rib cage with what felt like the force of a charging rhino. Pain exploded through her body and for a moment all she could see was stars.

A moment was all Jackson needed.

He followed the first blow with several others, slamming his fists into her face, stomach and rib cage, blow after blow landing against her unprotected flesh as she fought against the darkness to keep from blacking out.

She stumbled and then fell, landing on her hands and knees, gasping for breath.

Jackson stepped back and for a moment she thought he was going to give her a reprieve, but seconds later she found out how wrong she was when he landed a vicious kick to her rib cage and followed it up with another to her face.

The latter literally lifted her off the ground and flopped her down on her back, her head lolling.

She was in serious trouble and she knew it. Her mind was shrieking at her to protect herself, to get up and fight, but she couldn't seem to make her arms or legs work the way she wanted them to; it was as if all her muscles had turned to jelly.

"This time, I'll be sure to finish the job," he said as he delivered another kick to her ribs, then turned around, looking for his knife.

Get up! a voice screamed in the back of her mind, but she could barely focus on it. Everything was swimming around her—the floor, the walls, the ceiling. She didn't know which way was up.

Still, she tried.

She rolled partially on her side and tried to draw her legs up under her, but even that little effort took nearly all her strength.

Darkness threatened at the edges of her vision.

"I'm gonna cut you up!" Jackson snarled as he picked up his knife and started back toward her.

There was something she could do to save herself, she knew, but she couldn't seem to focus on what it was. Something she could use to keep him away from her, something...

Jackson loomed over her, knife in hand.

"Time to join the rest of your friends," he said. He bent over, grabbed her hair and hauled her up by it so that she was kneeling there in front of him, her throat exposed to his blade.

The pain from her scalp where he tugged on her hair cleared her head.

As Jackson drew his knife back, intending to slash open her throat, Annja called her sword to hand.

It slipped into her fist like it was made for it, materializing out of the otherwhere without warning.

She saw Jackson's eyes go wide at the sight of it.

Sword in hand, she thrust upward, impaling him on the weapon before his arm had even begun its downward arc.

He died with a surprised expression on his face, as if he couldn't understand what had happened to him.

Releasing the sword, Annja slumped forward onto her hands and crawled away from the body, gasping for breath.

She heard footsteps approaching and turned in time to see Griggs and two of his men rushing down the corridor toward her. He helped her to her feet, asking, "Where's Garin?"

Annja lifted her head toward the door at the end of the hall. "He chased Shaw through there."

"Go!" he told the other two, then, taking her elbow in his hand, he helped her along after them.

Behind the door was a stairwell. The sound of gunfire from somewhere above let them know that the men they were pursuing had gone up instead of down and they followed suit.

The stairs led up to the roof and they emerged into the night air on the far side.

Annja took it all in with a glance.

The case containing the old Soviet RA-115 lay a few feet away, as if tossed aside when Shaw had emerged from the stairwell.

Shaw was leaning out of the rear door of the Vanguard helicopter, gun in hand, firing at Garin Braden, who stood midway between Annja and the helicopter.

Garin was in the open, completely exposed, but that wasn't stopping him from returning fire, intent on preventing Shaw's escape.

There wasn't anything Annja could do; her only weapon was her sword and a fat lot of good that was going to do against a helicopter.

That didn't mean Griggs and his companions were helpless, however.

The three men added their gunfire to Garin's, unleashing a wave of bullets that sprayed across the open doorway where Shaw was crouched. As the helicopter lifted up off the pad and swung itself ponderously around in midair, intending to make a clean getaway, Annja thought she saw Shaw flung backward by the force of a shot, but she couldn't be sure.

He can't get away!

The helicopter was several yards above the building, the sound of the rotors winding to a higher speed as the pilot tried to get them out of there.

"We have to stop him!" Annja shouted over the noise, her fists clenched at her side in impotent fury.

As if in answer to her cry, a bullet from one of the guns finally found a vulnerable target, puncturing the fuel reservoir in the rear of the fuselage, which touched off a spark at the same time.

With a thunderous boom, the helicopter exploded in midair.

Griggs threw himself over Annja, taking them both to the ground, as shrapnel and other larger parts of the aircraft came whizzing back toward them, carried by the force of the explosion.

Thankfully none of them were hurt.

Griggs helped her up and the two of them were dusting themselves off when Garin walked over to join them.

"What happened?" Annja asked.

Garin explained how he'd caught Shaw at the top of the steps and how they'd fought over possession of the device. Apparently deciding that escaping was more important than retaining control of the suitcase bomb, Shaw cast it aside and ran for the helicopter.

While listening to Garin, Annja stepped over to the battered steel case and looked inside.

"It's not here," she said.

"What's not?"

"The torc."

Garin frowned. "Shaw must have had it with him in the chopper."

It was about the last thing Annja wanted to hear, but

she couldn't ignore the logic. Obtaining another suitcase nuke, while difficult, wouldn't be impossible, she knew. But gaining control of enough plutonium to activate it? That was something else entirely. Annja knew that Shaw likely would not have let something as precious as the torc out of his sight.

They'd search his office, but she didn't expect to find anything.

The torc was gone.

45

Two nights later, Annja was recovering at Roux's estate outside of Paris when Henshaw informed her that she had a phone call from Detective Inspector Beresford.

"How are you, Miss Creed?" he asked, once she got on the line.

"Doing better, Inspector. And you? I take it you survived the fallout surrounding the events of the other night?"

"Just barely," he said, but there was no disguising his satisfied tone. "I called to let you know that Shaw left behind a mountain of evidence regarding his work as leader of the Red Hand Defenders, more than enough to condemn him in any court of law three or four times over. We can tie him, and his henchman Jackson, to several car bombs and kidnappings over the past few years, never mind the attacks at Arkholme and against Sebastian Cartier. Given what we have, they'll probably cancel the inquest next week."

"That's great, Inspector." Annja hadn't been looking forward to having to explain it all over again to a group of magistrates; having done so for Beresford's final report was more than enough, in her view. Now it appeared she wouldn't have to.

"There's just one thing I don't understand," she told him, "and it's driving me nuts. How did Shaw know that the torc was plutonium in the first place?"

Beresford laughed. "I wouldn't want you to go crazy now, so let me answer that for you.

"Based on his journals, it appears he was aware of the legends behind the torc, about how the material from which it had been fashioned supposedly came from outside this world. He had men like Paolo Novick on his payroll searching for anything resembling the torc. When it surfaced, it was a simple matter for Novick to run a Geiger counter over it to determine that it was radioactive."

Annja wasn't surprised to hear there had been a spy in their midst at the dig site; it was the only way anyone outside of those present could have known they'd uncovered anything of value. She was dismayed, however, to learn that the spy had been Novick.

The loss of the torc in the explosion still pained her, but she supposed it was for the best. Having it loose in the world might just tempt someone else to try the same thing Shaw had.

They spoke for a few more minutes and then hung up. In a few days, Annja would be returning to the U.S. to get back to work on a new episode for *Chasing History's Monsters* and for once, she was actually happy to be leaving Europe behind.

It was time to go home, she thought.

Munich

THE MAN ENTERED the study with the swift sure strides of one who had done it a hundred, nay, a thousand times before. Despite the fact that there was only a thin slice of illumination coming in through the open doorway, he didn't trip over any of the furniture, nor did he hesitate as he made his way to the oak cabinet on the far side of the room.

He opened it, pressed six digits on a keypad set against the back of the cabinet and then waited patiently as the wall closest to him swung silently open, revealing another room behind.

The biometric lights came on as he stepped inside, closing the false panel behind him. The room wasn't large, not by modern standards, but it was fair-sized and comfortable. Shelves lined the walls and on them were displayed a number of valuable treasures. Artwork that was supposed to have vanished during the fall of Berlin, recovered from a warehouse in Argentina. A selection of ancient weaponry, each item more valuable than the last, not the least of which was a samurai sword known to some as Jucchi Yosamu, Ten Thousand Cold Nights. An illustrated Bible said to have been penned by the hand of an angel. A strangely shaped skull kept in a glass case, the three empty eye sockets staring out in silent accusation. The room was a veritable storehouse of some of the most valuable finds ever made.

The man ignored what was collected there, however. He'd seen it all before, many times. Instead he moved to a wooden cabinet against the far wall and opened one of its many drawers.

The drawer was lined with velvet and stood empty, just as the man knew it would be.

He removed a thin, slender box from the inside pocket of his suit jacket and open it gently.

Inside, on a bed of cotton, lay a black necklace with carved eagle heads as clasps.

He knew the legends surrounding it.

Fashioned from the tears of a goddess.

Carried by the warrior queen, Boudica, in her rebellion against Rome.

Rumored to provide the wearer with invincibility in battle.

As he transferred the Tear of the Gods to the storage drawer he'd selected to house it in, Garin Braden laughed.

To hell with the bomb! he thought. In the end, he'd come away with the only treasure that had been worth having.

* * * * *

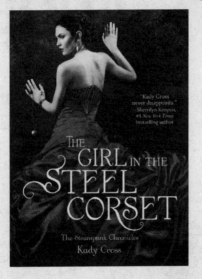